Stay Amazing

Shadows

JULES NELSON

WESTBOW
PRESS
A DIVISION OF THOMAS NELSON
& ZONDERVAN

Copyright © 2014 Jules Nelson.

All rights reserved. No part of this book may be used or reproduced by any means, graphic, electronic, or mechanical, including photocopying, recording, taping or by any information storage retrieval system without the written permission of the publisher except in the case of brief quotations embodied in critical articles and reviews.

WestBow Press books may be ordered through booksellers or by contacting:

WestBow Press
A Division of Thomas Nelson & Zondervan
1663 Liberty Drive
Bloomington, IN 47403
www.westbowpress.com
1 (866) 928-1240

Because of the dynamic nature of the Internet, any web addresses or links contained in this book may have changed since publication and may no longer be valid. The views expressed in this work are solely those of the author and do not necessarily reflect the views of the publisher, and the publisher hereby disclaims any responsibility for them.

Any people depicted in stock imagery provided by Thinkstock are models, and such images are being used for illustrative purposes only. Certain stock imagery © Thinkstock.

ISBN: 978-1-4908-4839-6 (sc)
ISBN: 978-1-4908-4840-2 (hc)
ISBN: 978-1-4908-4838-9 (e)

Library of Congress Control Number: 2014914577

Printed in the United States of America.

WestBow Press rev. date: 08/13/2014

*This book is dedicated to my Children,
Sabrina and Simon...
You have made me a better person
and inspire me to make this world a better place for you to live in...
I pray for God's guidance in your everyday life!*

*...and to my husband...
God's gift to me...*

"For I know the plans I have for you,"
Declares the Lord,
"Plans to prosper you and not to harm you,
plans to give you hope and a future."
Jeremiah 29:11

~Prologue~

August 1850...

She looked down as the purple flowers landed in the mud puddle. The pretty little petals disappeared as the horse's hind legs trampled them under the dirty water. Emma looked up as the horse raced away. Feeling her eyes fill with tears, she wiped them away in frustration.

"Jest leave 'em Emma! Ya can pick more on the way back ta the farm," her brother said impatiently. Mark had not wanted to take a trip to town that day. However, his father had taken one look at the blisters on Mark's pinched toes and told him to buy new boots before stepping one foot back in the fields.

"Those were the last ones. There won't be more 'til next summer," Emma replied, wiping at another tear. "I've been lookin' everywhere and finally found those." She had been so happy when she saw them growing beside the road that morning. The first happiness she had felt in weeks.

"Well there'll be more next year. Now, do ya need flour or not?" Mark asked as he pulled her arm toward the mercantile door.

"They were fer Mama," Emma stated softly. "They're her favorite."

"Oh," Mark stopped as the words sunk in. Emma saw her brother take in a shaky breath as he released the arm he was holding. Slowly, he turned to look at her. Sounding remorseful he offered, "I can help ya look again on the way back iffen ya want."

She shook her head. "They're the only ones I've seen in awhile."

Mark cleared his throat, "Look Emma, Mama isn't gonna notice one season from the next. We'll jest have ta get some other flowers this time."

Taking one last look at the muddy flowers, she followed her brother into the mercantile.

The rain had held off that morning, but the gloomy skies matched the atmosphere at the Wells' farm. Even Seth's usual whistling was absent in the house and yard. Emma found herself relieved that the sun stayed hidden. Almost like the sun couldn't bear to be happy either.

Going to stand near the counter, Emma waited for the store keeper to notice her. Mrs. Phelps filled orders for two other customers before she turned to her. "Good morning Emma dear. How are ya today? Do ya have a list fer me?" Emma handed her the paper in her hand and Mrs. Phelps read through the items quickly. "A good start, but I think yer gonna need lard and molasses. I'll put `em in. Don't be hard on yerself. If yer Mama was still here, she'd be teachin' ya how ta take proper stock of yer pantry." She turned to fill the order as she continued explaining her thoughts on necessary items to have on hand. Emma didn't try to reply because Mrs. Phelps rarely expected a response from her.

Mark met her at the counter with a pair of boots he found to fit his growing feet. He was relieved to have found a pair that fit. He had not wanted to make a trip to the shoe maker.

When Mrs. Phelps finished putting their packages into Emma's basket, she added up the purchases and Mark paid for everything.

"Thank ya, Mrs. Phelps," Emma called out quietly as she turned to follow her brother from the store. As they stepped outside, Mark took the basket from Emma and hurried down the walk. Emma paused once more to look at the drowned flowers.

Suddenly, little purple flowers appeared in front of her nose. Emma followed the flowers up an arm, to a boy not much older than her ten years. She found herself staring into a pair of dark gray eyes. Gray eyes that looked like they understood the sadness in her heart.

Reaching up, she took the flowers gently. "Thank ya," Emma said softly. "They're fer my mama."

With a nod of his head, the boy turned and disappeared between two buildings. He was gone so quickly that for a moment Emma wondered if she had imagined him. Looking down at her hand, she saw proof that she had not. She smelled the delicate purple flowers and then hurried to catch up with her brother.

Emma Fern

~One~

Eight years later..

The soft purple material was too pretty and too thin to be a serviceable dress for a farm, but Emma ran the delicate material between her fingers longingly. She couldn't help but wonder if she had enough money for it. With a shake of her head, she scolded herself for even considering it. Even for a Sunday dress, the material was too thin. But Emma ran her fingers across it one more time anyway.

"That bolt came by mistake. I never would've ordered such a one. It's too pale ta catch anyone's notice and far too thin ta be a suitable choice fer a farmer's daughter." Mrs. Phelps pulled the bolt of purple fabric away from Emma and placed three others in front of her. "If yer own mama was here she would do the choosing fer ya, but yer on yer own. I suppose ya should have some new under garments as well if yer dresses are wearing so thin. A bolt of this should suffice." The store keeper added a bolt of muslin and, to Emma's relief, removed the bolt of scratchy homespun. "I think this green is too bold fer yer soft coloring, so let's go with the tan and the blue." Without waiting for a reply from Emma, Mrs. Phelps started cutting the appropriate lengths of each and wrapping them for her. "These will make fine dresses. Do ya need thread? Jest reach yerself into that basket and get a couple spools. That should be enough fer these projects."

Emma didn't attempt to respond to Mrs. Phelps's questions. She had long since realized that answers weren't necessary and rarely heard. She watched as the storekeeper worked. Mrs. Phelps's round face gave her a soft look. But behind that softness was a firm disposition. She ran a neat and orderly store, and she tolerated no tomfoolery. Emma had seen her reprimand child and adult alike, more than once. She took no rude behavior from anyone.

Ever since Emma's mama had gotten sick, the storekeeper had taken it upon herself to school her in the things she thought a daughter needed to know. She knew the life lessons were kindly meant, but Emma felt her mother had done a fine job of preparing her for a life of caring for her father and brothers. Still, she held her tongue and thanked the kind storekeeper every time.

"Thank ya Mrs. Phelps," Emma replied when she was handed her packages. She turned to leave the store as her friend Abigail entered. When Abigail saw Emma, her face lit up with a smile.

"Oh Emma! I'm so happy ta see ya. Do ya have time ta stop fer tea?" Abigail asked as she leaned in for a quick hug. Emma suddenly felt grubby next to her friend's neatness. Abigail's dark hair was pulled back neatly and smoothly to reveal her clear skin to its fullest advantage. Emma knew without having to look at her friend's complexion that there still would not be a single freckle in sight. She also knew, without a doubt, that the heat would have turned her own hair fuzzy at the ends, and her nose would be dotted with freckles from working in the sun so often.

"Sorry, Abigail, I can't today. I plan on sewin' this afternoon, seein' I've a rare quiet day," Emma replied.

"Oh." Abigail's beautiful face turned down in a pout. "Next time ya come ta town, set aside an hour fer a visit. I've so much ta tell ya, and I want ta show ya the cradle David has finished fer the baby." As they walked out the door and down the dusty street, Abigail continued to tell her everything that had been done in preparation for the baby's arrival that fall. "And David tells me I'm even more beautiful each day, but I swear I'll not be able ta see my feet soon. So will ya promise?"

Emma looked over at Abigail, realizing she had stopped walking and was waiting for a reply. "Promise?" Emma repeated, not exactly knowing what Abigail had asked her.

Abigail's hopeful smile barely flickered as she clarified, "Do ya promise ta stop fer a visit?"

"I will when everything on the farm slows down."

"Oh Emma! Ya need ta have more fun. Relax a little and visit. All this work's makin' ya tired lookin'. How do ya expect ta catch a husband if ya have no time fer frivolities?" Abigail's dark brown eyes filled with excitement, "I should invite ya fer dinner and have David invite one of his brothers, or maybe wait 'til his cousins come ta town. We must get ya married before ya look desperate." With another hug, Abigail turned and hurried away.

Emma watched her friend return to the mercantile and disappear inside. She sighed at the turn of the conversation. With a family to look after, she felt her chances of getting married were small. She knew she should be grateful for her friend's attempts, but the thought of Abigail trying to arrange dinners sent a shiver down her spine. With a shake of her head, she turned towards the farm and ran right into a man. Blushing, she pushed away with a soft apology.

"Well hello there." A hand shot towards her arm to steady her. "Ain't ya a pert little thing?"

Dread filled her as she smelled the liquor on the man's breath. She turned slightly and confirmed that she was standing in front of their town's saloon. Even though it was early in the day, only her friend's distraction would have caused her to pause here. Her father once told her that even good men lose proper manners when possessed by liquor. With a deep breath, she pushed at the fingers. "Excuse me sir. My da is waiting fer me. Kindly let go."

"Let go? I think not," the amused voice slurred as he leaned closer. "I been lookin' fer ya Annie."

"Annie?" Emma asked, confused, as she pulled harder at his firm grasp. "Sir, yer mistaken me fer someone else." She couldn't help closing her eyes in dread. Before she could protest further, someone stepped between her and the drunken man.

"I found the man with the horses fer sale, Pa. Well, found the horses anyway. The rancher left them at the corral behind the blacksmith." The fingers loosened enough for her arm to be pried loose. Her eyes flew open in surprise. She stepped back. "There's only one black left though and someone is inspectin' it. We hafta hurry if ya want it."

"But Annie?" the voice slurred.

"'Tisn't Annie, Pa," the newly arrived man stated firmly but softly. Unexpectedly, he bent to retrieve Emma's packages and returned them to her arms. He kept his eyes turned away from hers. "Pardon us ma'am, fer takin' yer time." His lips turned up into a sad smile. Touching the brim of his hat, the man gave Emma a nod, then turned and strode away in the direction of the blacksmith. His arm propelled his pa along with him.

Emma watched him walk away for a moment before scanning her surroundings to see if anyone had witnessed her unfortunate situation. No one had stopped or slowed down to watch her. No one so much as spared a glance toward her. With a final look in the direction of the man who rescued her, she hurried down the street and out of the small town. She sent up a prayer of thankfulness that he had interrupted his pa from making a mark on her reputation. When she passed the last house, she finally slowed down. With a sigh of relief, she looked back at the town behind her. "That is why I don't like goin' ta town," Emma muttered. "It's far too busy fer my likin'."

Thinking of all the work waiting for her, Emma quickly walked the rest of the way home. The unexpected trip to town meant she would have to work faster if she was to have time free to sew.

As Emma arrived at the farm, her brothers were coming out of the barn. A scraggly dog ran up beside her, nudging her hand to be scratched. "Hello Dawg. Yeah, I see ya." With a few scratches behind his ear, the dog was content to run off.

"Hey Em." Mark called out to her. "Did ya find anythin' ya could use?" Emma looked up at her older brother as he walked closer. He was taller than their father now and looked more like him every day. The only exception was Mark's dark hair. The dark color came from their mother.

"Yeah I did. Mrs. Phelps helped me find a couple calicos," she answered. "Are ya lookin' fer lunch already?"

"We're comin' in ta make a couple sandwiches before we head out ta find Da. Seth finished weedin' the garden fer ya, and I split the kindlin' by the kitchen door. We wanted ya ta have the afternoon free fer sewin'." As they arrived at the house, Mark opened the door and stepped back to let her go first. With a chuckle he added, "We weren't sure when ya'd have more time ta make yerself presentable."

"Well thank ya," Emma replied, ignoring the reference to her dress incident from the day before. While weeding the garden, she had stepped on the hem of her dress, ripping off a section. Emma had not been surprised it had ripped. The dress was a little too small and had been washed thin. Unfortunately, Mark and Seth had been working nearby and witnessed her embarrassment. At dinner, they laughingly told the whole story to their father. Da had chuckled at their retelling of the story. Then he promptly told Emma to go buy some yard goods for two new dresses.

By the time Emma returned from putting her packages on her bed, her father was in the kitchen washing up as well. "So ya found material fer dresses? Good. Good. Me and the boys are set ta start clearin' that back field. We'll likely be kinda late workin', so we won't need much of a meal. Ya should have plenty of quiet time today and tomorrow. I imagine ya'll get quite a bit of sewin' done with us outta yer hair." He kissed the top of her head as he went to sit down.

Seth came into the kitchen with a ham from the cellar. Setting it on the table, the menfolk set about cutting slices for their sandwiches. Emma unwrapped a loaf of bread and put it out for them to slice as well.

"I won't need ta sew both dresses right away. Jest the one," Emma protested.

"Nonsense. Might as well sew them both while ya have the time. Harvest will be here before ya know it," Da stated.

"Me and Mark'll do yer chores in the mornin' too.. so ya can get back ta it after breakfast," Seth added proudly.

Emma smiled. "Thank ya." She rarely made herself any clothes. A couple summers before, she had simply put some tucks in her mama's old dresses to spare herself the work and the cost of new ones. Not that she didn't know how to sew. Just that she already had her hands full with the farm work, and with keeping up with her growing brothers. Luckily, their growth seemed to slow this last year.

They all seemed to be making an effort to give her time to sew herself something pretty. As she watched her family eat, they smiled and discussed what needed to be done to the new field. She cut the ham into some thin slices for herself.

"Maybe I'll ride into town tonight and ask James if he has time ta help us. We haven't seen him in awhile. Iffen he's game, working with two teams would make this go fast. We might even be done before harvest," Mark suggested.

Da nodded.

"With James helpin' out, maybe I can do some fishin'?" Seth put in hopefully.

Da laughed before replying, "No son."

"Rotten kid. Ya always try gettin' out of work," Mark muttered.

Emma smiled as she watched her family. She let her mind wander to what style dress she should make. It had been so long since she had a dress that was fit to her, she was excited to get them done. Suddenly, Emma realized how excited she was to get sewing. She finished eating her food and excused herself from the room. "I'll jest clean this up later," she assured them.

~Two~

Emma's family was true to their word. They took care of themselves so she could sew uninterrupted. She looked at her new things with a sense of pride. Picking up her worn skirt she realized she couldn't bear to throw it into the rag basket. Running her fingers across the faded material, she smiled. She could still remember her mama wearing it when the material had been new. Emma hung the skirt back on the hook and went to cook breakfast.

Holding onto the rail, she carefully went down the steep stairs. Suddenly, Emma saw her mother's face clearly. It was a memory from when she was eight. Emma had tripped coming down the original ladder. Her skirt had caught on her shoe and she had almost fallen to the ground. Emma had caught herself just in time. Heart pounding, she had scolded herself to be more careful.

But Emma's mother had witnessed the whole thing. She had been so frightened, she immediately stormed out to the barn. "Joseph Wells," Mama had stated firmly, "There WILL be stairs WITH a rail in this cabin, before anyone sleeps tonight!" It was the only time Emma had ever seen her mother demand anything.

Da had started on the stairs that very moment. He had given no argument. Mama had asked for so little, that anything she did ask for was immediately produced.

When Emma's father had brought his wife to the Michigan territory, he had promised their small cabin would only be temporary. He had planned to build a larger house like the one they left behind in Vermont as soon as the money was available.

But with each harvest there didn't seem to be enough money. Each year, something would happen to delay the building from going up. Then another reason and another. Year after year of disappointment. After years of waiting, Mama had finally informed her husband that she didn't want a new home. She stated that the cabin felt like home and it would be a shame to leave it. Emma's father had been upset with himself. So upset that he had let his wife down.

Then one day, Emma and her mother had returned from town with their supplies to find a beautiful white porch. Da and the boys had painted the porch and shutters with whitewash, while they had been away. When Mama caught sight of it, she froze with a gasp. Letting the tears streamed down her cheeks. Da had been so pleased with her reaction that every spring afterward, he had painted it all again.

"It's not a bad cabin," Emma thought as she looked around. The chinking wasn't brand new, but it was still white. The main rooms were joined together and let in a lot of light. To one side of the stairs, stood the door to her parents' bedroom. The bedrooms upstairs were very small. Emma had just enough space in her room for her bed and a chest. "I spend so little time up there though," she reasoned. "No need fer it ta be bigger."

Shaking her head, Emma cleared her head and set about making breakfast.

Deciding on flapjacks for breakfast, Emma quickly mixed up some batter. The flour bag was getting light, so she added it to the list for town. Once the skillet was hot, she poured circles of batter in. While that batch cooked, she set the table. Emma knew the maple syrup jug was mostly empty and wanted to save it for a special occasion. So instead, she decided to use molasses. But when she reached into the back of the pantry to grab the bottle, she realized it wasn't there. Spotting it on a different shelf, she picked it up to find it was empty. "Have ta put that on a list fer town, as well," she said to herself. She decided they could just use jam on their flapjacks. By the time breakfast was on the table, her list had grown. Emma knew she would be heading to town.

Her brothers came in for breakfast, followed by their father. After a quick prayer, the conversation turned to the work ahead of them.

"Ya want both wagons ta start with, Da?" Mark asked as he piled the flapjacks on his plate.

Da finished his mouthful, then answered slowly. "No. Let's jest take one taday. If we find need fer the second, we can bring it out after dinner."

A knock on the door brought everyone's heads up. A young man stepped into the kitchen. "Hey James," Mark called, "come have some breakfast. Emma made plenty." He pulled out the empty chair beside him.

James Abernathy had been Mark's friend since the first day they attended school together. Almost from that same day, James had been finding excuses to come help Mark on the farm. Her older brother had gladly started sharing his farm chores with his town friend. Emma had figured James's fascination for farm life would have long ago lost its appeal, but so far it had not. His light blue eyes came to life with the hard work.

"Are ya sure there's enough?" he asked, eyeing the food, and then looked to Emma. Her nod was all the approval he needed. He sat down in the chair Mark held out for him, as Emma got up to hand him a plate. With a quiet thanks, James filled the plate with flapjacks.

"It appears I'll be headin' ta the mercantile today. Anything ya be needin' ta add ta my list?" Emma asked as she retrieved her list from under the butter crock, placing it on the table.

Mark reached for the list and studied it. "It's odd that we're needin' both molasses and brown sugar after Seth spends one day cookin'."

Emma turned to see Seth's ears turning red. "Seth Wells? Did ya eat all those sweets?"

He laughed, "Would ya believe they jest walked out ta me?" His blond curls fell into his eyes, adding to his boyish charm.

"I should make ya go ta town," Emma groaned.

"I don't have time fer town today," Seth answered her, then offered, "But I'll fill up the water buckets before I head out ta the fields."

Emma let out a long breath and started gathering the empty dishes. She was almost finished washing up the dishes, when the men finished discussing their plans and headed for the door. Seth paused in the doorway to ask, "Iffen I promise ta stay outta the pantry, would ya make some of those ginger cookies?"

Mark pushed him through the door with a muttered, "Rotten kid." Da put his hat on his head with a chuckle and followed them all out.

Emma found herself smiling. Silently, she reminded herself to add ginger to the list.

Her kitchen was cleaned in no time. She climbed the stairs to her room to change from her work dress into her new one. Selecting a bonnet from her hook, she gathered her things for the walk to the mercantile.

Setting off for town, Emma found herself smiling again. There was a wonderful breeze. The weather had been a little warmer than she liked it to be. Putting on a bonnet for town was almost unbearable, yet necessary. She could imagine Mrs. Phelps's comment, and Abigail's horror, if she were to arrive in town with a bare head. "At least the breeze makes the walk tolerable," she thought.

The small town was already bustling with activity when Emma arrived. It was always busy on Saturday. Tethered horses lined each side of the street. Every shop had people standing out front. With miles between farms, there were not many chances for visiting. So when a trip to town was made, it was also a time to see other folks. Neighbors shared news with neighbors. Ladies tried to get their fill of female conversation. And during the summer months, kids had fun with their friends.

The noise alone made Emma cringe. She immediately wished she had waited until the following week. Surely they could get by until then. "I'm already here, so I may as well jest get the job done," she muttered to herself. Straightening her back, she forced herself to move toward the busy doorway of the mercantile.

As she reached for the door, it flew open and two boys ran around her. A hand shot past her to stop the door before it slammed into her. She pushed her basket back up to her elbow and looked up into a pair of deep gray eyes. Emma blushed as she realized they belonged to the same young man that had rescued her earlier in the week. He touched his hat with a nod, "Ma'am." She gave him a grateful smile as she hurried through the door.

She maneuvered through the crowded store, finding the things on her list. When she had everything she could get herself, Emma waited for her turn at the counter. She caught a glimpse of the man that stopped the door for her and studied him. "He looks very familiar," she decided. "I musta seen him around town and not realized it." She continued to watch him as he moved about the store. His dark hair was overgrown and waved slightly at the back of his neck. His tan face was clean and carefully shaven. However, it was his eyes that Emma kept being drawn to. The deep gray color was unusual in itself, but it was something more. When she had looked into his eyes at the door, they seemed to be telling her a story of their own. Almost like a storm of emotions.

As he moved around the store and around people, she was surprised by how graceful he was for being so tall. Unexpectedly, the man turned and looked at her. Embarrassed that she had been caught staring, Emma turned away quickly and almost collided with someone.

An arm steadied her, with a chuckle in her ear. "Careful now, Missy!"

Embarrassed again, she apologized and tried to move away. "Now wait jest a minute. I saved ya from a spill, least ya can do is talk ta me." Emma looked up. The man holding her arm was older than she was by a quite a few years. His fair hair was trimmed neatly and his bright eyes were amused.

"I thank ya fer yer help. I can stand on my own now," Emma stated politely, and tried again to move away.

The man laughed out right but didn't release her. "Imagine ya could, but ya can never be too sure." He looked around the crowded store, before settling his eyes on Emma again. "Are ya married little Missy? Are ya hidin' a man around here?" He looked around the store again. Emma was tempted to lie, but knew her Mama would not approve. Looking for help from someone she knew, she realized that she was so short that she was mostly hidden behind the barrels of vegetables. She could see no one from her corner. She focused her attention on trying to back away from the man holding her arm, prying at his fingers.

Emma didn't notice that she had been moved until she found herself fully in the corner, looking at a man's back. "Pardon me ma'am," came the familiar voice. Looking up, she recognized the man from the door. With a small smile in her direction, he turned his attention to the shelves of food along the wall. Reaching up, he casually selected a coffee tin from a high shelf. As he brought his arm down to study the tin, his gaze settled on her face for a moment. The gray eyes again looked like a storm of emotions were brewing in them. Turning to the fair haired gentleman who had cornered her, he spoke carefully, "Ain't seen ya around town before. Ya here lookin' at that shipment of horses?" Her rescuer studied the tin of coffee in his hand, pretending not to notice the other man's annoyance.

"I ain't here ta look at anythin', 'cept a farm," came the irritated reply. After a moment of silence, the fair haired gentleman grudgingly asked, "Where are these horses?"

"Over ta the blacksmith corral. Northern rancher breaks 'em in real gentle. No finer horses." The gray eyed man absentmindedly handed the tin to Emma, "Well bred and tough stock. Rancher only brings 'em this way every couple of years." She found the stormy eyes on her once again before he turned completely away, pointing toward the door. "I'm headin' back there now. Can show the way iffen ya want ta see 'em."

Emma held her breath as she waited for the fair haired gentleman to answer. "Much obliged," he finally replied. She released her sigh of relief a little too quickly. The older gentleman leaned around her rescuer and smiled at her. "We'll continue our discussion when we meet again," he stated before he sauntered out the door. The man with the gray eyes followed him without another glance in her direction.

She rubbed her arm before walking toward the counter. As Emma approached, she realized that Mrs. Phelps was looking at the door the two gentlemen had just exited. She hesitantly continued towards her, hoping she would not have to answer any awkward questions. But the store keeper never noticed Emma's anxiety.

She was still staring toward the door. "Hmm... I don't think I've ever heard that boy talk before. Wouldna be surprised iffen the bank was getting robbed and he's the distraction," she muttered absently. Turning to see Emma watching her, Mrs. Phelps smiled, "Don't worry ya none, yer family doesn't have money at the bank. It wouldna hurt ya at all." She reached out to take Emma's list. "What did ya forget? If yer own Mama were here, she woulda reminded ya ta make a thorough list before comin' inta town the first time. But ya'll learn. Ya'll learn." Mrs. Phelps started gathering her items.

The other lady's words were still going around in Emma's mind. "He's the distraction." While Emma doubted the man was robbing the bank, she had to agree with the storekeeper. Thinking back through her recent trips to town, she realized that she knew of at least three times this man had distracted trouble away from her. "How many times has he helped me and I haven't been noticin'?" she wondered.

Emma paid for her purchases and carefully arranged them in her basket. Making sure the weight of the heavy packages were balanced, she headed toward the door and back toward home. Weaving in and out the people carefully, she didn't slow down until the last evidence of town disappeared behind her. She released a sigh of relief. Reaching up to untie her bonnet, she let the breeze cool her head.

"Well here we are again," called out a voice behind her.

Stiffening, Emma froze before turning toward the voice. The fair haired gentleman from the store was leading his horse in her direction. Another gentleman sat astride his horse, leaning over the saddle horn in an amused manner. The second man kept riding forward until he positioned his horse behind her. "I shoulda kept on walking," Emma thought miserably. Closing her eyes, she took a deep breath to steady her nerves.

"I can't believe my luck. Sure was happy to see ya walk past my horse. I was jest leavin' town myself. Now I can escort ya home," the stranger continued happily.

"You'll hafta excuse me, sir, I must be hurryin'. My Da will be expectin' me ta have dinner ready soon," Emma stated.

"Well then, we musn't keep him waitin'," he replied. There was a chuckle behind her. The fair haired gentleman smiled in response to his friend's laughter. "I'll come along with ya. Ya can introduce me, so I can git permission ta call on ya. Official like. We can git our courtin' started today."

"I believe ya misunderstood me, sir," Emma replied appalled.

"Misunderstood? Na, I think not. I see that ya waited fer me outside of town, so that we could walk together without all those busybodies watchin' us and interuptin'." Smiling, the man reached for her arm. Emma stepped back and bumped into the horse behind her. Feeling panic well up within her, she looked around for help and was amazed to see a pair of stormy eyes walking towards her.

From behind, Emma heard the man on the horse cleared his throat in warning. The fair haired gentleman stiffened in irritation as he turned towards the approaching man, demanding, "What do ya want now?"

Emma could not take her eyes off the approaching help, even though she knew it was rude to stare. The gray eyed man did not look away from her as he answered, "When this young lady fergot ta bring me my coffee before she left town, I started in ta worryin'."

Looking down into her basket, Emma realized that she had indeed purchased the tin of coffee the man had intended only as a distraction. "I fergot," she said weakly, trying to figure out why he would want the coffee she accidentally purchased.

Coming to stop a few steps from Emma, the gray eyed man smiled at her. "Ya steal a man's heart and then ya steal his coffee, darlin'?" He winked at her. "Ya go too far." The smile that touched his mouth, did not reach his stormy eyes. They tried to convey a meaning to her. A meaning that Emma could not quite grasp. "Ya shoulda waited fer me ta walk with ya. I've been wantin' ta speak with yer Pa," he paused briefly before continuing, "before the weddin'."

Gasping as his plan dawned on her, Emma ducked around the fair haired gentleman and reached for her rescuer's arm. He weaved her hand around his tense elbow and held it there. Wanting to look convincing in her new role, she desperately tried to remember how

Abigail had looked at her David all those months while they were courting. Opening her eyes wide, she batted her eyelashes. "Oh do forgive me darling," Emma said, attempting to mimic Abigail's sugary tone. She hoped no one would notice how her voice quivered.

Her rescuer leaned forward and, for a split second, Emma feared he would try to kiss her. But before she could pull away, he simply leaned his forehead against hers. He looked into her eyes for a long moment before replying, "Course I forgive ya," patting the hand tucked through his elbow.

Emma thought she saw fear flash through his eyes, before the strength returned to them. He glanced over at the gentlemen on their horses, as if he had forgotten they were still there. "Oh.. I thank ya gentlemen fer offerin' to escort my lady home, but I'll see to it. I do apologize fer yer trouble." He turned back as if to look at her, but angled his eyes so he could watch the angry man mount his horse. The gentleman stepped his horse closer to where Emma stood with her rescuer. He hesitated a moment before he reluctantly turned to join his friend and they rode away.

Her rescuer released a deep breath in relief as he watched them disappear around the road bend. "I'm glad ya caught at my meanin'. I wasn't sure I coulda protected ya against both if it came ta a fight," he stated quietly. The gray eyes turned to search her face. "Yer shakin' pretty bad, did they hurt ya?"

She shook her head slowly, not trusting her voice to be steady enough to speak. He loosened the grip holding her hand to his elbow, preparing to move away from her.

"NO!" Emma called out before she even realized she was going to protest. Embarrassed by her outburst, she hurried on explaining, "Please don't let go… in case they come back." She did not wish to admit that she still felt weak. That without his arm to lean on, she might not be able to walk home. He seemed to understand. When he didn't move away from her, she relaxed her hold. He reached over to take the heavy basket from her other arm and she let him. They walked along in awkward silence until Emma finally quit shaking.

When she could see the turn off to the farm up ahead, Emma felt relief flood through her. Thoughts of all the possible things that could have happened to her, ran through her mind. She shuddered. "Thank ya Lord fer sendin' this man ta protect me," she prayed silently. She looked over at her companion. His dark hair was long enough that it covered his eyes from the side, shielding most of his face from her view. "May I have yer name sir?" she requested and then added with a half smile, "Since we are intended?"

The young man looked up in alarm. When he realized she spoke in jest, he smiled shyly, "To most I am Young Hawkins, but as we are 'intended'," he paused looking down, "ya can call me Thane," finishing with a lopsided smile.

"Thane?" Emma repeated his name, as if she was considering it. "Yeah, I could see myself courting a 'Thane'," she decided and was rewarded with another smile. "I thank ya Thane, fer helpin' me today. I don't know how ta repay ya fer all yer trouble."

"Weren't no trouble ta escort a pretty lady home," he stated softly. "Especially one who agrees ta marry me after jest one meetin'," he finished with another lopsided grin.

Emma laughed outright. "I musta appeared pretty desperate ta ya," she stated, glancing sideways in his direction.

"Ya looked a mite worried was all." She felt his arm tense up, but he didn't look at her again.

When she could see the cabin down the lane, Emma stopped and released Thane's elbow. "Well Thane, I can see my house up ahead. I thank ya again fer yer assistance." Turning to face him, Emma asked curiously, "Did ya find the horse ya were lookin' ta buy?"

Thane looked at her surprised, "I've no need fer a new horse." Handing her the heavy basket, he touched his hat and disappeared into the woods.

The suddenness of his leaving left Emma feeling a little disoriented. Shaking her head to focus, she turned back toward the farm. Something in the basket caught her eye. She still had Thane's tin of coffee.

~Three~

Emma took the last cookies out of the oven and looked around the kitchen. Her purchases had been taken care of. The dishes, from making cookies, were all washed and dried. It seemed that she had some time to spare before she needed to make the evening meal.

Removing her apron, Emma headed out the back door. She walked past the garden and down the short path to the creek. At the end of the path, an area opened up that was well hidden from the farm's view. On a small hill, overlooking the slow moving creek, was a giant rock sitting next to a gravestone. The clearing was guarded by the hills that rose high above them and was completely surrounded by trees. It seemed to be secluded from the rest of the world.

Emma crossed to the large rock and knelt beside it. Pulling some overgrown weeds, she cleared the front of the gravestone. Once all the letters were visible, she ran her fingers along them. "Hello Mama," she greeted the stone, as she sat down in the grass. "I've had myself an excitin' day today. It worried me some at the time, but mostly jest left me ta thinkin'," she laughed softly. "Remember how ya used ta tell me I reminded ya of Mary in the Bible.. because I pondered so much? Well, I haven't been changin' much. Seems my mind is always busy thinkin' on somethin'." She turned, leaning against the rock atop the hill, so she could face her Mama's gravestone. "I don't think I'll be goin' back ta town `til I have ta. `Twas real busy, when I went today. Seems always ta be busy of late." She relaxed into the rock with a sigh. "But I met Thane taday. Ya'd like him. He doesn't say much, but he has a nice manner. Even calls me ma'am." She smiled at the memory. "He has the strangest eyes. I think they're supposed ta be blue, but they look mostly gray. Might sound strange-- but they're very calmin' ta look at. They've such sadness in 'em though. Ya know, he seems familiar Mama-- like I should know him -- but I don't know the name. Hawkins?" Leaning her head back against the stone, Emma closed her eyes as she told her mama about her excitement. "I don't know why he keeps helpin' me. No one else in town seems ta notice me. But whenever I find trouble, he's there." Talking to her mother had always helped her relax. As she explained about Thane, about her difficult situation, she found the tension from the long day leaving her body. Emma could almost feel herself fall asleep. She allowed the peacefulness of the woods and the sound of the creek to soak in.

Just as she felt sleep pull at her senses, she was aware of a warm presence next to her. Thinking it was the dog, who frequently came to sit next to her on the hill, Emma automatically reached her hand out to pet him. But instead of fur, she felt a muscular thigh. Her eyes flew open as she snatched her hand away. Emma watched Thane sprawl backwards in surprise. Just as quickly, Thane jumped to his feet, "Beg yer pardon ma'am," he muttered and turned to leave.

Scrambling to her feet as well, Emma called, "Wait!" Thane stopped at the tree line but stood facing away from her. Tilting her head to one side she asked, "What brings ya here?"

Keeping his eyes on his feet, he turned half toward her. Quietly he replied, "I came ta apologize fer my behavior earlier. I don't know what came over me ta act so bold and familiar with ya."

Emma repeated his words in her mind a couple times, confused by their meaning. "Ya saved me from a bad situation with unpleasant people," she paused before continuing on softer, "I'm not sure what I woulda done without yer bold rescue. I find nothin' fer ya ta apologize fer, Thane."

"Thank ya, ma'am!" He tipped his hat and turned to leave.

Emma's soft laughter caused Thane to pause again. "This morning we're gettin' married and now it's back to ma'am? What changed?" she teasingly asked.

Thane turned then to look at her fully, "Ma'am?"

"See? It's ma'am again. Why not my name?" Emma asked curiously. Humor lit up those stormy gray eyes. "Well ma'am, ya haven't given me yer name."

"Oh!" She felt herself blush. "I'm sorry Thane—I mean Mr. Hawkins—I'm Emma Fern or Miss Wells—but ya can jest call me Emma."

"It's jest Thane, ma'am," he said with a smile. Tipping his hat to her, Thane disappeared among the trees.

~Four~

"Amazing Grace, how sweet the sound," Emma sang as she squeezed the water out of the blanket she just scrubbed. Not even the fact that Seth had made extra work for her by falling asleep with his boots on, could dampen her spirits.

"It was an amazin' service yesterday," she told herself. "That's the reason I'm so light hearted today." She would not allow her thoughts to stray to Thane. To wonder if she would see him down by the crick again. "No," she silently reprimanded herself. "This back achin' chore is goin' by quickly because I am singin' the hymns from yesterday."

"'Twas Grace that taught my heart ta fear and grace my fears relieved," she sang on. "How precious did that Grace appear, thee hour I first believed."

Struggling to keep the end of the blanket off the ground, while draping the other end over the line, Emma stood on her toes and stretched. But her arms couldn't reach far enough to keep it on the line and she almost dropped it in the mud. Heart pounding, she decided to just hang it over the porch rail, when someone lifted the heavy blanket from her arms.

"Here let me help ya," Thane said so close to her ear that Emma jumped. "Uh—pardon me. I didn't mean to startle ya Ma'am," he said softly, stepping away from her side.

"No, I'm jest not used ta anyone helpin' me durin' the day. It's always so quiet here." Then she smiled, "Here ya are savin' me and apologizin' fer it again."

A smile touched his lips as he finished straightening the blanket on the line. "I shouldn't make a habit of it, Ma'am."

"It's Emma," she stated, raising her eyebrows. "I know `twas rude ta keep my name from ya before, but now ya have it. I willna know yer speakin' ta me iffen ya call me ma'am."

"It's terrible forward ta call a young lady by her given name. `Specially when she isn't attached ta me," Thane said softly.

"Maybe I won't let ya save me from any more embarrassin' situations. Iffen ya keep callin' me ma'am?" Emma teased, trying to keep her lips from smiling.

"I'd best be callin' ya Emma then," Thane stated with the hint of a smile.

"That's better." Emma smiled and handed him a pair of wrung out pants to hang up. "Besides we are gettin' married, remember? And if my unfortunate suitors come back, ya'll have more practice with my given name."

"Ya'll be Miss Wells ta the likes of them," Thane replied simply.

"Of course," she laughed softly. "Very practical, my dear."

As Thane reached for a flannel shirt in the tub, it dawned on Emma that she was wringing out her nightdress. She blushed as she tucked it back in the tub. Reaching for anything that wasn't white, she saw there was only one more colored garment. Trying to hide her embarrassment, she continued. "Um.. I was figurin' on eatin' my lunch down by the crick while the wash dries. Would ya care fer a bite?"

Thane was silent for a minute before he answered. "Wouldn't want to impose. I jest came ta help when I heard ya--."

"Ya heard me singin'?" Emma interrupted, mortified.

"Like an angel," he smiled. "Yer voice echoes through these hills."

"Get out of here," she insisted, pretending to be offended to cover her embarrassment. She pulled the shirt from his hands and shooed him toward the path. "Go, so I can finish hangin' my laundry in peace."

Smiling, Thane reached for another wet clothing item. He froze when he saw that the remaining clothes were all white. Pulling his hand back quickly, he turned to leave with a quiet, "Yes ma'am."

Emma fairly flew through the rest of the laundry, hanging her white clothes behind Seth's quilt so they couldn't be seen from the tree line near the path. Flipping the metal tub over the stump to dry, she ran into the house to make sandwiches for her family. And a picnic for two.

"I wish I had something delicious baked up," she thought to herself. Shaking her head to clear the regret, she reprimanded herself. "No use worryin' `bout what I can't change."

Grabbing the basket, she headed for the back field where she could hear the men working. As Emma passed the water bucket, left by the edge of the field, she noticed it was empty. She set down the basket, exchanging it for the bucket and headed back toward the house. She wondered if Thane would wait for her as she pulled the heavy bucket of water out of the well. Filling the bucket as full as she dared, she poured the rest back into the well. Mark met her to relieve her of the heavy bucket. She had no sooner retrieved the basket before it was gently taken from her as well. James smiled at her before he turned to follow her brother across the field to Da and Seth.

"Do ya think we should set fire ta that stump? It's not budgin' with the team," Mark asked their father as they approached. He took a sandwich from the basket and sat in the shade.

Da nodded, "It'll slow us down some, but be savin' the horses in the end."

"Our backs too," Mark agreed.

They continued to lay out their plans as they ate their sandwiches. Emma collected their towels into her basket and headed back toward the house.

By the time she walked back from the field and made it to the hill by the creek, she had convinced herself that Thane would have left by now. When she arrived, it was indeed vacant. Emma sat down in disappointment, but intent on looking carefree. "Well Mama, it looks as if I brought ya a sandwich."

"Ya've already given my sandwich away?" asked a voice that made her jump guiltily.

"Ah—No, of course not," Emma replied, willing her heart to slow down. "But I almost dropped it in the water, ya scared me so," she scolded. Thane sat down a couple paces from Emma. She handed him a sandwich, wrapped in a towel.

Thane took a bite of the sandwich. Looking thoughtful, he asked, "Ya gonna introduce me ta yer Mama?"

Emma looked up at him. She couldn't decide if he was making fun of her. Finding no hint of teasing in his face, she replied, "Mr. Hawkins meet my Mama, Lilliana Wells. Lily, to those that loved her. Mama, this is Mr. Hawkins.. He's taken ta savin' me lately. Even promised ta marry me ta protect me from an ugly mess," she ended with a smile.

"Pleasure ta meet ya ma'am. Please call me Thane."

"Mama wants ta know where ya come from that we shouldna know ya already? We thought we knew everyone here in the valley," Emma asked innocently.

"Well ma'am, I live in those hills," nodding his head across the creek, "tucked in a valley. I come this way a couple times a year but spend most my time on the trail huntin' and trappin'."

"So yer a trapper?" Emma asked between bites.

"Yes, ma'am."

"Call me Emma –," she reminded him.

"Beggin yer pardon, ma'am, I thought I was talkin' ta yer Mama," he said with a lopsided smile.

She chose to ignore his teasing and looked toward the hills.

"Yer mama seems ta belong in this spot," Thane observed.

"She does," she stated simply. "A fever took her and my baby sister ta heaven a few years back." Her final words were barely above a whisper.

"I'm sorry," Thane said softly.

Emma blinked back a tear before she looked at him.

"Where is yer sister's stone?" he asked.

"Isn't one. She was so small, I couldna bear fer her ta be put by herself. Mama had wanted her so. And Da-- well he couldna bear ta name her. So she sleeps in Mama's arms, here in Mama's favorite spot." She waved her arm to indicate the hill top overlooking the little creek. "Da brought this rock here. When he dug it up outta the cornfield – he decided ta roll it here so Mama wouldna have grass stains on all her skirts. She always was sittin' in the grass. She tried ta make them stop before they hurt themselves. But Da had jest teased how "embarrassed" he was ta have a wife with green dresses. She finally relented then...but wouldna come down here fer weeks," Emma laughed sadly. "But when she did, she sat on the rock." She paused, remembering. "She kept one skirt with an especially bad grass mark though. She hung it right in their room. It's hangin' there still. Da won't even let me wash it." She didn't notice the tears on her cheeks until Thane handed her his towel.

"What about yer Ma?" Emma asked, trying to lighten the mood as she dried her cheeks. "Will I know her if she's in town? Or will I have ta wait `til the weddin'?"

Thane looked back towards the hills. "Awhile beyond that, I expect," he answered softly. "My Ma died when I was young. We went out trappin' and when we returned.. she was gone."

"Oh," Emma replied, not knowing what to say. "How old were ya?"

"Not sure really. Probably 9 winters ago."

"Ya don't know how old ya are?" Emma asked incredulously.

Thane shrugged his shoulders. "Pa doesn't keep track of such things-says they're nonsense. I stopped askin'."

Wiping her eyes again, she cleared her throat. "Maybe we should jest start plannin' our weddin' before I start cryin' again."

Thane nodded. He picked a nearby weed and slowly peeled it.

"We should wait till after Harvest," she said jokingly.

"Probably best," Thane answered, following her lead. "At least with no sisters ya won't have ta worry about anyone being prettier than ya."

Emma turned and studied Thane's face carefully before she answered him. "I'm content being plain, ya know."

"Plain?" he asked, tilting his head in question as he looked up at her.

"Yup plain. Not pretty enough ta talk ta but not ugly enough that dogs bark," she laughed.

"Ya aren't plain," Thane spoke a little lower than normal. "Who would say that ta ya?"

"I figured it out on my own. No one notices me unless I talk or move. Kind of like a shadow. I don't stand out. My coloring isn't light enough ta be called fair, not dark enough ta be pretty. Even my eyes don't have enough of a color ta stand out." Emma shrugged as she turned to look at him. "I'm jest plain."

"They don't notice ya? I've seen plenty of men notice ya," Thane pointed out. She noticed that he looked almost angry.

"Thane, I like bein' plain. I never wanted all the extra attention other girls asked fer. I like the solitude," she assured him.

Thane studied her face before looking around her hill, at her mama's grave and then back to Emma. "Ya seem lonely to me."

Emma was surprised. No one had noticed her mood before. She looked away. "It does get lonely. But havin' people around me doesn't make me feel less lonely. Only-," she paused, "only more plain."

They sat in silence. The only sound was the water in the creek.

Finally, Thane cleared his throat, "Maybe we should go back to plannin our weddin' – before I get any more angry." Repeating her phrase from earlier, he tried to lighten the mood.

Emma started to laugh but stopped as she looked toward him. He smiled back but she noticed it didn't quite reach his eyes. "Oh… Thane. Please don't be angry with me," she quickly pleaded with him, "I need ta go in soon and it would ruin this lovely day."

"Emma," Thane started, but stopped himself. He clearly wanted to say something. Watching her closely for a moment, he seemed to change his mind. "I could never be angry with ya."

She let out a sigh of relief, as she started folding the towels to put back in the basket. "So I guess ya jest need to decide if ya need ta have a bride in white or would settle fer a simpler dress that could be worn again?" She stood up and shook her skirt.

Standing, Thane lifted the basket and handed it to her. "I'll be leavin' that decision ta you… As long as ya let me know when yer goin' ta town again. I may need ta get some supplies," he said with a small smile.

"Yer jest worried that someone else'll try ta walk me home," Emma accused him playfully. Carefully balancing her basket on one hip, she tried, unsuccessfully, to keep the smile from her face.

"Yes ma'am," he admitted easily.

She studied his face a minute, "Well, I don't go ta town every week, but when I need ta, I like ta go on Thursdays."

"Thursdays?" he repeated in question.

"Yes sir, Mr. Hawkins," she stated with a smile.

Thane asked curiously, "Why Thursday?"

Emma was startled by the question. She was not used to anyone asking her why she did things. "I guess it's because it isn't as busy as Fridays or Saturdays, but late enough in the week so I can have a good list. I can do my shoppin' without all the fuss."

Thane nodded in understanding. "Thank ya fer the picnic lunch." Tipping his hat to her, "Good day, ma'am."

She watched him walk toward the trees, until she felt rude for staring. "Good day, Thane." Turning, she headed up the path to the house. When she reached the bottom step, she realized she still hadn't given him his coffee.

~Five~

The snap of a stick broke the silence. Emma's head jerked up as she looked toward the path. But the pathway was empty. The woods around the path were empty as well. Blowing out her held breath, Emma turned back to the sheet she was pinning to the clothes line. It had been a week since she had shared a picnic with Thane on the hillside. For that week, she had turned hopefully at every sound. But every time she turned, she found nothing. "Goodness," she chided herself silently. "He never said he was comin' again."

"Emma?" called a voice uncertainly.

Emma stepped out from behind the sheets on the line. "Yes?" Looking around, as she answered, she finally saw James standing near her wash tub.

His uncertainty changed to a relieved smile as she stepped into view. "I'm headin' back to the shop jest now. Yer Da said fer ya not ta bring dinner out ta the fields today. They'll be in ta eat before they start cuttin' hay." James laughed nervously. "Ya had me alarmed when ya weren't in the kitchen," he admitted.

"Can't scrub clothes in the kitchen," Emma stated simply.

"Thet's true," James agreed with another laugh.

Emma grabbed the last sheet out of the washtub. "Yer not stayin' ta eat with us?" Disappearing behind the line of sheets, she flipped the last sheet over the rope. Slowly inching it down until it was smooth, she pinned it in place.

Emma stepped back into the open, not sure she would find James still there. But there he stood, twirling his hat in his hands.

When he saw her walking toward him, he placed his hat back on his head. "Naw, I'm not needed fer hayin' today. I'll be headin' back ta help my Pa."

"If yer sure?" Emma reached for the washboard to prop it next to the back steps. Turning back around she saw that James was already carrying the heavy washtub to the woods to empty it. "Why thank ya James! Emptyin' that tub is such a chore after all the scrubbin'." She took the empty tub from him and flipped it over the stump to dry.

"Ya should jest leave it fer one of us ta get then," James suggested. "It's too heavy fer ya ta lift by yerself."

Emma laughed, "I've been liftin' it since I was eleven or so. Not gonna hurt me none, I reckon." She turned toward the house again. She picked up the washboard and hung it over the nail on the outside wall. "Will we be seein' ya tomorrow?"

"Yea, I'll be back ta help stack the hay tomorrow."

"Good day ta ya then, James." Emma gave him a wave and turned toward the door. She needed to start cooking if she wanted dinner ready before her family came looking to eat.

"Emma?" James called out suddenly.

Curious, she turned around again. His hat was in his hands again. The twirling motion made her think he was nervous. "Yes?"

"I was wonderin'," he began. "I-." He stopped to clear his throat, before he tried again. "I noticed that yer big pot has a loose handle. I'd like ta take it with me ta fix. Iffen ya can spare it, that is."

Emma blinked her eyes in surprise. "Ah, yeah. I can spare it." A little embarrassed that he knew how rickety her pot was, she went on, "I tried ta fix it, but couldn't figure it out. Was gonna ask my Da ta look at it."

"I can fix it up fer ya. I'll bring it back ta ya in the mornin', most likely," James offered, helpfully.

"Jest let me go git it fer ya, then." Entering the kitchen, Emma grabbed the pot off the stove where she had set it to dry. Returning outside, James met her halfway and reached for it.

"What are ya doin' Emma?" James and Emma turned to see Mark walking their way. "James is busy enough without lookin' at yer pot."

"He offered ta fix it," Emma replied, feeling offended that her brother assumed she had prompted it. "I wouldna have asked him ta do it."

James interrupted her brother's reply. "I saw that it's been gettin' looser every day. I know how ta fix it."

"Ya offered ta fix her pot?" Mark repeated with a suspicious smile.

"Yea," James answered, his ears turning red.

Emma looked between the two boys confused. Shaking her head, she finally stated, "I'm goin' in ta cook. See ya in the mornin' James." With a nod in his direction, she turned for the house.

"He's fixin' yer pot and ya won't even invite him ta stay ta dinner?" Mark asked incredulously.

Emma froze on the steps.

James interrupted, "Emma already asked me ta stay, I told her I needed ta get back ta town."

"Yea, so ya told me. Yet I find ya still here. Offerin' ta fix a pot," Mark said.

Emma studied her brother's face. She was confused by the whole conversation. Not wanting anyone to think her rude, she repeated her offer from earlier. "Would ya like ta stay ta eat with us, James? It wouldna be any trouble ta set another plate?" Her eyes never left Mark's face. She didn't see James studying her. Jest found herself more confused by her brother's raised eyebrow.

"That'd be fine. Iffen it's no trouble?" James answered.

"No trouble at all," Emma stated. Relieved that James staying seemed to please her brother, she turned to go inside. Suddenly exhausted, she couldn't wait for dinner to be over, so she could relax by the creek before taking the laundry down.

~Six~

The smell of smoke reached Emma's nose. Confused for a moment, she looked around the farmyard. "Where's it coming from?" she wondered aloud. As the words left her mouth, she remembered the cookies she had put in the oven. "Oh no!" she gasped. Emma quickly headed for the door and raced inside. Her broom hit the floor as it missed the chair she tried to prop it against. Grabbing a towel, she pulled the cookies through the small oven door. Just as she feared, they were dark brown.

Emma's mind had been far away all morning as she had gone about her morning cleaning. She had forgotten to take the broom outside with her to beat the rugs that were hanging on the line. She had forgotten to take the bowl of corn to the coop with her to feed the chickens. And she had completely forgotten the cookies she had been baking. Dumping them onto the plate with the first golden brown ones, she pushed the pan to the back of the stove so it would not burn any worse. Emma pressed her hands against her forehead in exasperation.

"Is there something wrong with the stove Em?" her brother asked as he came into the kitchen. Seth was heading straight for the washtub when he saw the plate of cookies. "Cookies!" he exclaimed and grabbed one. He paused from taking a bite when he noticed the color. "Oh! They're burnt? Need me ta look at the stove after dinner?" he asked around bites.

"Dinner?" Emma jumped into action. The cookie mess had distracted her from what time it was.

"Jest make somethin' cold, then I can be fixin' the stove when we're done eatin'," he suggested, taking the plates from Emma and setting them on the table.

She was tempted to use his suggestion as the explanation for the burnt cookies but knew her Mama would be disappointed. Emma shook her head. "There's nothing wrong with the stove, Seth. I jest got busy beatin' the rugs and fergot ta remember the time," she explained without meeting her brother's eye.

Seth stopped moving and turned to Emma. "Ya fergot?" he echoed back to her. "Ya never ferget," he stated while studying her. "Ya never burn anythin'."

Her cheeks reddened, as she replied simply, "I was distracted." She focused her concentration on getting the ham sliced so it could be frying.

"Distracted?" he repeated slowly. "Yer never distracted."

"It happens..," Emma said with a shrug. "Ya fergot ta latch the gate one night and let all the hogs out, if I remember? They got inta the corn. We had ta round 'em up by lantern light," she pointed out, finally looking up at him.

"Yeah," Seth agreed. "But that's me. I ferget stuff all the time. Ya never ferget ta do anythin'," he stared at her curiously until she turned away to finish setting the table. "Well, since dinner isn't ready ta eat yet, I'll go back an' help. I'll take some cookies out ta – ah -- distract them all from hunger," he chuckled as he went out the door, letting it slam shut behind him.

Emma blew out the breath she had been holding. She had fought the distraction all morning and not won against it. "Thank the good Lord rugs can't get burned on the line and ya can't wear a hole in the floor sweeping the same spot over and over." She kept finding herself wondering if Thane would walk up. When he didn't show up day after day, she found herself wondering where he was, and what he was doing. Wondered if he wanted to stop by.

She shook her head to clear it and focus. "It's not as if we are actually gettin' married," she reminded herself. "Thane told me he only comes ta town a couple times a year. He never said he was comin' back." Emma forced herself to think of the meal she was preparing. She couldn't be standing in the same spot when Mark came back in with the other men. She would never hear the end of the teasing if she was.

The men came in for their meal just as Emma finished frying up the ham slices. They were full of laughter as they washed up. Seth started in on teasing her about being distracted and "those poor burnt cookies." The others soon joined in. Only James refrained from teasing her. But he joined their laughter easy enough.

On the way out the door to return to the fields, Seth took a cookie from each pile. He winked mischievously, "I won't be neglectin' these cookies the way ya did." Mark and Da laughed at her embarrassment. They each grabbed cookies as they followed Seth out the door. Only James hesitated slightly before taking cookies with him. She shooed them all out the door so she could clean up.

She would have things straightened in no time, she decided. As long as she kept herself from wondering about Thane.

~*~*~*~*~*~*~*~*~*~*~*~*~*~

The next day came with more sunshine and a cool breeze. She managed to cook breakfast without burning anything. After scrubbing the pans, she decided to walk down and sit on Mama's hill. She dumped the dish pan water out in the brush and set it on the step to dry in the sun. Wiping her hands on her apron, she slowly walked down the path. Emma slowed her step as she sensed movement from the hilltop. As she peered around the last tree, she saw Thane setting something against her Mama's stone. He squatted in front of the gravestone looking closely at it. She stopped moving to watch him until he turned.

When Thane caught sight of her, he stood up, pulling off his hat. He motioned to the purple flowers he had placed on the ground and stepped back. "I was thinkin' on what ya asked. I think that a simple weddin' dress, like the color of that pretty flower, would be best. Then whenever ya wore it again, yer man would remember yer happy day. A white dress would jest stay in the bottom of a trunk somewhere an' wouldn't mean as much."

Thane spoke so softly, that Emma wasn't sure she heard him correctly. She was surprised that he had remembered her off-handed question. He had obviously put a lot of thought into it. She repeated the words over in her head, before replying. "It sounds as if ya've been in love before."

He looked off toward the hills, "No ma'am. Can't say I know what love looks like."

Emma walked over to her mother's rock. She reached over and picked up the flowers as she sat down, tucking her dress around her ankles. "I always think love looks like my parents," she smiled softly as he finally looked her way. "Doing the small stuff every day happily. Like my Da rolling a rock ta a hilltop. Or Da painting the shutters white on the cabin, when he realized they weren't goin' ta be able ta build a bigger house. My Mama always baking Da's favorite food. Never complaining when we did without."

Thane sat down a short distance from her. He looked very thoughtful. "My Pa loved my Ma somethin' fierce. When she died, so did he." He plucked a long blade of grass and slowly pulled it apart. "He started drinkin' and never stopped. Put everything that reminded him of her inta a trunk and hid it away. It's the only look at love I've ever had."

Emma watched Thane's face as he talked and felt the sadness of every word. "Is that the Annie he's lookin' fer?" she asked, even though she was fairly sure she already knew the answer.

When he turned to find her studying him, he cleared his throat and looked out over the hills. Nodding he answered, "Her name was Annabel. Only Pa called her Annie."

Emma remained quiet for another minute. She wasn't sure she could speak around the lump in her throat as she ached for this young man. Finally, she spoke, "My mama always said that everything has a season, everything has a reason. Even when we don't know the reason, it happens as part of God's plan. When she got sick, she said it more. 'As for God, His way is perfect,' she would quote." The wind blew the strands of hair that had fallen with her morning work. She tucked them behind her ear. "When she died, Da said we'd live so she'd be proud of us, until we could be see'n her again in Heaven. That's how we've lived ever since."

She followed Thane's gaze towards her Mama's stone. "Ya believe there's a Heaven? That there's a God?" he asked.

"Yes," Emma stated simply, then quietly added, "Mama said God is always there. That His hand shapes our lives fer a purpose. Everythin' has a reason, guidin' us along God's unknown path."

"Everythin' fer a reason?" Thane repeated. "So what would be our reason fer meetin'? The reason fer talkin' about God by a crick on a summer morn?"

Emma checked to see if there was teasing in Thane's face. When she found none, she answered, "Maybe it's ta show me that yer pa is proof my Da was right. Ta never let us give in ta our grief. Maybe it'll somehow shape our days in a way we'll never know." A smile played at her lips, "Maybe God sent someone ta ask me tough questions ta keep me lively in my Faith."

"Maybe it's fer me," Thane commented softly.

"Could be," Emma acknowledged.

"Never had anyone ta talk ta. I always wondered if I thought God was real only cuz I needed someone. Always wondered iffen He was really there."

"He's real," Emma confirmed. "And only God knows the reason for the path He puts us on. The reasons fer the gifts He brings ta us," she paused before adding, "Or takes away."

Thane nodded. After a couple minutes of comfortable silence, he rose and dusted off his clothes. "Best be goin' about my work or God'll be thinkin' I'm takin' His gift fer granted."

Emma laughed, "I don't think He'll be mistakin' ya fer lazen about." She started to stand when Thane offered her his hand. She accepted it, and he easily pulled her to her feet. She gave his callused hand a slight squeeze, to thank him, before releasing it.

"Ma'am," Thane said, with a nod of his head and a touch to his hat. He turned and entered into the woods.

"Thane?" Emma called out to him. "Do ya -?" but then paused embarrassed.

Thane stepped back into the clearing. "If yer worried 'bout offendin' me.. ya needn't be. Jest ask. I'll answer ya."

Emma looked down at her hands. They were pressed against her stomach. Trying to appear more relaxed, she moved them to her sides. "I was jest wonderin' when ya'd have time ta visit again."

His chuckle warmed her cheeks. She looked up and saw a smile twinkling in his eyes. "Are ya askin' me ta be knowin' God's unknown plan?" Thane asked.

Emma returned his laugh, "Guess I was."

With a tip of his hat, he answered, "As soon as God permits." And then Thane disappeared among the trees.

Emma watched the trees sway in the wind near where she had last seen him. She looked down to the purple flowers still in her hand. Mama's favorite flowers. "Best be gettin' these in water," she thought, and turned towards the house.

As she approached the back stairs, something wet touched her hand. "Hello there Dawg." Emma bent to scratch behind his ears. "Are ya done in the fields fer today then?" The dog sat contentedly by her leg as she looked toward the barn to see if her family had returned from the fields as well. "Come on Dawg," she called as she set off for the barn.

She could hear voices, before she could see anything in the dark barn. She blinked her eyes three times to help them adjust from the bright sunshine.

"Ya needin' help Em'?" Mark asked from the shadows.

Rubbing her eyes, she headed to the back corner of the barn where her brother's voice came from. "No. I was jest comin' ta see what brought ya in so early," she replied. As her eyes became used to the soft light, she could see that all four men were looking into the corner stall.

Mark stepped closer to her side, "Da's worried about ole' Bess. She seems ta be havin' a hard time with this calf. He's not sure it's turned," he explained quietly. Just then the cow let out a loud bawling sound.

"Oh!" Emma could feel her stomach tighten. "I'll be lettin' ya get back ta it then." Turning quickly, she fled the barn. Once she was in the bright sunshine, she took a deep breath. It wasn't until Mark laughed that she realized he followed her outside.

"The cow'll be fine, Em'," Mark stated. "Ya worry too much."

Seth came through the barn door behind Mark, squinting in the bright light. "Why'd ya run out Em'?" Seth teased. Both of her brothers knew that Emma couldn't stomach seeing the animals in pain. Mark was more sympathetic than Seth. But not by much.

"I wish I could stay out here so ya could tease me more, but I've some flowers ta put in water," Emma stated.

"Never did understand yer likin' those flowers. They're a weed. We pull 'em outta the fields all season," Seth laughed.

Emma looked at her little brother closely. "They were Mama's favorite," she explained, "She used ta say how much she admired 'em. That, even though, no one pampered them or took care of them, they fought ta grow anywhere their seeds landed. Whether or not they were near water, or had enough sunlight. No matter iffen they were crowded or all by themselves. Mama always said we could learn a lot from 'em," she finished barely above a whisper.

Her older brother nodded thoughtfully as he listened. "Maybe ya should hang them ta dry. That way ya can keep them longer than a day or two," he suggested quietly.

Emma smiled, "Maybe I should." She lifted the flowers to her nose to smell them. "Well, I'd best be getting supper ready." She turned toward the house, to go inside.

Seth's voice stopped her. "Why is it yer rememberin' Mama lately? More'n ya used ta?"

Emma stood quietly while she repeated his question in her mind. Turning her head to the side, she answered over her shoulder. "I've always been rememberin' Mama," she stated slowly. "Maybe because I spent every day with her? She was always sharin' her thoughts on every day chores – everyday problems. So I see her in everythin' I do, everywhere I go. An' now, -- now what she was sayin' is startin' ta make sense ta me." She looked down at the flowers in her fingers. "Mama always said that we live in the sunlight but are guided by the shadows. I think I was livin' in the shadows -- missin' the sunlight. It's like how the sun is blocked out by the trees – and a shadow is left behind. That's what it was like fer me –losin' Mama -- like the sunlight was blocked by the trees – and all I'd left were the shadows."

No one spoke. Only quiet met Emma's ears. She continued on up to the house. When she put her foot on the bottom step, her brother cleared his throat.

"I guess ya never saw it," Mark responded quietly. "We did. Mama left her light in you."

Emma's eyes filled with tears. Not trusting her voice to speak, she nodded her head to acknowledge that she had heard him. She climbed the stairs and went into the house.

When she reached the kitchen cupboard, she pulled out a ball of string. The ball was made up of the different sized string that had held together packages from the mercantile over the years. The ball that Emma's mother had taught her to wind. She unwound a small piece and tied the stems of her flowers together. Then making a loop in the other end, she slipped it over the nail holding up her Mama's homemade curtains.

Emma smiled for a moment, remembering Mama telling her about the many uses of string. Then she stoked the fire and set about getting supper on the table.

~Seven~

Gathering all her supper scraps into her scrap bucket, Emma headed for the chicken yard. Easily opening the gate with her free hand, she stepped into the fenced area. Grabbing a handful of green bean snips and potato peels, she tossed them gently out onto the ground. "Here ya are ladies. Yummy treats fer ya," she laughed as two young hens struggled with the same peel. Tossing another handful near them, both hens let go and grabbed something new. Shaking her head at their nonsense, she was startled by a peck at her boot. Jumping to the side, Emma scowled at the rooster standing where her feet had been. He reached over and again pecked at the buttons on her boot. "Ya dumb bird. I'd think - by now - ya'd know they're jest buttons. Ya can't eat 'em."

"Ya'd think - by now - that ya'd know it makes no sense ta try ta reason with them birds," Mark laughed. "I still see ya try every day though."

Emma turned with a scowl. "He's gonna ruin my boots." Looking down at the young rooster, she warned, "Yer gonna end up as dinner iffen ya do." Just as she finished her threat, chaos broke loose in the chicken yard. The dog ran past her, barking loudly. Chickens went flying in all directions, colliding with each other and into Emma. The chickens finally escaped into the coop, leaving a cloud of feathers and dust behind them.

Seth's boisterous laugh brought his sister's full attention to him. "Ya shoulda seen yer face, Em'," he choked out between the laughter. "Yer eyes were as big as those chickens dashin' about."

"Seth Wells! Did you open the gate fer THAT Dawg?" she demanded.

"Naw, I jest gave it a nudge. He mostly had it worked out hisself," he insisted, taking a deep breath. He turned his attention to something behind her. "Look at that."

Turning back, she saw the young rooster circling the dog. In spite of the warning growl, the rooster was ready to defend his yard. He boldly lunged toward the dog's nose. When the dog lunged at the same moment, snapping his teeth in a bark, the rooster spooked and ran for the coop door.

Seth erupted in laughter again. Mark joined him as he watched the retreating chicken.

Trying to look stern, Emma scolded her brothers, "Iffen they lay no eggs fer yer breakfast tomorrow, ya've no one ta blame but yerselves." Turning away to shoo the dog out the gate, she found it hard to contain her smile.

"Maybe that rooster'll finally learn not ta peck at yer boots," Mark suggested.

~*~*~*~*~*~*~*~*~*~*~*~*~*~

The next morning, Emma mixed up a batch of flapjacks to go with the usual scrambled eggs. She washed her dishes as she went along, so that cleanup after breakfast would go quickly. She wanted to make it to town and back before the day could get too hot.

The boys ate quickly, without much talk that morning and joined their father in the fields. Emma finished up the chores and changed her clothes to head to town.

She read through her list one more time. Double checking anything the boys could have gotten into. Satisfied that it was complete, she grabbed her basket of eggs.

Regardless of the chaos in the coop yard the day before, the chickens continued to produce more eggs than her family could eat. Even with James buying eggs from her every week, the extra eggs that the spring chickens were laying left Emma with a basket full left over. She decided it was time to take them to town with her to see if Mrs. Phelps would buy them.

Tying a bonnet on, she stepped out into the sun. Usually Emma dreaded going to town. But today the thought that Thane might be there looking out for her, made it seem less threatening. Smiling as she thought of all the times she had seen him around town, not knowing who he was then. Emma wondered if she would see him today.

The road before her curved away from the farm and toward town. Her house disappeared from view behind the trees. The trees were starting to look dry from the warm weather. As the wind blew softly, it kicked up a small cloud of dust. Emma fanned her hand in front of her face, careful to not disturb the eggs in her basket. She watched as a hawk circled above her. It let out a loud call. The call was meant as a warning, but Emma let the sound echo through her mind. It sent a thrill through her. "Wonder if he's tellin' me I was too close ta his nest," she thought.

"Appears it's God's plan that I go ta town taday," Thane said as he fell into step beside her.

Emma jumped at his sudden appearance, not hearing his quiet step. She pressed her hand to her mouth to keep from crying out.

"Pardon me, ma'am," Thane apologized as he moved back a step. "I didn't mean ta scare ya."

"Well Mr. Hawkins," Emma stated pointedly, "I'm not used ta people sneakin' up on me."

Thane gave her a lop-sided smile. "No sneaking necessary. Ya were deep in thought."

"I was watchin' the hawk fly over me," Emma retorted. "Musta got too close ta its nest."

Thane shaded his eyes to look up at its retreating form. "He likely thought ya'd be a good meal. Until he saw he couldn't carry ya away."

"So what brings ya ta town?" Emma asked as they resumed walking.

"Besides coffee?" he teased.

"Oh," she cried out. "I never gave ya yer tin of coffee."

"Twern't mine. Ya paid fer it with yer family's money," Thane corrected. "I can repay ya fer it, iffen ya won't be needin it."

"That tin wouldna last long with my Da and brothers. Especially with James eating near every day. Ya're welcome ta it," Emma assured him.

He nodded. "I'm needin' ta visit the blacksmith. An animal keeps knockin' my trap apart. This time it broke the pin. I'm hopin' he has somethin' that'll fit it. I need ta be gittin' it set back up," Thane paused, running his hand on the back of his neck as he looked at her. "I suppose trappin' isn't proper ta talk about with a lady. Sorry."

Emma looked at him thoughtfully. "I don't see any harm in it. I'm not squeamish," she paused, "I could ask in town iffen it's proper discussion fer a lady?"

His chuckle brought her focus back to him. "That'd be an interestin' talk, wouldn't it?"

She smiled at his laugh. "Indeed."

"So what kind of cookies did yer brother ask fer this week?"

Emma blushed as she remembered her burnt cookies. "None this time," she answered truthfully. "He seems ta be busy with other things." Not caring to explain Seth's almost constant teasing, she instead explained all the work the men were doing to the new field.

Thane listened carefully, only asking occasional questions. "Is James a cousin?"

"No. He's a friend of Mark's from their school years. Loves ta come out and help farm. Guess it gives him a break from town," she said with a shrug, too confused at the fascination herself to offer a better explanation.

"Seems like a lot of work fer ya ta be feedin' an extra mouth every day," Thane stated thoughtfully.

"Well he does a lot of work every day. Seems like the least I can do. `Sides he doesn't eat as much as Mark or Seth. Mostly, I cook the same, jest with none left after the meal is over," she replied, realizing that no one ever asked her if she minded the extra work. "Only difference bein', James is more thankful than the others."

Thane nodded. They grew quiet as they approached town. When Thane turned onto the blacksmith's path, Emma watched him until he disappeared through the door. She looked around guiltily to see if she needed to explain why she was walking with a man in town. But no one seemed to notice.

Emma continued on to the mercantile. Soon her eggs were sold and the purchased pantry items tucked in their place in the basket. Emma turned to leave the store with a quiet, "Thank you," to the storekeeper. Thane opened the door to enter, just as Emma was approaching it to leave. Realizing she was finished, Thane stepped back outside to let her pass.

Before she could step through, her friend Abigail hurried into the store and stopped directly in front of her. Emma felt her smile freeze on her lips. Abigail reached out, taking Emma's hand in hers. "Oh Emma! How are ya today? Can ya believe how hot it is this week? I've been jest miserable, but I'd never tell David. When ya plan ta start a family, make sure it isn't in the summer. I'm sure it'd be worse fer ya as a farmer's wife. But I can't complain, I'm so excited. Ya need ta stop by and see all of the adorable things we've been collectin' fer our little man." She leaned closer to Emma, "I'm so sure that it'll be a little man after all. David says he won't mind a girl, but I know he really wants a boy ta tag along side him," she giggled and leaned away again.

Emma smiled in response. Abigail took her smile as encouragement and continued to catch her up on everything new in her life. After several minutes of listening to her friend's happiness spill into her words, Emma shifted the heavy basket in her hand. Watching Abigail wave her hands gracefully as she talked, reminded her of their childhood friendship. Emma remembered how happy, clean, and beautiful her friend had been every day. Abigail always had boys vying for her attention. She had sometimes thought Abigail had preferred her as a friend because she didn't have to fear competition with Emma's plain looks. Her eyes wandered over to where Thane was looking at hardware. She wondered if he agreed that she was plain next to Abigail's dark haired beauty. When Thane looked up and caught her gaze, he smiled before moving to the counter.

"And ya need ta promise me that ya'll come over and hold my baby all the time, until ya get one of yer own," Abigail words brought

Emma's attention back. She finished up with a sympathetic squeeze to her still captured hand, "Cuz no one knows when that'll be."

Thane's quick glance her way caught Emma's attention. Puzzled by what he was thinking, she returned her friend's squeeze and pulled her hand free. "When Harvest is over, I'll come over and ya can show me everythin'. We'll have a nice long visit then. But I really must be goin'."

"Ya MUST come fer the whole day when ya do come. Ta make it up ta me fer makin' me wait so long," Abigail said with a pout.

"I'll do my best." Emma responded politely, sounding stiff even to herself. Promising to see her soon, she stepped around her friend and walked out of the store.

Thane quickly fell into step with her once they were in the street but waited until they left town behind before he spoke. "Do ya not like children?" he asked softly.

Surprised, Emma turned to him, letting the question sink in. Turning back to the road, she continued walking. "I like children jest fine. I don't spend much time with them, but I don't mind 'em."

"Do ya not want kids of yer own?" he rephrased his question.

Emma took a slow deep breath and pressed her hand to her stomach. Thane reached over and took the heavy basket from her. "Ya don't have ta tell me." He turned his attention ahead, wishing he had not asked what was on his mind.

Emma looked over at Thane. She could see his embarrassment. Drawing in a shaky breath, she explained quietly, "Having kids of my own makes me nervous. The last childbirth I saw didn't end well. I know that there is a season fer death—and a reason— Still it makes me nervous," Emma smiled weakly at him. "I guess it's okay ta discuss this with ya, since we're intended," she teasingly added to lighten the mood.

Startled, Thane looked over at Emma. He rubbed his neck, embarrassed again. "Sorry, I'm not used ta talkin' ta anyone polished."

Emma laughed aloud, "A farmer's daughter is hardly polished."

"Anyone proper then," Thane amended with a lopsided smile. He took a few steps in silence, before asking again, "Are ya worried about yer friend's condition?"

Emma looked over at Thane, then back ahead again. Guessing that he had heard a great deal of her conversation with Abigail, she responded carefully. "I'm worried enough about her, I guess. But mostly, I'm a selfish creature, and a little too proud," she paused in her explanation, keeping her eyes straight ahead. "Abigail brags about all that she has while remindin' me that I may never have a family. I've accepted that my chances at marryin' aren't good. I jest choose ta avoid Abigail because she takes pleasure in pointin' it out." Emma pressed her hand to her stomach again. Realizing she wasn't being fair, she knew she needed to change her statement. "Of course, she doesn't really take pleasure in it. My pride's jest hurtin'. I need ta keep prayin' fer my heart ta be more forgivin'," Emma finished softly.

Emma could feel Thane's gaze on her, but she couldn't bear to see what he thought of her confession. The silence between them was accented with the sound of their steady footsteps.

Finally, Thane broke the silence. Clearing his throat, he started speaking, "It'll be a few days before I return this way. I have ta fix my trap so I can re-set my line. And keep an eye on 'em."

Emma closed her eyes and nodded. She could feel his disappointment at her selfishness. They both continued on in silence. When they reached the farmhouse, Emma reached out to take the heavy basket from Thane's outstretched hand. When he didn't release it right away, she looked up at him questioningly.

"Emma yer heart isn't selfish," Thane said softly. "It's jest hurt that a friend would be so cruel, even if she feels it ta be the truth." Emma felt her eyes fill up with tears. He let the basket rest on her arm and let go. "I'll be back when my traps are taken care of." He touched his hat and disappeared into the woods.

As his shadow disappeared into the trees, Emma felt alone.

~Eight~

The reading at church, that Sunday, was from the prophet Jeremiah. It reminded the captives that God had plans for them. The words in the Bible said He has plans to give everyone hope and a future. Emma felt that the words were directed at her that morning. She could hear the words echo through her mind, long after service was over.

Once outside, the boys had gathered next to the church steps to make their plans. They weren't the same plans that the Bible referred to in the reading that they just heard though. The boys were all planning the Harvest Church Social.

"I'm still thinkin' we should hold it before Harvest gets here," Seth reasoned. "That way we can be thinkin' on our happy times, while we're workin' hard."

Mark laughed, "Ya never work hard!" James joined in the laughter.

"I don't mind when it is," another boy stated. "I'd jest rather have a picnic than dancin'."

"That's cuz ya can't dance, George! I look forward ta the dancin'," Seth argued. "Only time ya can hold hands with the girls."

"That's a terrible reason," James hushed Seth. He threw a glance toward Emma to see if she had heard.

But Emma hadn't been following their conversation. She had no interest in the popular event and had never gone. As soon as the boys started talking about the social, she turned her thoughts to her week ahead. She listed out the projects she needed to get done, but her thoughts slowly turned to Thane. She looked down the road in the direction of the hills, as if she would be able to see what Thane had been doing the last few days.

"What do ya think, Emma?"

Emma turned her attention back to the group surrounding her brothers. She blushed as she realized she didn't know what they had asked her. "About what?" she asked softly.

James turned to her quietly, repeating what she had missed, "The plan is ta have a picnic along with dancin' for the social, instead of jest one or the other. Do ya think it's too much?"

Emma looked around the group of faces waiting for her reply. "I wouldna know," she admitted, "I've never been ta one."

Seth laughed, "Yes, ya have."

"No she hasn't. You and Mark have always come on yer own," James pointed out.

George itched behind his ear, thinking. "Can't say I remember her ever comin' neither."

"There's always too much fer me ta do," Emma explained simply.

"All the more reason ta have it before Harvest, and not after," Seth decided.

Emma listened for a couple more minutes before excusing herself to Mark. "I'm gonna head back, I'll probably catch up ta Da." Her brother nodded and turned back to the group.

"I'll walk with ya," James offered.

"I've no wish ta take ya away from the fun," Emma protested. "I jest have ta go check on the roast."

"A roast?" James smiled as he walked along side of Emma. "I'm wishin' it were tomorra now so I could taste that."

Emma laughed easily, "Ya'd think you'd be sick of my cookin' by Sunday."

"Sick of it?" James shook his head. "Me and Pa are sick of our own cookin'. It's the same three meals over and over."

Emma looked over at her brother's friend. She had forgotten that without a woman in the house, they would be cooking for themselves. "Ya know, the roast is plenty big. Why don't ya go ask yer Pa ta come ta dinner with us?"

"Are ya bein' quite sure?" James asked hopefully.

"Yeah I'm sure," Emma reassured him. "Go along with ya." Shooing James back toward town, she turned to continue her walk to the farm.

"Emma?" James called out to her.

She turned back, "Yes?"

"Won't ya think on comin' ta the social with us?" James asked her, stepping closer to Emma. "Wouldna be the same without havin' ya there with us."

Emma put her hands on her hips. "James Abernathy! Yer jest afraid I won't send along a picnic lunch."

James smiled, "I'm sure we could get along without a picnic iffen we start storin' up now," he stated as he patted his lean stomach.

Emma laughed outright at that.

"Jest think on comin'?" he asked again.

Emma nodded. "I'll be thinkin' on it. Now go git yer Pa, so I can check the roast."

James gaze drifted up the road, "You'll be alright walkin' by yerself?"

Emma jest laughed again and turned toward the farm. The only part of the road that worried her, was the part closest to town. James had already walked her past most of it. The rest of the walk home went quickly.

When she reached the cabin, she pulled the roast from the oven and spooned the juices over the top. Making sure the roast looked moist, she set it back inside the oven door.

Emma untied her bonnet and slipped it off her head. Walking toward the back door, she hung the bonnet on the hook and grabbed her apron. Slipping it on over her Sunday dress, she headed to the garden to see if there were enough ripe vegetables hanging on the bushes.

By the time her brothers and James returned from church, Emma had the vegetables in hot water. She had found a few potatoes sticking up from the soil. Even though there weren't very many, these would be the first fresh potatoes they had eaten in months. She couldn't wait to taste them.

"Hello James," Emma's father called from the yard. "What brings ya by today?"

"Our Emma invited him and his Pa ta dinner," Seth called back joyously. "Must be she's cookin' somethin' good."

Emma dried her hands on her apron and stepped through the door onto the front porch. She had forgotten to find her father when she had returned. She should have let him know that she had invited company.

Her father stood halfway up the stairs with his back turned to her. "James, I'd think ya'd be stayin' far away from here on this Lord's day of rest," he replied with a laugh.

"Emma's roast sounds heavenly when comparin' it ta our pork'n beans, sir," James insisted.

"I'm glad you've come then," Da stated. "Seth said yer Pa's comin' too?"

"He'll be along shortly, sir," James answered.

"Well ya all stay out of the barn, no workin' today," Da reminded them, giving his sons a hard stare.

"We're gonna ask Em' iffen we've enough time ta check the honey tree before dinner," Seth stated, looking past their Da in her direction.

Emma smiled at him. Every year, Seth ended up with more than a few bee stings. He could never seem to wait for fall to taste wild honey. "Go on with ya, jest be careful." She turned back inside to finish preparing dinner.

Da followed her inside. "Ya invited him fer dinner?" he asked her curiously.

"Ya," Emma nodded. "I know I shoulda asked ya first. I jest thought with all the helpin' James has been doin', he deserved a nice unhurried meal." She looked up at her father, "With it bein' Sunday, I extended the invitation ta his Pa as well."

Da nodded in understanding, "An' ya have enough?"

"Ya, there should be plenty," she answered.

He reached up to rub his chin thoughtfully. "Can't remember the last time we had company... 'Sides James that is." After a moment of silence, her father left the kitchen.

Emma was left to her thoughts. He was right. The only other person that had eaten in the Wells kitchen was James. For as far back as she could remember. Even her friend Abigail had never eaten a meal in the cabin. She tried to search her memory back to before her Mama had taken sick, but she still couldn't remember anyone else sitting at their table. Not even the reverend.

Before she could dwell longer on it, Emma was startled by a knock. She turned toward the open door to see James's Pa standing there awkwardly.

During the day, Emma propped the doors open to cool the kitchen while she cooked. The boys just wandered in and out. James's Pa didn't seem to be as comfortable. He stood in the doorway not knowing what to do.

"Come on in, Mr. Abernathy. Roast isn't quite ready so the boys are off lookin' fer honey," she offered him a tentative smile to make him feel more relaxed. "Would ya care fer some coffee?"

"Some water would suit me fine, jest now," Mr. Abernathy answered gratefully.

Emma filled a cup and set it on the table.

"Have a seat," she insisted. "My Da will be back around shortly."

James's father pulled out the chair and sat. Awkward silence filled the kitchen. Emma tried to think of something to say to fill the time, but she couldn't come up with anything.

"It's awfully nice of ya ta invite us bachelors ta dinner with ya," Mr. Abernathy surprised her by breaking the silence. "Roast's a welcome treat fer us."

"I wish we woulda invited ya sooner than," Emma smiled. They settled back into awkward silence. As she started gathering the dishes to set around the table, she offered, "Let me finish settin' these out and I'll go ta find my Da fer ya?"

"I can go search fer him in the barn. I know yer busy," he stated. "It's real nice talkin' ta ya, Emma."

"It's my pleasure, Mr. Abernathy," she replied easily.

"John – it's jest John, please," Mr. Abernathy insisted.

Emma hesitated. "I'm not sure, Mr.-,"

"Ya can call him John, Emma girl," her father interrupted, as he entered the kitchen. Walking over toward the table, he reached out to shake Mr. Abernathy's hand. "John, how've ya been?"

"Stayin' busy Joe. I'm hopin' this heat will break soon," he replied.

Da sat down at the table across from their company. "Could go fer awhile yet. Wouldna complain about gettin' some rain soon, though," he commented. Emma brought him a cup of coffee and offered one to Mr. Abernathy as well. They settled in to talk town news and Emma sank happily back into her own thoughts.

When she finally decided the roast and vegetables were ready, she headed to the porch. Banging the striker loudly against the side of the triangle, she hoped the boys could hear it. The honey tree was located in the tree line, furthest away from the back field.

Stepping back into the kitchen, she was startled by the boys coming in the back door. "Guess I need'nt have worried about ya hearin' the dinner bell. Coulda saved my arm."

Everyone laughed.

"I could hear that bell ringin' anywhere in this valley," Seth stated enthusiastically.

"Works better than me callin' fer ya ever did," Emma insisted.

"I don't remember ya ever callin' fer me," Seth said as he washed his hands in the wash tub.

"That's because James felt sorry fer Emma and brought her that bell. Saved her the trouble of ya ignorin' her at chore time," Mark reminded him.

Emma remembered the day she had called and called for Seth, only to find him hours later asleep in the hayloft. The following day, James had brought her the triangle shaped bell and hung it by the front step. She shook her head slightly, "I still don't understand why that customer brought it back ta ya. It's done a proper job here and we've been ringin' it fer years."

"Brought it back ta us?" Mr. Abernathy repeated. He looked toward his son confused.

Emma saw James freeze. "I--," he started to say something to his Pa, but stopped.

"Isn't that the bell ya stayed up all night makin'? Shapin' it 'til it was perfect?" Mr. Abernathy insisted.

Mark burst out laughing! "Maybe ya shoulda shared yer secret with yer own Pa," he playfully smacked James on the shoulder as he settled in his chair.

"Yer secret?" Emma asked James. She was confused by the whole conversation.

James's face turned a bright red. "I didna think ya'd take the bell iffen ya knew I made it fer ya," he cleared his throat uncomfortably. "So I said it was unwanted."

Emma sat down in her chair, wide eyed, trying to understand what he was saying. "Ya made it fer me?" she asked finally. "Why?"

James's face flushed with color again.

Mr. Abernathy laughed loudly at his son's discomfort.

"Let us thank the Lord fer the food you've graced us with, Emma," Da requested. "Then ya can continue ta pester our guest with questions."

Embarrassed to be called pestering, Emma immediately bowed her head.

"Father, who art in heaven, we thank ya fer this wondrous feast our Emma has Blessed us by preparin'. We thank ya fer providin' good food and good company fer us this day! Amen!" Her father's voice had such a deep rich tone to it. Often as a child, Emma would delight in its sound.. and forget to listen to the prayer.

A chorus of "Amen," echoed around the table. Da offered the first piece of roast to Mr. Abernathy. Emma took the opportunity to look across the table to study James's face. He looked up to find her watching him. Smiling awkwardly, he turned to her brother.

"Seth only earned four stings taday," James stated a little too pointedly, nudging Mark under the table.

Her brother turned toward James, raising his eyebrow. After a silent stare down, Mark laughed at his friend. "Well Seth won't be satisfied until he's tasted the honey every time. Serves him right."

James visibly relaxed as the conversation turned away from him. The boys playfully retold their afternoon adventure, teasing each other as they went along.

Emma shook her head in amazement. She decided that she would never understand any of them. She tried to focus on the conversation, but found her thoughts drifting away. Her thoughts wandered up into the hills, and Emma began to wonder what Thane was doing.

Before she knew it, dinner had been eaten and the men folk went out to the porch to talk. Emma was left on her own to wash up. She was grateful for the solitude. Being by herself, she could finally relax. Putting water in the roast pan, she set it on the stove to loosen up the baked on food. With the plates in the wash tub to soak, she began scrubbing. Emma sang softly as she worked. First one song and then another. She started singing Amazing Grace again as she turned to wipe down the table and chairs. Grabbing the broom, she moved around the kitchen sweeping until she caught sight of James watching her from the steps outside. He sat with his head leaning back against the rail as he followed her movements. His expression unreadable. Startled at being watched, Emma stopped singing. James gave her a forced smile and turned back to listen to the talk on the porch.

Emma lifted the washtub and headed out the back door. Pouring out the water, she left the tub on the back step and headed down the path to the quiet hilltop. She lowered herself to the ground and let out a long sigh.

"Hello Mama," Emma said softly as she leaned against the giant rock. "It's been a lovely day of rest on this Sabbath day. Wasn't much of a service today, since Reverend got called away fer a funeral. We had a reading from Jeremiah, which reminded us about the plans God has fer us. Then we had some hymns and they closed with prayer." She leaned back and closed her eyes. "The boys are all fired up about the church social. 'Specially Seth. I don't plan on goin', so I paid no attention ta 'em. Although I did promise James I'd think on goin' with them." She paused for a little while, listening to a bird close by. Turning back to her mother's headstone, she continued, "I invited James and his Pa ta share our dinner roast. I never thought about them havin' ta cook fer themselves until today. Can't imagine iffen Da and the boys had ta do their own cookin'. They probably'd get used ta it I imagine. But it felt strange havin' someone we didn't know very well ta dinner. We don't have much practice talkin' with anyone who's not family. James is different. He's always here. But his Pa... Well, Mark and Seth did most of the talkin' with James. It went easy 'nough I suppose." Emma looked down at her hands and smiled softly, "I kept thinkin' back ta Thane all day. Wonderin' what he was doin' today. I realize I'm not knowin' a lot about him really. I don't know if he even keeps the Sabbath day." She looked toward his hills.

~Nine~

The silence was broken by laughter. Strong, loud, boyish laughter. Emma looked up from her plate and around the table. All eyes were on her. "I'm sorry, did ya ask me somethin'?"

Seth laughed harder. Mark and James looked at each other and smiling. Da repeated in an amused voice, "I asked ya if yer going ta town today?"

"No... it's only Wednesday," Emma replied slowly as she shook her head. "Besides, I went last week."

Da smiled. "I've a few tools ta add ta yer list fer when ya do go. No hurry. Jest don't want ya ta waste a trip."

Emma pushed her chair back from the table and retrieved the list she had started. Handing it to her Da, he neatly wrote down the items he needed. Seth leaned over the list, studying it. "No sweets?" he asked disappointed.

She ignored Seth's pleading tone. Da handed the list back to Emma when he was finished. She moved to slip it back under the butter crock before she sat back down in her chair at the table. Her thoughts returned to Thane. She wondered what he would be doing on this day.

"Somethin' troublin' ya, Emma Fern?" her father asked concerned. All the heads at the table turned in her direction.

She looked up surprised. "Ah.. Jest worryin' a bit about a friend is all," Emma replied, forcing herself to smile for her Da. She realized they would all think it was Abigail she was worried about, instead of Thane, but was satisfied that she hadn't lied. Her father was satisfied with her answer and they went back to discussing the day's goals.

Emma looked around the table. She watched as her father and the boys made their plans. They all joked with each other. James seemed to be relaxed today. Much more relaxed then he had been in the weeks since he came to help this time. "How long has he been helpin' Mark this time?" she wondered to herself. Trying to count back, she guessed it had been at least three weeks. Before this summer, James would spend only a few days at a time helping at the farm before his father would need his help back at the shop.

"How is it that yer Pa can spare yer help still, James?" she asked him suddenly. The question surprised Emma as much as everyone else at the table. The conversation stopped abruptly at her interruption. Everyone turned in her direction. She felt her cheeks heating up, embarrassed for her outburst.

James looked surprised at her question. He opened his mouth to answer her, but his eyes darted back to Mark uncertainly.

"I didna mean that yer not welcome company. Ya know that we enjoy havin' ya here. It's jest-," Emma hurried on apologetically. "Jest seems that it'd be a busy time fer ya." She looked around the table to see that everyone was still staring at her in shock. She closed her eyes, wishing the question hadn't slipped out.

James cleared his throat, "Well my Pa believes it too hot ta work with the forge in the heat of the day. So we do most of our work early in the morn or at night." He looked back to meet Mark's gaze before he returned his attention to Emma again.

Emma watched him explain himself, and felt terrible for making him uncomfortable. She forced herself to smile, hoping it would help him feel more at ease. "So ya work here all day, an' then go home ta blacksmithin' in the evening?" she asked incredulously.

"Sounds about right," James admitted with an uncomfortable smile. He moved the food on his plate around with his fork absently.

Emma turned to Mark, "Why don't I see ya goin' ta help James at the end of the day, Mark Wells?" she asked.

Mark's face broke into a smile then, much to Emma's relief. He reached up to rub the back of his neck. "Well, let's jest say blacksmithin' isn't as appealin' ta me, as farmin' is ta James," Mark chuckled as he raised an eyebrow to his friend. Emma felt there was a hidden meaning behind the words that he wasn't going to share. She figured it wasn't any of her business anyway, since James was Mark's friend.

James laughed outright. "Pa wouldna let him near the forge anyhow." He smiled at Emma as he continued, "He could clean our stalls, I suppose. That wouldna be too difficult fer him." Mark threw his napkin at James and the three boys erupted in boyish laughter.

"Doesn't exactly seem fair ta me," Emma replied thoughtfully. She turned to her Da, finding his gaze had not wavered from her. She could almost feel her Da's disappointment in her at being so outspoken. Again, she regretted her questioning James. Uncomfortable, she rose to refill their cups with coffee and then started to clear the dishes to scrub.

Silence reclaimed her kitchen as Da and the boys journeyed out to the new field. Emma let out a sigh of relief. Never could she remember being so embarrassed. She intended to keep a better hold over her tongue. She set about finishing her cleanup work. Scrubbing the dishes, she dried them and returned them to their cupboard. Emma swept the floor and shook out the rugs. Grabbing the dishpan, she stepped outside to empty it.

A sudden movement caught her attention. In the corner of her garden stood a doe with her fawn. "No!" She dropped her dishpan on the back step and shooed them out of her vegetables. "Git on with ya. Go!" They took one glance at Emma and ran off. Looking down at the plants they had eaten, she admitted to herself, "I guess I can't blame 'em none. This garden does look like a field of weeds." She went in search of the hoe, chiding herself for not keeping up with the weeding better. Tucking her skirt between her knees, she found she could move easier. Emma had not even finished one row when she felt a blister forming by her thumb. Sighing, she put the hoe aside and started pulling weeds by hand. She tried to keep her skirt off to the side so she would not step on it.

Her hand froze as she saw a purple flower growing among the weeds. It was one of the purple flowers Thane had brought her the week before. One of Mama's favorites. Not able to bring herself to pull it, she skipped to the next weed. Emma thought about the long week since she had seen Thane. She wondered if she should take her short list of things to town, to see if Thane'd be there. Thinking better of it, she reminded herself to not be silly – shaking her head to rid it of the wayward thought.

A soft chuckle startled her and Emma lost her balance. Reaching around for something to catch onto, she realized she was going to fall. Strong hands caught her before she flattened the bean plants behind her.

"Ya really should look around more often, instead of arguing with weeds," Thane stated amused, from behind her.

"I wasn't arguin' with weeds," Emma denied. "I was pullin' them."

"Yer shakin' yer head at 'em – almost scoldin' them fer growin' in yer garden," he added with a quiet laugh.

Emma opened her mouth to deny it, but realized there wasn't anything she could say to defend herself. She laughed, "I neglected my garden so long, the deer thought it was part of the field. I was scoldin' myself fer lettin' it git that bad."

Thane gave another soft laugh. He retrieved the hoe from the ground nearby. "Why don't ya rest yer blisters and pick those beans. Must be 'nough fer yer family ta eat," he suggested. She looked at the plants and realized they were very full. She would have to start canning them. "What ya been doin' this week?" Thane asked as he worked.

She settled on her knees, started picking the beans and gathered them in her apron. "Well let's see. I checked the berry patch. I picked enough ripe blackberries for a dessert but I'm gonna go back today ta git enough fer jam," Emma paused, thinking about her week. "I aired out the rugs and such. Trying ta get ahead on chores and bakin', getting ready fer harvest time. Not a moment too soon, it seems. From the looks of these bean plants, I think I'll be cannin' pretty quick. That usually keeps me busy fer a couple weeks." Moving to the next couple plants, she continued. "Our Sunday services were cut pretty short this week. Reverend Keyes was called away suddenly, fer a funeral in a neighbor town. Not sure where. So we jest sang some hymns and had a reading."

"I wondered if there wasn't more ta service than that," Thane commented thoughtfully. Kneeling down, he pulled a patch of weeds from the base of a potato plant.

Emma stopped and looked up surprised. "Ya were there?" When Thane nodded, she smiled. "Why didna I see ya?" she wondered aloud.

"Ya were surrounded by people and I didn't want ta intrude," he stated simply as he continued to chop the weeds with the hoe.

"They were jest my brothers and their friends – They're plannin' the Harvest church social," Emma explained absently. "Why didna I see ya though?"

He paused, leaning his elbow on the top of the hoe. "'Cause no one was talkin' ta ya. An' when no one talks ta ya, ya lose yerself thinkin'." Thane took his hat off and wiped his brow, before continuing. "I find myself tryin' ta remember all the things I want ta ask ya every day. Then I watch 'em stand right next ta ya and not sparin' ya more'n a glance," he started to hoe again, shaking his head.

Emma gave him a half hearted smile, "Now who's arguing with the weeds?" Turning back to the plants, she continued snapping beans. "People do talk ta me, they jest find me dull."

"Dull?" Thane repeated, standing up and looking at her. "I haven't heard one person ask ya a question and wait fer a reply. That friend of yers jest keeps on talkin' as if ya had no voice."

Emma couldn't think of anything to reply to that. She had thought it herself more than once.

They continued on in silence for most of a row. Emma looked over at Thane, and asked softly, "What have ya been doing since our trip ta town last Thursday?"

He was so quiet, Emma wasn't sure he had heard her. Wondering if she should repeat her question, she continued to watch him. He looked uncertain, but finally he cleared his throat to answer her.

"I trapped a couple of coyotes and finally found the culprit of the trap smashin'. 'Twas a young bear. I took care of him," he stated simply as he continued to hoe, "I stopped by a couple times but I know how busy ya are. Knew ya'd be with yer family on Sunday. I didn't come by on Monday, 'cause I wasn't sure what ya'd be washing. I could smell yer bakin' all over these hills on Tuesday. So I saved my visit fer today," Thane paused in his explanation. "Ya seem ta have a break on Wednesdays. Otherwise, I hate ta keep ya from yer family."

"Nonsense," Emma said without looking up. "I miss our visits when yer away. Yer never a bother." She felt his gaze on her as she continued. "So coyotes, church and ya took care of a bear?" she shuddered at the thought. "Sounds busy."

"Not busy enough," Thane replied quietly. "Cause I'm back here again. Can't find enough work ta keep me away."

"Well then," she smiled impishly, "I hope ya have a very borin' summer, so ya can come back every day."

Thane stopped moving then and looked over at her. Emma denied the impulse to see what he was thinking. As he started hoeing again he asked, "Where is this blackberry patch?"

And her heart soared.

~*Jen*~

*E*mma wasn't sure how much of his own work Thane finished during those following days, because he was always with her. He left for a couple hours in the afternoon to check on his traps and returned for the late afternoon hours to visit by the creek before heading home in the evening. Then he was back again, as soon as she was done with breakfast.

Before he went home that Wednesday, he helped Emma pick blackberries. Both of the buckets they took with them were filled to overflowing. They set them in the kitchen to keep for overnight.

The ripe berries were too irresistible to Seth when he came in for supper that evening. Emma took after him with her wooden spoon more than once and threatened him with no jam. Yet her brother's fingers were still stained when they sat down to their evening meal.

When Thursday morning came, Emma was up, before the sun, getting ready for her day. By the time the sky began to lighten, she knew it would be a hot day. She rinsed some berries and sprinkled them in the flapjacks while they were frying. Hiding the buckets under towels, Emma managed to keep the boys out of the remaining berries.

The kitchen was quiet as everyone ate. Her father was the first to finish eating and head for the barn. Mark and Seth met him as he was hitching the horses. The sound of the wagon became quieter as it headed for the fields. Emma looked out the window above her washstand to see Thane coming up the path from the creek. In his arms he carried an arm load of twigs.

"What do ya have there?" Emma asked curiously, as she stepped out onto the porch.

"Got ta thinkin' it might be easier ta make the jam outside, with it bein' so hot today," Thane answered.

Emma readily agreed. Thane started a fire, letting it burn high in the beginning to build up some good coals to work with. Finding a couple green logs to balance the pot on, they set about boiling the berries. While she was getting the jars cleaned and ready, Thane kept an eye on the fire, making sure the flame stayed steady as the jam boiled. They set the pot out to cool once the jam was thick and dark. They took turns spooning the hot jam into the waiting jars. Emma put the wax in a small pot and set it inside a larger pan of hot water. She explained how to tell when the wax was ready to seal the jars.

"Let me try pourin' it," he asked. Carefully taking the melted wax from Emma, Thane tried to pour the wax in the first jar. He missed, spilling a little bit of wax down the side of the jar and burned his hand. "Ooo," he exclaimed with a sharp intake of breath.

Emma took the pan from him to pour wax in the remaining jars. "Ya can tighten the lids down fer me. Try not ta tip 'em. The wax needs ta cool against the glass," she instructed. "Then ya can stick yer burn in the crick."

"It's nothin'," Thane insisted.

"How do ya put yer food up at home if ya never used wax before?" Emma asked curiously.

"We salt cure everythin'," Thane answered simply.

"Even yer beans?" she asked, astonishment showing on her face.

"Can't say we've ever grown beans," he admitted.

When the jam jars were all sealed, Emma went to retrieve a basket to collect beans in. When the basket was full, Thane revived the flames in their fire. Emma washed the large pot they cooked the jam in. Then Thane filled it with fresh water so it could be heating, while she started snapping the beans. Once the water started boiling, they carefully dumped the beans in the water. Emma prepared the jars and filled them with the cooked beans.

Again, they warmed the wax. "I think I'd like ta try my hand at pourin' again," Thane insisted. He managed to pour wax into the first jar without spilling any. Emma laughed at his triumphant smile.

"Ya'll need ta be hurryin'. It'll harden pret' quick like," Emma reminded him. She found herself laughing again at his look of concentration.

Once they were done, Thane cleaned up outside. He stacked the jars on the porch steps to cool before they took them to the shelves in the root cellar. Emma disappeared into the kitchen to make a cold picnic for the men working in the field. After she delivered it, she met Thane down by the creek. She found him laying in the shade with his hat down over his eyes. She paused, trying to decide if she should disturb him. "Are ya too tired ta eat?" she asked softly.

"Never too tired ta eat," Thane said adjusting his hat and sitting up. She handed him a thick sandwich and went to sit down near the big rock.

"I brought ya yer coffee, as well," Emma stated, pulling the tin from the basket.

"Well so ya did," Thane gave her a lopsided grin as he reached to take it from her. He got to his feet and retrieved a sack from behind a bush. It was made out of buckskin and looked incredibly soft. Emma reached her hand out to feel it.

"I didna know ya had a bag there," Emma said distracted by the detail along the edge.

Thane laughed softly at her expression. "I tuck it outta the way, so I won't ferget it when I leave," he explained. He pulled a small pouch out of his sack. Opening the drawstring, he pulled out a coin and dropped it into her basket. Lifting his bag, he held it out for her to take. Emma flipped it over, looking at the stitching, and ran her fingers along the soft material.

"Did ya make this?" she finally asked.

Thane nodded.

"I tried ta sew some canvas once and made a mess of it. Finally gave up on it. I can't believe how small yer stitches are on this," she stated approvingly.

"It jest takes practice," Thane replied quietly.

Emma ran her fingers over the soft material one last time and handed the bag back to him.

He walked over and dropped it behind the bush again.

Coming back to the hill, Thane lowered himself back in the grass. He picked his sandwich up again to finish eating.

Emma reached for the small coin in the basket, rolling it between her fingers. "That first time I met ya, ya said ya only went ta town a couple times a year," she stated quietly. "Yet ya were in Vermontville twice that week?"

Thane looked over at Emma's face, then looked away.

"I assumed ya were lookin' ta buy a horse, but later ya denied it," she watched him curiously. She noticed his back was stiff. He seemed embarrassed. Realizing she was making him uncomfortable, she tried to change the subject. "Not that it matters why ya were there. I was jest thankful," she stammered, dropping the coin back in the basket.

Thane continued to sit with his back to her. Emma rubbed her eyes. "I shouldna said anythin', I'm sorry Thane," she apologized.

"Don't apologize," Thane insisted quietly. "Ya've done nothin' wrong." Looking down at his sandwich, he took a bite and chewed it slowly. "My Pa needed a horse. We'd heard from another trapper that a shipment had come ta Vermontville fer a time. But when we got ta town, my Pa got distracted. Fer four days he was distracted. We'd barely enough money left ta buy the Black," Thane paused. "That's why ya found me still in town when ya came back days later."

Emma nodded. Clearing her throat, she offered, "Maybe God knew I would need ya, so he sent the distraction." Even as she said it, she doubted God would use liquor as part of his plan.

"Could be," Thane agreed. He looked up suddenly and met her gaze. "Ya went ta town twice that week too," he realized. "What brought ya back?"

Emma laughed awkwardly. "It's a mite embarrassin'," she replied.

"More embarrassin' than my reason?" Thane asked, raising his eyebrow.

"Ya shared no blame in yer Pa's distraction," she pointed out.

"Will ya tell me?" Thane asked again.

Emma took a deep breath. "Well it started with me steppin' on the hem of my dress. I was pullin' up weeds in the garden, when I tripped. Made a horrid rippin' sound," she laughed as she remembered her shock. "Course that horrid sound brought Seth an' Mark a runnin'. After they'd a good laugh, they told Da." Emma continued on with the events of that week so long before. She spared herself no embarrassment. Hoping, she could make him forget how uncomfortable she had made him. Thane joined in her laughter several times during her story.

"So what started as a dress needin' ta be replaced, ended with me meetin' ya," Emma concluded with a full smile. "Talkin' about God's plans fer us."

Thane nodded in agreement. Then with a look to the sun, he stood to his feet. "It's close ta yer supper time," he stated.

Emma pulled a couple jars out of her basket. One of jam and one of beans. She held them out to him, "Take these home with ya," she insisted.

"I couldn't take yer food," Thane stated, eyeing the jars she held out to him.

"Course ya can," she repeated, putting the jars in his hands. "I want ya ta have 'em." When he looked up at her, his mouth broke into a smile that was so full of joy, her breath caught.

~Eleven~

Friday dawned with a gentle breeze. Emma could feel it through the open doors as she cleaned up the breakfast dishes. She saw Thane coming up the path as she put the last coffee cup back on the shelf. She walked outside to greet him.

"God has sent ya a gift today," Thane called out quietly. "He sent one of those breezes ya love."

Emma smiled at him, "Ya noticed I enjoy a good breeze?"

"Hard ta miss," he admitted.

"I wonder if anyone else notices I like breezes," Emma thought to herself. With one more smile, she rolled up her sleeves.

They started in to work before it got any hotter. They finished pulling the vegetables from the garden. Thane climbed down into the root cellar and brought up the barrels. They turned them over to dump the old contents out. Thane hauled water from the well to wet the pile of sand by the cellar doors. Then they carefully layered potatoes and carrots with the damp sand.

They went back to the garden to check the beets and onions. Thane broke up the ground around the plants with the hoe. Emma went behind him, kneeling down to gather the vegetables.

Again, they poured damp sand between each layer, packing it down. When the barrels were full to the top, Emma tried to move one. She couldn't even budge it. Thane laughed heartily at her attempts. Then he carefully maneuvered the barrels back down the steep stairs.

When they stopped for dinner, Thane left to check on his traps. Emma went in to start cooking for the men. She decided that she would whip up some sweet biscuits to go with the fresh jam as a treat.

"Sweets with our dinner?" Seth asked excitedly, as he entered the kitchen. He hurried to wash his hands in the washtub. The other menfolk followed close behind.

Mark shared a smile with James. "What're we needin' ta do ta be deservin' this? I suppose it means yer potatoes are ready ta be dug up tonight?"

Emma shook her head, "Naw that job's done. I jest thought I'd fatten ya up before Harvest," she stated simply, trying to hide her smile.

James laughed aloud, "I'm gonna need new clothes then. I'm already wider than I was last spring," patting his lean stomach.

"The only one gettin' wider here is Seth. Eatin' more than all the rest of ya together," Emma retorted.

Mark and James laughed loudly at that.

After the men folk had eaten their fill, they headed back to the fields. Emma dished up the remaining biscuits and jam. Packing them with the simple lunch she had made to share with Thane, she walked outside. By the time Emma travelled down the path to her Mama's hill, Thane was already waiting for her.

When he heard her footsteps, Thane turned toward her. "How did yer Mama jest know what God thinks? How could she know fer sure?" Thane asked curiously.

Emma paused at the unexpected question. "She read her Bible everyday and jest remembered the words I suppose," she answered thoughtfully. Sitting on the grass, she began to spread out the simple picnic.

"So the talk about the Seasons and everythin' havin' a Reason is in the Bible?" Thane asked again to clarify.

"I always believed so," Emma stated carefully. She tried to remember for sure if her mother had read it to her out of her Bible. "I'll have ta look in Mama's Bible fer it tonight ta be sure."

Thane nodded in understanding. He took a bite and chewed it carefully. Looking at the gravestone, he asked hesitantly, "Do ya find yerself fergettin' yer Mama?"

Emma looked at him before she replied. "Yeah I do. Lil' bits at a time. I realize I can't remember her smell or the sound of her voice."

She looked down at the food in her hand. Swallowing the lump in her throat, she continued, "But then somethin' happens that brings back a memory of her. A memory so strong, thet I ferget she's gone. It's easier ta remember her fer a time after that."

"Tell me one," Thane prompted, "A memory of her."

Emma put a bite of her food in her mouth and chewed slowly. By the time she had swallowed her bite, she had decided which memory she would share. "The summer before my Mama got sick," she began with a small smile, "I was itchin' ta be outdoors. I was watchin' my brothers runnin' alongside the hay wagon, yellin' and hollerin' the whole way. They'd come in fer dinner laughin' and carryin' on. It looked ta be more fun than I ever had in the cabin workin'," she paused to take another bite.

"Hayin' looks ta be a fair amount of work ta me," Thane observed.

"I 'magine it is. Sometimes my family comes in fer the night and they barely make it ta bed before fallin' asleep," Emma agreed before she continued with her story. "But that Seth made everythin' look fun. And as they headed out ta the fields that day, I decided I couldna handle it anymore. I stomped my foot and told my Mama that I couldna understand why those boys got ta have all the fun, while I was stuck inside ironin' their clothes. I put all the hatred I could inta that one word -- ironin'-. I waited fer my Mama ta send me ta my room, or tell me ta apologize ta her fer yellin'. But she smiled. Looked out the window after my brothers and smiled like she wished she was out there too. Almost like she knew the feelin'. I felt sorry then. "I'm sorry Mama," I said ta her. "I know yer stuck here too, I shouldna yelled." I felt like cryin'. And she jest smiled.. and kept ironin'." Taking another bite, Emma looked up at Thane. She smiled absentmindedly, "When I started ta ironin' again, my Mama finally spoke ta me. She said, "Don't be sorry fer yer feelings, Emma girl. Jest make sure they're fair. It sure is a nice day out, I'm wishin' I was out in that breeze myself. But yer brothers aren't ta blame fer our work. They aren't takin' pleasure at ya bein' in here ironin' instead of bein' out there with them. Besides, they've plenty of work themselves that they don't care fer." She let that sink in and then she put her iron back on the fire ta gather me in her arms.

"What yer wantin' is an adventure outside these walls. So that's what ya need ta be sayin'. That way I know what yer thinkin'." After we finished our work, she took me down here ta the creek. We took off our shoes and stockings ta walk in the cool water. We splashed and laughed until it was time fer supper." Emma stared at the creek as if she could see her Mama standing there. "I never complained again after that. But I would tell Mama my frustrations every so often. And I can see her perfectly, as she would smile at me. As if she knew exactly how I felt."

"Yer Mama sounds pretty special," Thane commented.

Emma nodded, swallowing back the lump in her throat. "So tell me a memory of yer Mama."

Thane turned toward her. "I don't remember much. An' what I do remember doesn't always match up ta what my Pa says." He looked deep in thought.

"I thought yer Pa didn't talk about her much."

Thane returned his attention to her, "He doesn't unless he's been drinkin'. Guess that's what confuses me the most. Either I'm rememberin' it wrong or my Pa is."

"Tell me," she prompted.

Thane took a minute before he started, "Well I remember my Ma havin' brown hair, but Pa – he insists it was blacker 'an mine. He told me she loved havin' it down and free, but I only ever saw it knotted." He paused thoughtfully, "Pa will tell how she was so full of life and love. I jest remember her sad like. He said how he couldn't take his eyes off my Ma. But I don't have any memories of them talkin'. I find myself forgettin' how she looked."

The pain in his voice made Emma's throat hurt. "I'm sorry Thane."

Nodding absently, Thane was lost in thought for a few minutes. Finally, he looked over to Emma and smiled. "Do ya have any more memories of yer Mama?"

Emma laughed easily, "I could talk about my Mama all afternoon."

Thane leaned over on his side, using his elbow to prop himself up. "I best get comfortable then."

~*~*~*~*~*~*~*~*~*~*~*~*~*~

Emma smiled triumphantly. "There it is!" She had brought Mama's Bible down the stairs with her after she had washed her hair. She had flipped through the marked passages as she allowed her hair to dry. The gentle breeze felt good blowing through her damp hair. She worked through the tangles in her long hair as she slowly rocked on the back porch.

"What did ya find?"

Emma looked up to see that Mark and James stood nearby watching her curiously. The smile returned to her face. "Somethin' Mama used ta say ta me. I couldna find it fer the longest time."

"An' now ya have?" James finished for her.

She nodded without looking up, "Jest now I did. I was afraid it'd take awhile ta find it," her voice drifted off as she read the passage silently.

"I had no idea yer hair was that long," James stated thoughtfully.

Emma's hand flew to her hair. The motion made the Bible slide from her lap, and she almost dropped it. Blushing, she closed the Bible and pulled her hair back. It was still too wet to braid, so she tucked it behind her back. Looking at Mark she explained, "I thought everyone was in the house fer the night."

"It's jest hair Em'," Mark retorted.

She laughed softly. "True. Jest my plain ole' hair."

"It's beautiful!" James disagreed. Both Emma and Mark turned to stare at James. He kept staring at Emma, until she looked away uncomfortably. "With the sun shining through it, like that, it looks like honey. It's glowing. And the waves.. ya canna see the waves when ya have it pulled back."

Mark burst out laughin' and pounded his friend on the back. "Ya should see yer face, James."

Emma smiled, "So I jest need ta carry a lil' sunshine around ta be beautiful?" she laughed lightly as she stood to her feet. "I'll keep thet in mind. Good night ta ya, James." Taking her Bible, she went in through the kitchen door to go up to her room. Her thoughts went back to Thane. She couldn't wait to share what she had found.

~Twelve~

Saturday morning came with clouds and thunder. Emma waited all through breakfast for the rain to fall, but it seemed to be waiting for something.

"I'm gonna head ta James's shop after I'm done here," Mark stated as he sat down at the table.

Da looked up, "We won't be getting' much done in the fields here from the looks of it. We need the rain though. Good day ta work under a roof," he said nodding in approval at his son's plans.

"Bout time ya're payin' James back fer all his help these last weeks," Emma teased her older brother. With a smile, she asked, "Are ya muckin' stalls then today?"

Mark threw his napkin at his younger sister and she laughed aloud. When her father's watchful stare caught her attention, she quieted herself to finish eating.

They all hurried through breakfast. Mark headed out to saddle a horse before Emma had finished eating. "Hopin' ta beat the rain ta town," he explained.

Her Da and Seth finished shortly after. Emma's family left her sitting at the table. She didn't take her time though. She hurried to gather dishes in her washtub. By the time her kitchen was straightened up, it still hadn't started raining. So Emma grabbed her Bible and headed for the hill. Soon after she sat down, Thane stepped out of the trees.

"Looks like I may get wet on the way home today," Thane commented.

"If the clouds ever get ta work," she agreed. Then with a smile she added, "I found it. It's in Ecclesiates 3."

Thane settled on the ground facing her rock. Leaning back on his hands he said, "Will ya read it ta me?"

Emma opened her Bible, and started reading softly. "To everything there is a season, A time for every purpose under heaven:
A time to be born, And a time to die;
A time to plant, And a time to pluck what is planted;
A time to kill, And a time to heal;
A time to break down, And a time to build up;
A time to weep, And a time to laugh;
A time to mourn, And a time to dance;
A time to cast away stones, And a time to gather stones;
A time to embrace, And a time to refrain from embracing;
A time to gain, And a time to lose;
A time to keep, And a time to throw away;
A time to tear, And a time to sew;
A time to keep silence, And a time to speak;
A time to love, And a time to hate;
A time of war, And a time of peace.
What profit has the worker from that in which he labors? I have seen the God-given task with which the sons of men are to be occupied.

He has made everything beautiful in its time. Also He has put eternity in their hearts, except that no one can find out the work that God does from beginning to end. I know that nothing is better for them than to rejoice, and to do good in their lives, and also that every man should eat and drink and enjoy the good of all his labor – it is the gift of God.

I know that whatever God does, It shall be forever. Nothing can be added to it, and nothing taken from it. God does it, that men should fear before Him."

Emma put the Bible down on her lap, but kept it open. Her gaze stayed on its pages still. She was deep in thought.

"Thet's a lot ta think on," Thane said softly. "Do we have ta be goin' through all those 'times'?"

"I hope not," Emma answered. Thunder rumbled nearby and she looked up at the sky.

Thane leaned forward, pulling a stalk of grass up. "The part nearin' the end, the words that say 'Nothin' can be added ta it.' What's that meanin'?"

Emma reread the part he spoke of. "I'm not sure. My Mama always said that God has a plan from the beginnin'- his perfect plan - and no amount of pleadin' will change his mind for the path he has fer us. Maybe that's the same thing?" Her eyes still skimming the page.

Thane laughed, "A time ta rain."

Emma looked at him confused, "Ya mean weep? It says a time ta weep, but no rain."

"Naw, I mean it's gonna rain Emma," Thane stated as he stood to his feet.

"Oh," Emma exclaimed as she felt a raindrop hit her nose. She quickly closed the Bible and slid it under her apron. The clouds looked dark and angry above her suddenly.

"Thanks fer findin' the words fer me. Now git inside before yer soaked," Thane pleaded. Gathering the basket up, he handed it to her.

Emma nodded to him and ran for the house.

~*~*~*~*~*~*~*~*~*~*~*~*~*~

The next morning, all signs of the storm had disappeared. Except that the crops all stood a little taller. Emma looked for Thane at church and found him easily. He slipped in just before the service started and he sat in the back of the church. His face broke into a smile when he looked up and caught her gaze. She smiled back happily.

Emma found herself turning to Thane whenever she heard something in the sermon or the reading that she found interesting. She turned again when they started singing her favorite hymn. He returned her smile each time.

When the service ended, Emma headed toward the door hoping to get a chance to speak with Thane before he left. Her escape was blocked as James stepped near her to talk with Mark. She leaned around her brother's friend looking for Thane. She caught a glimpse of him as he disappeared through the doorway. She sighed in frustration.

A laugh next to Emma startled her. "Ya don't like fishin'?" James asked amused.

"Fishin'?" Emma repeated absently.

Seth laughed at her, as they patiently waited in line to go through the door. "Emma doesn't go fishin' with us."

"Ahh," James said.

As they stepped outside, all signs of Thane were gone. She tried to keep the disappointment out of her face as she greeted the Reverend.

Her Da and brothers left for fishing that afternoon as soon as Emma fixed them dinner. They asked her to keep it simple so that they would have longer at the fishing hole.

When silence filled the cabin, Emma took her Mama's Bible and a picnic down to the creek. She wasn't disappointed when Thane showed up soon after.

"I wondered if ya'd be here with yer family gone fishin'?" Thane said with a smile.

"Ah.. Ya heard 'em talkin' at service," Emma realized.

"Yer brother couldn't be missed. He's very loud," he pointed out.

Emma had to smile at that.

While they ate their simple meal, Emma asked Thane what he thought of the service. He took the opportunity to ask who certain people were and why things were done the way they were. Emma answered the best she could.

"Is it disrespectful ta talk ta a young lady in church?" Thane asked.

Emma looked up curiously at his question, "No one has mentioned it ta me."

"It's jest that no one spoke ta ya until they got outside," Thane explained. "Thought maybe it was a rule."

Emma laughed softly, a little embarrassed that she had been caught daydreaming, "I jest don't listen ta 'em. I'm usually thinkin'."

Thane smiled at her answer. They sat in a comfortable silence, listening to the sounds of the woods around them. A woodpecker called shrilly above them. The wind blew softly, moving the branches of the trees.

"Would ya mind readin' Ecclesiastes 3 ta me again?" Thane asked suddenly, breaking the silence. Emma opened her Bible and started reading the passage once she located it. When she finished reading, Thane looked toward Emma. "I understand where yer Mama gets the Seasons. But where does it say there is a Reason fer everythin'? Am I not understandin' it?" Thane asked.

"I think that's jest what it meant ta Mama. 'Everythin' beautiful in its time.' Meaning that there's a reason behind everythin' that happens? Or that somethin' good comes from everythin'. Even if we can't understand why things happen," Emma replied uncertainly. "I imagine everyone who reads the words in the Bible, hears them a little bit differently."

Thane nodded toward the Bible. "Can ya show me where ya found it in there?"

Emma turned the Bible, angling it to show Thane. She showed him how it was broke into the different books. She explained how it was laid out. "The Old Testament is in the beginning and the New is at the end. There is a list of the books in the front. Genesis is the first book. Tells how God created everythin'. Ecclesiastes is pert near the middle of the Bible."

"What else did yer Mama read ta ya?" Thane asked. Leaning back, he propped himself up on his elbows to relax while she read.

Emma flipped through the Bible she held. She read a few passages from Jeremiah and then the whole book of Ruth.

"So this Ruth, she followed whatever God planned fer her and He blessed her?" Thane asked.

"That's what this seems ta be sayin'," she replied, not quite sure.

"Seems like Ruth went through most of the Seasons," he said rubbing the back of his neck. "I can't decide if that makes her more Blessed or Blessed the same as everyone else?"

"Close ta all the seasons that's fer certain. It doesn't really tell of her bein' Blessed. Jest Naomi." Emma flipped through the pages again. "Does seem like Boaz is Blessed too. Maybe God is sayin' ya Bless yer loved ones by followin' His plan?" Emma gave a short laugh, "When I was a girl, I jest thought it was a lovely story. I never gave a thought ta the meanin'."

"Emma?" A call came from the distance, interrupting her thoughts.

"Oh they must be back from the fishin' hole," Emma stated, closing her Bible.

Thane stood to his feet. "I won't be keepin' ya from yer family then." Smiling as he touched his hat, he hesitated just a moment before he turned to cross the creek and disappeared.

Emma gathered the remains of their picnic and put it in the basket. Standing up, she dusted off her skirt. As she walked up the path, she saw Seth standing on the back porch. "We brought company home fer supper. Hope ya have enough," he called out as she got closer to the cabin.

"Am I cookin' the fish ya caught?" Emma asked.

"Na," Seth laughed. "It was too hot fer the fish ta bite."

Emma followed him into the kitchen. Her Da and Mark sat talking to James and his Pa. "Hello Mr. Abernathy, how are ya? Hello James." James looked up as she entered and his face broke into a smile. Seeing his hopeful look, she had to laugh. "I hope ya weren't countin' on another roast, because the plan was fish fer supper. With our fishermen comin' back empty handed, it looks like yer stuck with fried chicken."

Seth's whoop filled the kitchen. He ran out the front door, flying off the top step, and headed in the direction of the chicken coop.

Everyone laughed at Seth's enthusiasm. "Guess we better go help pick 'em out James," Mark suggested to his friend.

"Yeah, wanna make sure he gets a young rooster and not an old hen," James agreed as he slid his chair back.

"Don't let him terrorize my hens," Emma warned good naturedly.

The boys laughed as they headed out the door. "Maybe we can figure out the one thet pecks Emma's buttons," Emma heard James suggest to her brother, before they travelled out of ear shot.

Emma found herself smiling. It had been a wonderful day. She tried to remember the last time she had felt completely content. She looked over to see her father watching her. She smiled in response, "Ya may want ta move ta the porch Da. Nothin' warms up this cabin like fryin' chick'n, and it's already hot in here. Do ya want me ta fetch the checkers down? Ta entertain ya while ya wait?"

Da's mouth spread into a slow smile. "That sounds nice, Emma girl." Sliding his chair back, he insisted, "I can run up there though, while yer gettin' ready in here."

As her Da climbed the staircase, Mr. Abernathy turned to smile at Emma, "I've been rememberin' yer good food all week. Was so happy ta be invited back again."

"Invitin' ya ta eat with us is the least we can do. James has been workin' as hard as anyone here, and ya have ta do without him durin' the day," Emma smiled. "Jest wish I could do more fer him."

Mr. Abernathy watched Emma for a moment before chuckling, "Not sure he's needin' anythin' more. 'Sides yer Da offerin' James a portion of his crop sales, it's really answered our prayers."

"Da is payin' him?" Emma asked, looking up in surprise.

Mr. Abernathy nodded, "James – he's been savin' fer a place of his own," he explained carefully, watching her face as he shared the information.

"Well that explains why he doesn't mind comin' around so much," Emma stated absently. "Explains why he's eager ta work such long hours."

James's Pa watched Emma closely, "It's part of the reason. I think he jest enjoys bein' out here on yer farm."

Emma shook her head slightly, "I've never understood why he enjoys it. Mark may be fine company, but the work he does when he's here? It's hard work. I don't know why he keeps on comin' back."

"Don't ya now?" his amused chuckle confused her.

Emma didn't have a chance to wonder at his words. Her father returned with the checker board, so the two men retreated to the front porch chairs. Emma took care of her picnic supplies and went to change. Fryin' chicken was messy work and she had no intention of ruining her new dress.

~Thirteen~

Monday dawned bright and hot. Emma found herself wishing for a breeze as she flipped the bacon. Laundry was going to be a burdensome task she realized.

"'Mornin' Emma," James called out.

Emma turned to see her brothers coming in from chores, followed by James. "Yer here early, James," she smiled happily at his cheerfulness.

"It'll be too hot come mid-day ta do much. Might as well get a jump on workin' in the morning' coolness," he answered.

Her father came in from the barn soon after, "Ya must be eager ta git ta yer laundry today, Emma girl," Da said as he moved to the washtub.

She shook her head in confusion at his words. "Not in this heat, I'm not."

"Ya already got yer water toted," Da stated. He nodded his head toward the kitchen window as he continued to scrub his hands.

Emma looked out the window and saw that the washtub was indeed sitting on her stump filled to the top with water. She turned to Mark in question.

"Don't look at me, it was James's idea. Said it was too hot ta make ya do it all by yerself."

Surprised, Emma turned to James. "Well, I thank ya, James. It is a hard chore fer such a hot day. But ya already have hard work ahead of ya. Ya needn't have wore yerself out doin' mine." She turned away before she saw his smile broaden.

"I was up early anyhow. Sheriff woke me early. He asked me ta help him move a man outta the street. He wanted him moved before the streets filled up," James commented as he sat at the table.

"Sleepin' in the wrong spot was he?" Mark laughed.

"Sheriff said he was waitin' fer the hotel ta open," James answered. "I feel fer the man. His hand's gone. Looks like a trap took it off."

Emma gasped. What would Thane do if he lost a hand in a trap? "Was it a recent injury?" she asked with a shudder.

James looked up at her and shook his head. "No it was healed. Looks like it happened before we got a doctor in the valley. It's pert rough."

"Boys," Da interrupted James. "Not the kind of talk intended fer my lil' girl."

"Sorry sir," James apologized quickly.

Emma wrapped an arm around her ribs to fight the feeling of heartache she felt for a man she had never met. She finished serving up breakfast so she could get to her laundry before it was too hot.

Wearing her patched up dress, she set about gathering all the laundry she needed to wash, and headed for the washtub. She had two of Seth's shirts scrubbed when Thane stepped out of the woods. "Oh!" she said, surprised. "I was hopin' ta have these all washed before ya found yer way here."

"Iffen it's alright with ya, I was thinkin' ta sit over here and listen ta ya talk," Thane suggested hopefully. "Or I can come back after yer done."

"Yer welcome ta sit," Emma smiled. "As long as yer keepin' yer back turned." Thane laughed as he remembered the first time he had helped her with laundry. How embarrassed they both were by the time he left. So he turned his back while she hung up the wash. All the while, they talked.

"So it's you and yer brothers. Mark's older'n ya, and Seth's younger?" Thane said, repeating back part of the story she had just told him.

Emma nodded, then remembered he had his back turned and wouldn't be able to see her head move. Smiling at herself, she replied, "Yea. My baby sister woulda evened out the numbers."

"Do ya have any other family round these parts?" he asked curiously.

"No," Emma said, wiping the sweat off her forehead with her sleeve. "My Mama's family was mostly gone by the time they left Vermont. Da's family is still there farmin'."

Thane picked at the grass by his feet.

"Didya ever go ta school, Thane?" Emma asked, "I don't remember seein' ya but I didna go much after Mama got sick."

"Na," Thane replied. "My Ma taught me ta read and write some. Enough ta get by." He paused for a moment. "Then after she died, Pa didn't go in much fer schoolin'. Mostly jest taught me figurin'… taught me how ta trap and survive on the trail iffen I had ta."

"So ya jest started trappin' when yer Ma died?"

Thane shook his head, "I've been out trappin' with my Pa since I can remember. An' I can remember pret' far back."

Emma had a picture flash before her eyes of a small child working on traps. A shiver went up her spine. "James was tellin' of a man in town that lost his hand in a trap," Emma said softly. "Is that common? Getting' hurt on a trap?"

Thane turned to look at her then. "My Pa hurt his hand in a trap when he was a boy. It's easy ta trigger one on yerself if yer not careful. My Pa taught me young ta be aware of the danger. And I listened real close, seein' his hand like it was every day."

Emma swallowed hard.

Thane looked away toward her cabin. "When was James tellin' ya about this man who lost his hand?"

Emma finished hanging another pair of pants, before she could reply. Taking the clothespin from between her lips, she answered, "It was this mornin' at breakfast."

"What did James say the man was doing in town?" Thane asked more specifically.

Emma blinked a couple times, "I can't remember. James said the sheriff asked fer his help movin' him."

Thane rubbed his hand over his face. "Well I best be getting back ta my work." He stood up and dusted off his pants. He nodded to Emma and walked down the path to the creek.

Emma watched him walk away, before she turned back to her laundry. She was surprised that Thane had come for such a short visit. Usually, he would have waited until afternoon if he had work to do. Shaking her head to focus back on her work at hand. She couldn't spend much time worrying about his sudden departure. She had a lot of laundry to hang up before she needed to start dinner.

~*~*~*~*~*~*~*~*~*~*~*~*~*~*~

When Thane returned in the afternoon, Emma was just heading off to pick more blackberries. He reached over to take the buckets from her. "What're we pickin' today?" he inquired.

"Blackberries. Or at least see if there are any left. The critters may've cleaned 'em out," Emma answered with a smile. "I'm jest needin' a walk ta work the kinks outta my back. So I figured I'd check the berries one last time."

Thane nodded in understanding. He stepped back to allow her to lead the way.

Emma looked at Thane thoughtfully. "Was that yer Pa in town?" she asked softly.

Thane turned to her in surprise. "It was," he replied with a nod. "Did ya know it was him this morning? Did ya know it was him, when James was talkin'?"

Emma shook her head. "All I was worried about was how you'd still be able ta trap iffen somethin' happened ta yer hand or arm. It's a harsh injury," she replied quietly, looked away before continuing, "It wasn't until ya left, so suddenly, that I remembered meetin' yer Pa comin' outta that same hotel. And – and I worried it was him again."

"Meetin' my Pa?" Thane repeated with raised eyebrows. Chuckling in amazement, he remarked, "Emma Wells you're the most forgivin' lady I've ever met."

Emma felt her face flush. "My Da says the liquor is ta blame. He says even good men forget their manners when they're full of liquor. That we should pray fer 'em instead of hatin' 'em." She gave Thane a half smile before turning back to the trail.

Thane nodded as he swallowed the lump in his throat. They travelled in silence for a few minutes, each absorbed in their own thoughts.

"So ya were sayin' Seth has more schoolin' ta go?" Thane asked, remembering a comment she had made earlier in the day.

It took her a moment to take in the change of subject. "No, his schoolin' is done. I was jest sayin' I think he'll miss it more'n Mark or I did. Seth really liked school. He liked the visitin' and gettin' away from farm," Emma said with a short laugh.

Thane smiled at her, "Maybe ya can send him ta the mercantile each week. It'd save ya the hassle."

"True. But instead of bringin' me lard and lye, I'd get brown sugar and ginger," she stated in amusement.

~*~*~*~*~*~*~*~*~*~*~*~*~*~*~*~

The next morning, she came outside while she waited for her bread to rise and she found Thane hoeing her garden for her.

"Good mornin' ta ya," Emma called.

Thane looked up and gave her a smile. "Thought I'd break up the potato plants and turn the dirt fer ya. Since ya were bakin' when I got here."

"Thank ya," Emma replied. "I came out ta gather some of the bigger corn ta put in the root cellar. I've a little time before the bread rises enough ta bake."

He nodded and continued to hoe the dying plants.

Emma walked over to the corn stalks and searched for the ears that were the most plump. In no time, she had filled her basket full of corn. She turned toward the cabin to take them down to the cellar.

Thane reached around her to take the heavy basket. "Ya know I've always pitied my pa. Pitied him fer missin' my ma so much he had ta drink. But I never thought ta pray fer him. And I never gave any thought ta forgivin'." They stopped in front of the cellar doors as Emma pulled one open for him. "I didn't even think about needin' ta forgive him. Yet you-," Thane turned to look at Emma, "Ya forgive him fer manhandlin' ya.. no hesitation. Yer amazin'." He looked away again, embarrassed by his open praise. "I was thinkin' on it all night."

Emma studied his downcast expression thoughtfully. "My Mama said that forgiveness sets ya free ta live. It pulls ya outta the shadow of anger an' hatred," she replied quietly. "It's jest the Wells way."

Thane nodded then, and carefully climbed down the steep steps. He put the basket high on a shelf that Emma had described and climbed back up.

They headed back to the garden. "It looks like the dry beans can be picked ta dry. Let me fetch a basket.. and I'll check on my bread."

In the cabin, Emma saw that her bread needed more time to rise. Grabbing a basket, she headed back to the garden. Thane was hoeing the corner of the garden where the beets had been. It was the last part of the dirt to be turned over. Emma knelt down next to the first bean bush. She started pulling the beans, dropping them into the basket.

Thane leaned the hoe against the rail of the porch and headed for the well to pull up a drink. Refreshed, he joined her in the dirt.

Emma watched him pluck the bean pods from the bush quickly, choosing only the ones ready to be picked. "Ya seem familiar with dry beans," she said with a smile. "Yer faster at pickin' `em than I am."

He smiled at her teasing tone. "It's `bout all we grow."

"They're easy ta keep, long as they stay dry," Emma stated. "We ate them fer a month straight, a few years back. Rot set inta the potato barrels and we could eat none of them. So it was dry beans with everythin'.. until spring brought the woods back ta life."

Thane nodded, "We have salt pork and beans all winter."

"That month was long `nough fer me," Emma said making a sour face. "The complainin' from Seth alone, sets my hair on end jest rememberin'."

Thane laughed softly. When they had picked all the beans that were hanging, Emma put the basket by the kitchen door so they could be shelled later in the week when they dried.

"I best get the bread ta bakin'," Emma stated reluctantly. Knowing it wouldn't be proper to be indoors alone, Thane had never accompanied her in the cabin for more than a moment. And she had never suggested it.

"I'm needin' ta finish some jobs at my cabin," Thane responded quietly. He seemed hesitant to leave.

"I'll have a couple hours ta jest sit an' visit before supper tonight," Emma suggested. "Iffen yer finished by then."

Thane nodded in response. He touched his hat and turned toward the path to the creek.

Emma watched him walk away with a smile. Then she forced herself to turn toward the cabin and all the bread that needed to be baked. Inside, she selected the loaf that had risen the most and put it in the small oven.

Then she set about making a big dinner. She fetched some potatoes and carrots from the root cellar. Putting them in a pot she set them to boiling. When she went to cut a chunk of ham, she realized they would have to think about smoking more meat soon. Hopefully they would make it until after the harvest.

When the vegetables were almost tender, Emma went out and rang the dinner bell. "Everythin' will be done by the time they make it in from the field," she figured.

"I made it in time fer dinner?" came a voice close by.

She turned in the direction of the road to see James walking toward her. Emma laughed at the hope in his expression. "It's like you've a clock in yer belly."

"Is yer family still in the field?" he asked.

"Yea. I canna leave my bread bakin' ta take them lunch today," she explained. "They should be in shortly."

"Anythin' ya need help with or should I head out ta meet 'em?" James asked.

Emma thought about his question. "I've only the wash tub ta refill, if ya want ta make sure my Da and brothers heard the dinner bell ringin'," she suggested.

"Seth can hear that dinner bell over any sound, no matter how quietly ya ring it," James said with a laugh. "Let me go check ta see iffen they're headed in, then I'll fill the wash tub fer ya."

"Thank ya," Emma said. She returned to the kitchen. She could smell that her bread was done baking, so she pulled it from the oven and set another loaf in its place. Then she drained the vegetables, replacing the lid to keep them warm until the menfolk came in. She had just set the plates around the table, when James came in toting a bucket full of water for the wash tub.

"They are headed in. Should be close ta the front field by now," James reported as he headed out for the door with the empty bucket.

"I'll dish it up when they come in."

"It sure smells good," James said eagerly.

Emma laughed softly, "Now ya sound like Seth."

James laughed too, as he left through the door.

When James returned again, her father and brothers were with him.

"Sorry ta make ya come in fer dinner. I couldna leave my bread bakin'," she explained to her family.

"We were needin' a break from the sun, Emma girl," Da answered.

"This smells better than a picnic lunch anyhow," Seth decided, inhaling deeply.

Emma met James eyes and they laughed. Seth's words were almost the same as the ones James had used earlier. Da saw the shared joke and raised his eyebrow at James. Emma had turned back to start serving up the plates and missed the exchange.

Once everyone was seated, her Da blessed the food and everyone started eating heartily.

"We noticed the raccoons are back in the fields. They did a fair amount of damage ta the cornfield by the woods last night," Da told Emma. "So we'll probably be sittin' out there tonight."

Nodding in understanding, Emma started planning what food she would send out with the boys.

"Ya interested in joinin' us, James?" Mark added.

James agreed easily. "Wished I woulda known earlier, I could've jest stayed on inta the night."

"We could send Emma inta town with a message fer yer Pa," Seth suggested.

"I'll not ask her ta make that trip in this heat," James said. "Besides she's bread ta bake."

Emma gave him a thankful smile. She was already dreading the trip to the mercantile that she knew was coming up. An added trip was not appealing to her.

"Speakin' of bread," Seth said suggestively. "Can I have a slice with my dinner?"

Emma put her fork down and pushed her chair back from the table. Reaching for a loaf that was cool enough to slice, she heard a whispered comment that made her smile.

"Rotten kid. Let her eat her food while it's warm," James said.

"Jest asked fer bread," Seth responded confused.

Their father laughed at his expression.

"It's fine," Emma insisted. Setting the plate of sliced bread on the table, she sat back in her chair.

Just as she was putting a bite to her mouth, Seth asked with a impish smile, "Could I have butter on mine?"

Emma froze mid-bite, just in time to see Mark smack Seth in the back of the neck. James slid his chair back and retrieved the butter crock before she could even respond. She tried to keep her smile hidden as Seth rubbed the back of his neck. "Never dull at mealtime," she thought to herself.

When their plates were empty, Da and the boys headed back to the fields. She put the last loaf of bread in to bake and set about cleaning the kitchen. As she lifted the washtub to empty it, she smelled that the bread was just about ready. Stepping outside, Thane stood up from the step he was sitting on.

"Yer back," Emma noted.

Thane answered with a nod. He reached up to take the heavy tub from her.

"Jest let me take my last loaf from the oven," Emma said, turning back inside. She pulled the loaf out and set it with the others to cool. She untied her apron and hung it on the hook by the door.

Thane handed her the empty washtub for her to put inside on the washstand. They walked toward the creek and had a seat on the grass.

She handed him the basket that held his dinner. "Normally it'd be too cold ta enjoy, but in this heat it didna cool off one bit," Emma said with a smile. She shared with him what happened at dinnertime earlier and Thane smiled.

"Never knew what I was missin', not havin' a big family. Listenin' ta yer stories, makes me realize how quiet it is ta home," Thane commented.

Emma thought about his words a moment. "Never thought about life without Mark or Seth. It would be quiet," she realized. "Course there'd be less work ta do, but I guess I don't mind it much."

When Thane finished eating his food, he leaned over in the grass, laying on his side. "Will ya tell me more stories of yer growin' up years?" he asked. "Stories of yer brothers and you?"

Emma smiled. "Ya want me ta tell ya how Seth startled the cow while I was milkin' her, so Da made it his chore? Or about the time Mark and James tied the outhouse shut on George because he wouldna stop pullin' my braids?"

Thane laughed, "The cow first... then tell me 'bout this George."

Emma told story after story from her childhood. Thane laughed frequently, but rarely interrupted her. When she finally stood to head up to the cabin, her cheeks hurt from all the smiling.

As they approached the end of the path, Thane wished her a good evening and turned back to the woods.

"Jest a minute," Emma ran into the cabin and returned with a loaf of bread wrapped in the towel. "Ya can bring the towel back ta me tomorra."

"I can't take yer bread," Thane stated. Even as he said the words, his hands reached for the loaf.

Emma laughed. "I've seen how ya enjoy bread when I bring it out ta ya. I made this one fer ya ta take," she insisted as she thrust it the last few inches into his hesitant hand. "Jest fer ya."

He looked up from the bread and a smile lit up his whole face. Once again, she found her breath catch at the joy in his smile.

~Fourteen~

After breakfast was cleaned up and the kitchen was set to right, Emma took her list to the back porch to finalize it. She was sitting in her mother's rocking chair when Thane strolled up.

With a smile he announced, "I found blueberries!"

"Where?" Emma asked, as she looked up from her list.

"About 30 paces off the road, where it branches off toward town," Thane replied with a smile.

Emma looked in the direction he spoke of. "Isn't that the Williams land?"

He shook his head, "Jest before the Williams land. 'Tis the abandoned farm jest ta the West. No one has picked the berries in a while. They've gone wild."

"Let me fetch the buckets then." When Emma returned, he took the buckets from her. She didn't start toward the road. Waiting for Thane to turn toward her, she hesitantly asked, "Do ya have traps over there?"

"No Ma'am," he answered easily. "I wouldn't let ya get hurt."

"I didna think ya would. I jest don't want ta see an animal hurtin'," she shrugged. "Sounds silly I know."

Thane smiled, "I wouldn't want ya ta see that either."

They followed the road to the bend and then Thane lead Emma down a simple patch. She could see that Thane was right. The patch was untouched and ripe. They would easily pick their two buckets full.

"How did ya know this was here Thane?" Emma asked curiously.

"I remembered picking blueberries here with my Pa when I was a child. It's one of my good memories. One of the only times Pa talked about Ma with a clear head." Thane smiled at the memory. "I've searched all over lookin' fer `em."

Emma watched him as he shared the memory. She saw that his face didn't immediately regain the shadow of sadness that it usually held. When he noticed Emma watching him, he smiled. She felt her cheeks burn as she went back to picking blueberries.

Stretching to reach the far bushes, Emma felt the branches pull at her skirt. She stepped back, not wanting to damage it. Seeing an opening on the other side, she looked for a way to get over to it. Emma decided if she moved around the large tree at her side, she would be able to reach the other berries easier. As she moved around the tree though, she found herself in a small clearing. "Oh there's a house," she exclaimed softly. Feeling awkward that they were on someone else's property, she turned to Thane, "Should we be here?"

Thane stepped into the clearing with her and looked towards the rundown building. "No one's lived here fer years. Fer as long as I can remember. My Pa said the farmer went back East fer some reason and always planned on comin' back." They both watched the house in silence before Thane turned to look at Emma. "I won't let anythin' bad happen ta ya. Ya don't need ta be worryin'," he added softly.

She saw his gaze rested on the arm she had wrapped around her ribs. Quickly moving it to her side, she turned back to picking the berries from the bushes. Some of the blueberries were over ripe. Their fingers were stained with the purple juice in no time.

When the buckets were full, Thane led Emma past the abandoned building and down a short path to a creek. They bent down to rinse their hands, but the stains were stubborn. Emma took a handful of sand and rubbed it onto the stains. When they were satisfied with their hands, they sat on a fallen log to rest in the shade.

"This crick runs deeper than the one by Mama's hill," Emma remarked.

Thane glanced down stream, "Tis the same crick. It splits off a little ways downstream. If ya follow the lil' branch it'll lead ya ta yer hill." He turned to Emma, "We can walk the crick back iffen ya'd like ta."

She nodded and got to her feet. "It's probably time I was headin' back."

Thane stood and stepped, easily, over the log they had been sitting on. He held his hand out to help Emma over. Realizing it wasn't going to be easy for her to do, she handed her bucket to him. She sat back down on the log, and attempted to lift her legs over to the opposite side while keeping her skirt close to her legs. She was halfway around, when she felt herself being lifted down. Thane quickly released her and then retrieved the buckets. Handing her one, he turned to follow a narrow path next to the creek. Emma followed him in comfortable silence. After a few minutes of walking, Thane turned to hold her elbow as she climbed over a large rock in their path. When she stepped down, Emma saw that the creek branched off up ahead.

"You seem ta know this crick pretty well," Emma observed.

Thane looked at her for a second before he turned to look back the way they had come. "If ya follow it the other way, it'll lead ya ta my cabin. Deep in those hills."

Emma smiled. "So if I ever need ta find you, I can jest follow the crick?" she asked following his gaze into the hills.

Laughing softly, Thane nodded, "Yup, jest follow it upstream. Follow it fer miles an' miles. It's pretty deep in the hills." As they approached the fork, he reached back for her bucket and set both buckets on the opposite bank of the smaller branch. "It's easier walkin' on the other side." Bracing his foot on a large stone in the water, he easily lifted her over the creek. Flustered by his ease in lifting her, she reached for the buckets only to have them taken from her carefully. "It should be easier fer ya now," Thane assured her.

Emma's face flushed, realizing Thane probably travelled much faster without her. "I'm slowin' ya down."

He looked back at her, "I'm in no hurry."

"Seems like it's a mite shorter travellin' this way," she observed.

Thane nodded. "The water cuts the quickest path outta the hills. Makes the shortest road. My Pa taught me that," he paused to look back past her. "When my Pa would have a drinkin' spell, I would follow the crick and explore it. Shortly after showin' me the blueberry patch, he had a bad spell. I set out ta find that house 'gain. But I overshot it and ended up here at the Fork," Thane looked at her awkwardly. Clearing his throat, he continued, "I stood here not knowin' which way ta go. Not rememberin' the crick branchin' off this way. An' then I heard a voice talkin'," he looked away from her then and continued slowly along their path. "I followed the voice ta yer hill. I stood there a listenin' ta ya talk ta yer Mama. I stood there till ya went back up the path," he finished softly.

Emma froze in horror. In the early days without her Mama, her talks on the hill had been emotional and filled with loneliness. Thane stopped walking too, waiting for her to say something. She glanced at him to see his back stiff and his head hung in embarrassment. She blew out the breath she was holding. "Ya musta thought I was plumb crazy."

Surprise flashed through Thane's eyes as he turned to her, "I had lost my Ma. I thought ya were the only person that made sense." He looked ahead again. Emma followed his gaze and saw her Mama's hill rising above the crick. She glanced back at Thane, who was deep in thought. She wondered what he was thinking as he continued to stare toward her hill.

He shook his head, as if to clear his thoughts. "I learnt better than ta listen in ta yer talkin'." Taking a deep breath, he looked down to the buckets in his hands, "I beg yer pardon fer listenin' when I was too young ta know better."

Emma studied his face. "Why did ya never speak ta me?"

"Wouldn't have dared ta. I was a filthy boy from the hills. Not yer kind."

"Nonsense," she scoffed. "My brothers were always filthy. No difference."

Thane chuckled, "Not exactly my meanin'." He continued along the path until they reached the clearing with her Mama's hill. He set the buckets down and lifted her across. Once her feet were under her, he handed her the blueberries. "I must be gitten back," he said quietly. Touching his hat with a "ma'am," Thane turned back to the path they had just followed.

Taken aback by the suddenness of his leaving, she watched Thane move easily and quickly into the woods. Finally, Emma turned up the path to her house. She couldn't keep herself from wondering how different life would have been if he had talked to her that day long ago. How it would have felt to have a friend.

Emma set the buckets on the back step, as she retrieved the stew pot from her kitchen. Filling it with water from the well, she rinsed the blueberries and set them to boil. She had the jam ready to go into jars by the time the men came in from the fields looking for their dinner.

~Fifteen~

Thursday morning dawned hot and sunny. As Emma came out the door with her list for town, Thane was waiting for her. She felt a smile expand across her face. "I wasn't sure ya were goin' ta be able ta escort me ta town today."

"Leave my intended ta fend off the wolves by herself?" he asked, with his lopsided smile. "Not a chance."

She laughed easily. Thane reached for her basket and they set off for town.

"I'll be headin' away fer the next couple days. I need ta work on some skins and tend ta some chores at my cabin," Thane spoke quietly as they rounded the bend toward town.

"I understand," Emma replied. "I can't expect ta have yer help all the time I guess."

Thane walked quietly the rest of the way to town. Emma couldn't think of anything to say. She was already missing him. The trip was eerily quiet. Without the wind blowing, the quietness of the forest was easily heard. Emma noticed the absence of the birds chirping or any animals moving about. The stillness made her shudder.

As they neared town, she expected Thane to duck into a shop as he had done before. He surprised her as he walked on ahead to hold the door open as she went into the mercantile. He wandered over to inspect the tools needed on her list. Emma found herself standing next to the fabric, while waiting for Mrs. Phelps to fill her order. She easily located the bolt of her favorite soft purple material. She ran the edge between her fingers gently.

She was startled as the bolt was pulled out of her fingers and put on the top of the stack. She looked up to see Thane's stormy eyes studying it. "It's the same color as yer flowers," he uttered in amazement. He looked up to see Emma watching him. "It'd be perfect fer ya."

Not trusting herself to speak past the knot in her throat, she just nodded. For once, Emma felt like someone saw something the same way she did.

"Emma dear, what can I get ya today? Don't tell me ya need another dress already?" Mrs. Phelps said, not taking any notice that Emma was having a conversation. Emma moved reluctantly away from Thane and handed the store keeper her list. When she looked back towards Thane, he slid the tools he had gathered into her basket and motioned that he would be right back. She smiled at his consideration.

"Corn meal, flour,.. I heard that ya've been feeding the Abernathy boy every day. No wonder yer goin' through so many supplies." Mrs. Phelps continued to talk while gathering the items on the list. Emma remembered Thane's expression when he had held the purple cloth. She was still trying to decide why it meant so much to her, when the store keeper finished rounding up the items on her list. She added the tools that Thane picked out for her Da, and paid for it all.

She thanked Mrs. Phelps and wandered outside to look for Thane. Instead of Thane, she saw Abigail walking towards her. Emma smiled a genuine smile for her friend. After her talk with Thane about Abigail, weeks before, she had spent a great deal of time in prayer about her friendship. The more Emma prayed, the more she realized that the fault lay with herself. She began to see that she had been letting envy of her friend's marriage and happiness cloud their relationship. She wanted to make it right.

But before Emma could greet her friend, Abigail spoke first. "Emma, I am so glad I found ya today. There's someone I want ya ta meet." The excitement on Abigail's face made Emma's mouth go dry. Emma tried to protest but was twirled around slowly by a strong arm. "Emma this is Allan Nash, he bought the Williams farm a couple weeks ago. He's lookin' ta get settled here. Mr. Nash this is Emma Wells. Her family owns the farm down the road from yers."

Emma recognized Mr. Nash immediately as the fair haired gentleman who had so long ago been too familiar with her. His closeness was making her nervous. "Well, I do believe it's a pleasure Miss Emma."

She pulled her arm away from his grasp and replied, "Nice ta meet ya Mr. Nash." Taking a step away, she stood next to Abigail, "I hope ya enjoy our town."

Abigail looped her arm through Emma's, trapping her from escaping. "Emma is the best person in this whole town," Abigail released an exasperated sigh, "But she needs ta be findin' a nice man ta take care of her."

Emma opened her mouth to quiet her friend but was talked over.

"I was under the impression that Miss Emma was plannin' ta be married soon," Mr. Nash replied surprised, looking closely at her face.

Emma smiled. She had wanted to make that impression.

"Not Emma!" Abigail laughed. "No, she takes care of her Da and brothers. She's much too busy ta court."

"Abigail!" Emma gasped.

"Emma-," Mr. Nash started to speak, but she quickly interrupted.

"It's Miss Wells ta ya. Look, I don't know ya and did NOT give ya leave ta use my given name." Turning to Abigail, "And you, my friend, haven't even asked me if I had a beau, so how can ya be sure?" Stepping away from them, she nodded politely, "Good day ta ya both."

Walking quickly out of their sight, Emma kept her eyes on the road straight in front of her. Thane caught up with her as she passed the blacksmith's. He watched her with concern as she all but ran to leave town.

"Emma!"

Her heart froze. The call did not come from Thane, but from the town she was leaving behind. Reluctantly, she turned back toward the voice. Seeing James's Pa walking to meet her, she forced herself to smile. "How are ya, Mr. Abernathy?" Emma searched his face to see if the man had noticed Thane walking with her. A stranger to her family. She looked for any sign that he would reprimand her. She saw none.

"Fine, Emma girl, jest fine," the blacksmith called back to her cheerfully. "Was wonderin' iffen ya'd tell James I'll be needin' his help this afternoon? Mr. Moore brought us some work that'll take the two of us together. Jest tell him it canna wait until the day cools." Mr. Abernathy dabbed at his forehead with a kerchief to emphasize the heat of the shop.

"I'd be happy ta. I'll fetch him from his work as soon as my purchases are put up," Emma offered helpfully.

"I thank ya, Emma." Mr. Abernathy gave her a grateful smile and turned back to his shop.

She turned back around and continued on her walk out of town. Thane stepped up beside her, almost immediately, and reached for her basket. She let him take it. She would not meet his eye, as her thoughts returned to what happened outside the mercantile.

Thane noticed her hands shake as she pressed them to her stomach. "Emma, what's wrong?" he asked quietly.

Emma took in a slow breath, trying to steady her voice. She slowed her step to match Thane's before answering. "My friend jest told a gentleman that I was desperate ta be married. Unfortunately, it was the fair haired gentleman from the mercantile. The one who followed me down the road, earlier this summer. The one on his horse." She tried to smile, but the quiver to her voice showed how upset she was. "He's the man ya rescued me from. Abigail introduced him as Allan Nash." Emma subconsciously reached up to rub the arm Mr. Nash had grasped.

Thane turned her toward him gently. She wouldn't meet his eye. She didn't want to see what he was thinking. "Did he touch ya?'

"He was holdin' my arm. It wasn't hard – jest too familiar fer my likin'," she answered softly, looking down.

"I don't trust him," Thane uttered. Looking back toward town, anger flashed across his face, and he clenched his fist. "If ya go ta town while I'm away, take someone with ya." When she didn't answer him, he insisted, "Promise me ya will." The raw sound to his voice made Emma look up then. The frustration she saw on Thane's face, brought tears to her eyes. She nodded.

They turned to continue on toward the farm. They were both silent for the return trip as well.

As they neared the back porch, Thane handed her the basket. He looked into her eyes and Emma thought he was going to say something. But then with a touch to his hat, he turned to leave.

As Emma watched him disappear along the path, she felt the familiar loneliness settle around her. A day that had started out with such promise, had changed in such a short period of time.

~Sixteen~

The dog barking brought Emma out of her thoughts. She could hear her Da talking close by. "I wonder if they're done bringin' the haystacks in," she wondered. She wiped the sweat from her forehead as the kitchen door opened. She sat back on her heels to look up. Mark was standing in the doorway studying her. She knew she must look a sight. Trying to keep busy all day, her current task was scrubbing the kitchen floor. A task much better suited for a cool morning or a fall day. She pressed her arm to her forehead again and then looked back at her older brother. "Are ya lookin' fer supper already?" Emma asked trying to see the clock on the mantle from where she sat.

"No, it's still early yet," Mark replied, looking behind him before returning his attention to her. "Da asked me ta fetch ya."

"Ta fetch me?" Emma repeated uncertainly. Her father never asked for her help. She stared at her brother confused.

"Yea," Mark paused before continuing hesitantly, "There's a man here askin' after ya."

"A man?" Even more confused at hearing this, Emma rose to her feet.

"I've never seen him before," he said slowly, watching for her response.

Emma crossed to the washtub and splashed water on her face. Using the towel to pat it dry, she turned to follow Mark out the door. "What does he want?" Rolling her sleeves down as she walked, she buttoned them around her wrists.

"Ta court ya..," came her brother's reply.

"Court?" Her heart started to pound foolishly. As they rounded the corner of the house to where she could hear voices, Emma's feet stopped. Her father stood next to a man with short pale hair. When he looked up at her, the man turned to greet her. "Ahh, here's the little Missy now."

Emma felt her mouth go dry. Refusing to be scared on her own land, she straightened her back and forced her hands to drop to her side. "Hello Mr. Nash," she greeted him with a steady voice.

"You've met this gentleman?" Da asked slowly. His words had an edge of disapproval that Emma could not ignore.

"Abigail introduced us when I went ta town yesterday," Emma explained. She felt uncomfortable under her father's gaze.

"Mr. Nash here has asked fer permission ta come courtin' ya," Da stated as he continued to study her reaction. "Says he bought a farm in the area and wishes ta settle down." Emma felt the color drain from her face. "He's waitin' fer yer answer," her father's voice sounded cold.

Taking a deep breath to steady her voice, she tightened her hands into fists to keep them from shaking. "I'm honored ta be considered, Mr. Nash, but I canna accept yer attentions." She sent up a prayer of thankfulness that her mother had schooled her in the proper response for unwanted suitors.

A shadow of anger crossed Mr. Nash's face, before he allowed his confidence to return. "Now that I know yer not promised ta be married, as ya led me ta believe, I'll try again another day. Eventually, you'll grow tired of waitin' fer yer reluctant young man."

Emma felt her face flush again, but everyone's attention turned to her father. "Well she gave her answer and 'twas mighty clear. My lil' girl knows her own heart," Da stated clearly, leaving no room for dispute.

Mr. Nash squared off to Emma's father. "Yer girl ain't so little. And every lady wants ta be pursued. She'll change her mind."

Her breath caught as she saw her Da's jaw lock. A sure sign that he was losing his patience. She felt her feet step forward to object, only to be blocked by the two towering bodies as they stepped in front of her. Emma felt someone step up close behind her, as well. The hammering in her ears drowned out her father's response.

When she finally heard horse hooves riding off, she released the breath she had been holding and felt herself sway. Arms steadied her from behind. As Emma felt her hand pulled through an elbow, she leaned into the strong arm for support. The bodies in front of her stepped aside as her father approached.

"Iffen ya only met the man yesterday, why'd he assume you'd accept his attentions?" Da asked softly.

Emma shook her head. "Abigail introduced him outside the mercantile. I told him I hoped he liked our town, then excused myself ta come home." Not wanting to share the rest of the details, she added softly, "I didna encourage him, Da."

Her father studied her face carefully, then nodded slowly. "I believe ya, Emma girl." Da looked around him to the three men that surrounded her. "If Emma leaves this farm, someone goes with her." He settled his gaze back on Emma, "Even ta the berry patch."

She swallowed hard as she nodded in understanding. Voices of agreement surrounded her. Emma leaned her head against the arm that supported her and closed her eyes. When everything became quiet, Emma opened her eyes again to see if she was alone. Instead, she found her father studying her closely again. Then turning on his heel, Da walked toward the barn.

Emma felt her heart sink. "Things'll be different now," she thought. "I can feel it." She turned toward the house still leaning on the strong arm. "I can help ya with supper if ya need the company," offered a voice near her ear.

Startled, Emma loosened her grip on the arm she held as she looked up into James's bright eyes. She was surprised to realize it was James's arm she leaned on. "Oh you gave me a start," Emma gasped. She turned to see that Mark and Seth were watching her closely. Turning back to James, she explained, "Pardon me James - - I thought - - I thought ya were my brother." Looking back to her brothers again, she saw Mark smiling at her.

James tucked her hand back into his elbow. "No Emma. I'm not yer brother."

Too tired to make any sense of their behavior, Emma let herself be led inside.

"Go help Da finish up in the hayloft, Seth. We'll be helpin' Emma make supper," Mark said with a smile.

The humor in Mark's voice made Emma's heart sink even further. "Definitely different," she told herself.

The boys helped her set the kitchen to right so she could get to the cooking. James took the heavy pail of scrub water, out back, to dump it. Mark brought the rugs in for her, shaking each one first. After bumping into James twice, Emma shooed them both out of the kitchen insisting that she was fine on her own. They were headed toward the door when James stopped to look at her again. Mark laughed a full loud laugh and playfully pushed his friend out the door. Emma pressed her hands against her forehead and took a deep breath before finishing up dinner.

She was almost ready to ring the dinner bell, when James stuck his head in the door and asked if she was ready for them. She nodded without turning to him. He rang the bell and stepped into the kitchen. After washing up, he held out his hands to take the stack of plates from her. She handed them to him and reached back to get the remaining plates from the cupboard. As she turned around to hand the second stack to James as well, they slipped from her shaky grasp. James's hand wrapped around hers just as she caught the plates with her other hand. Closing her eyes, she took in an unsteady breath.

"Are ya all right?" James asked softly.

Not trusting her voice, she nodded. Forcing her eyes open, she was surprised at how close James was to her. He reached a tentative hand up to tuck a stray hair behind her ear. Emma froze in confusion.

When they heard footsteps on the porch stairs, James stepped back, taking the stack of plates with him. Emma turned to lean on the cupboard while he finished spreading the place settings. She had herself under control and was setting bowls of food on the table, by the time her family finished at the wash stand.

When everyone was seated, Emma carried the last bowl to the table. Da blessed the food, and asked God for guidance in all things. With a chorus of Amen's, she looked up to find her father's gaze on her again. Uncomfortable, she looked down and concentrated on picking at her food.

~Seventeen~

"Guilt's a terrible friend," Mama had often said. "Never feed it."

Emma finally understood those words. She rubbed her eyes, before lifting the churn handle again. She had laid awake well into the night, trying to decide if she should tell her father the whole truth. Tell him the truth about Mr. Nash's unasked for attentions, and Thane's protecting her. But a nagging voice stopped her from doing it. A voice that told her everything would change. That Thane wouldn't be allowed to visit anymore. The little sleep she did get wasn't restful. She covered the yawn that snuck out of her. The truth was, she had not slept well since Mr. Nash broke the peace on her farm. Her father watched her endlessly. Her brothers laughed at everything she did. And James? James's behavior confused her. He was near her whenever she turned around.

And it had been four days since she had seen Thane. "When Thane gets back, I'll explain it all ta him. He'll help me figure what I should do," she decided as she covered another yawn.

"Looks like ya need some sleep Emma girl," Da stated as he approached. He sat on the step, next to her rocking chair, and watched her churn for a moment.

She nodded slowly as she continued to churn the butter. Uneasy, she waited for her father to speak. Emma could only remember one other time that her father had spoken to her on her own. When her Mama kept getting sicker, Da had fetched the doctor. After the doctor finished examining Mama, Da had found Emma at the clothes line. Heartbroken, he told Emma he needed her to stay home from school for awhile. He had explained, with a quivering voice, that her Mama was going to need her help. It was not a happy memory.

Her father leaned an elbow against his knee, watching the wind blow through her little garden. "I've been noticin' yer a lot happier of late. I found myself watchin' ya.. an' watchin' ya. It took me a lil' bit but I figured out why."

Emma almost knocked the churn over in surprise but managed to respond calmly. "Why is that?"

"The boys and I, we've been talkin'. We decided if yer weddin' can wait 'til fall – 'til after the harvest- then Seth could learn some basics of cookin' and keepin' house from ya," Da suggested.

Emma's hands froze, but her father didn't seem to notice. She tried to figure out how he could have learned of her assumed wedding. Dread filled her heart as she worried for Thane. "My weddin'?" she asked casually.

Da laughed softly. "We've all seen how James makes ya laugh and smile. Took me a mite long ta admit it. But we've all seen it."

"James?" Repeating the words back to herself again, hoping she had misunderstood him. "James Abernathy?" she asked again.

"There's been no other James comin' around here. Day in and day out. Fer years on end. In fact, there ain't been any other young fellas comin' round at all." Emma's mind was spinning. Da looked down and studied his hands before continuing. "Truth is yer mama didna want ya ta marry young. So at first, we discouraged any young man from lookin' at ya. Then, when yer mama took sick.. we was jest too busy." He paused, "or maybe I jest ignored yer growin' inta a young lady cuz I didna want ta lose ya too." Emma's father looked up at her. "Then James, - well he's been takin' some teasin' from yer brothers fer some time now. Teasin' him fer comin' round so much. They've accused him more'n once of tryin' ta steal their sister away. I guess havin' another man come around askin' after ya, jarred him some. Made him realize he was gonna need ta speak of his interest in ya. I'm still thinkin' of ya as my lil' lady. But James, - he argued that all yer friends are married and hav'n babies of their own. That woke me up," smiling sadly, Da continued, "Seems he'd like ta save my pretty girl from a spinster life of carin' fer her old Da."

She finally found her voice, "Da, I don't -," but her father interrupted her, raising his hand to stop her.

"Ya won't be abandonin' us none. We've us a plan ta keep ya close by. We jest have ta work it out with James. Told him it'll be easier fer ya ta bring us bachelors treats this way," he said with a smile that didn't quite reach his eyes.

Emma studied her father. "Are ya gonna ask me what I think?" she asked around the lump in her throat. Her hands still held the dasher, but were frozen in place.

Her father smiled and shook his head. "I see what ya think in the bounce of yer step, in yer singin', yer smiles... and yer burnt cookies. I see ya takin' an interest in his life. I see ya sharin' jokes with `im. Yer laughin' and teasin'. `Tis lovely ta see. Jest lovely ta see ya in love." Da stood up and kissed her hair. Then he strode off to the barn.

Emma watched her father walk away, too numb to move. How long she sat there in the rocker, she wasn't aware of. Finally she got up to scoop the butter into its crock. Needing to be away from the house, she walked down the path to Mama's hill.

She lowered herself in front of her mother's gravestone. Emma tried to form words. Tried to talk out her heartache. Her confusion. Craving the feeling of calm that came with sharing her problems with her mother. But Emma just sat there in silence, overwhelmed by the ache she felt. "Oh Mama," she whispered, "I wish ya were here." Carefully, Emma moved over and leaned her cheek against the giant rock. She let it cool her head.

When a shadow fell over her, she felt her eyes fill up with tears. "How do ya know?" she asked. Looking up, she saw Thane standing over her, concern in his eyes. "Whenever I need ya, ya jest appear. How do ya know?" her voice cracked and she closed her eyes to block out the pain.

"Emma?" Thane squatted close to her. "What's wrong?"

She felt a laugh burst from her throat. It burned as it escaped. "Yer the first person ta notice how I feel. First person ta ask me what's wrong. Ya ask me questions and ya listen ta me." Emma felt tears trail down her cheeks. She was beyond caring who saw her tears. "Yer the only one."

Thane stood to his feet and walked to the creek edge. When he didn't respond, Emma opened her eyes to see if he had left her alone on the hilltop. But she saw him at the water's edge. His hands fisted in his hair. When he turned back to face her, the emotions in his face made her chest ache more.

"Emma?" his gray eyes pleaded, "Please tell me." He walked toward her slowly, as if not to spook her. "Tell me what's happened?" Thane brushed her skirt closer to her so he could kneel in front of her.

Emma closed her eyes as her emotions caused the pain to expand in her chest. Closed her eyes as she struggled to breathe through the pain.

"Yer scarin' me," Thane whispered.

Taking a deep breath, Emma spoke through the emotions burning in her throat. "My mama once told me it was so easy ta fall in love, with a girl in love. That her joy-," her voice caught and she had to clear it before continuing. "That her joy – shines from her face and – and makes her irresistible. Mama said that once a girl falls in love, she should steer clear of all men folk, -- Or hearts will end up broken."

Emma felt Thane move to sit closer to her knees. His legs stretched out passed her side. She felt his warm callused fingers turn her face gently toward him. She opened her eyes straight into his. "Yer in love?" he asked softly, his stormy eyes questioned hers as they searched her face for answers.

Emma looked away as she wrapped her arms around her ribs.

"Emma?" his voice pleaded with her.

Clearing her throat, Emma took a deep breath. "Mr. Nash stopped by Friday afternoon." Thane stiffened beside her. "He came ta ask my da fer permission ta court me. I told him I couldna accept his attentions." Taking in a slow breath, she continued. "Mr. Nash told Da he's confident I'll come around given time. And now that he knows I'm not promised ta anyone, he's content ta wait."

Thane lifted her chin, so he could see her eyes. "Was yer Da angry?"

Emma shook her head. "He was confused. He asked if I had encouraged Mr. Nash. I told him I hadn't. I waited fer him ta ask me about Mr. Nash's words. Ask about his mention of my weddin', my bein' promised, my man... I didna know what I was gonna say. But Da never asked." Emma shrugged helplessly, "He jest walked away." Reaching up, she captured the hand under her chin so she could look away. But her hand didn't release his once the contact had been made. Their hands came to rest on the grass between them.

"I can see there's more," Thane encouraged quietly, breaking the silence.

A sad smile stretched across her lips. "My behavior of late has change. Since I met ya in town that day, I've been happier," she admitted looking up at him. "I didna know I was different. But my family noticed. Noticed and teased me. They assumed the changes were from havin' James at the farm every day." She looked out toward the hills, away from Thane's gray eyes. "Mr. Nash's suggestions that I had a reluctant young man, confirmed that they'd assumed correct." Pulling her hand away from Thane's, Emma wrapped it around her ribs. She squeezed tightly. Trying to stop the hurt. "They shoulda asked me about it. Shoulda talked ta me." Unshed tears choked her voice and made her stop.

Squeezing her eyes shut, she took a deep breath. "But what else were they ta think. As far as they knew, James was the only one around. They never suspected ya ta bein' here at all." She turned to Thane then. "It's my fault really. I shoulda brought ya out ta the field that first day. Shoulda introduced ya ta my Da. Explained what happened. Explained the honor ya did fer me." Looking away again, Emma continued softly, "I didna think of it then. Guess I didna figure ya'd be back. I didna think I'd see ya 'gain. And now-," her voice caught.

Thane reached over tentatively to reclaim the hand wrapped tightly across her chest. "And now?" he prompted softly.

Squeezing her eyes closed, "These last couple days, I kept tryin' ta decide if I should tell Da. But if I introduce ya now and explain how I feel- - I fear it would look improper. Like we've been sneakin' around these last weeks." The pressure on her fingers increased, reminding her that Thane still held her hand. "Instead of bein' thankful as they should be-," Emma cleared her throat, "-They'd never accept ya now. They'd likely run ya off. Never let ya come 'round here again." She looked at him then, tears pooling in her eyes.

The emotions playing across Thane's face were so raw and intense that Emma could not look away. "Are ya sayin' that ya love me?" he asked, his voice thick with emotion.

She nodded and tried to look away then. But his hand reached up to keep her looking at him.

"Ya love me?" Thane repeated.

Emma nodded again.

Thane's eyes mirrored his joy and sadness. He slowly brought the hand, he was holding, up to his cheek. Closing his eyes, he pressed it lightly there. She reached over with her free hand to move the hair that fell over his eyes. He captured that hand as well. He pressed a kiss to the palm of her hand. Keeping hold of her hands, he lowered them to the grass between them.

"The fault's mine," he stated hoarse with his emotions. "I never thought ya'd be lovin' me. But I did know that no father wants the likes of me fer their daughter. So I avoided the proper callin'. I shoulda tried fer yer sake."

Unable to speak, she gently squeezed his hand. Thane leaned over her fingers and pressed them to his lips again. Emma leaned forward and pressed her forehead against his. Time froze as she leaned on his strength for comfort. Too soon he pulled back, letting their hands rest in the grass.

Clearing his voice, Thane asked, "This James. Is he kind ta ya?" His eyes studied her face.

"Kind enough," she nodded.

"An' yer family thinks he'll take good care of ya?"

Again she nodded, not trusting her voice.

"They think he's asked fer yer hand?" Thane's voice deepened with emotion.

Emma shivered as his fingertips traced her ring finger. "They're plannin' their world around it." She could not meet his eyes. She did not trust her emotions.

Thane brought her hand back up to rest on his cheek, "And what we've been doin' would tarnish yer name?"

Turning her head away, "We've done nothin' improper." Anger gave her voice a bitter edge.

"But they'll think it?" Thane's fingers turned her face back toward him.

A deep sigh escaped her, "That they can't be sure what we've been doin'? -- That'll put a shadow on it," Emma nodded, barely moving her head.

Thane closed his eyes then. Anger flitted across his face. He shot to his feet and strode over to the creek edge. Again, his hands went to his hair and balled into fists. Emma wasn't aware she had followed him to his side until she reached out to touch his elbow. She ached to wrap her arms around his waist and lean into his chest. Wanted to feel the comfort she knew she would find there.

At her touch, Thane turned toward Emma, dropping his hands to her shoulders. His gray eyes were full of sadness and resignation. "Emma, I-," he cleared his throat to continue, "I wish you every happiness-." The thickness of his throat made him stop. He squeezed his eyes shut. Leaning forward, he pressed his lips to Emma's forehead. As a tear fell on her cheek, her breath caught in her throat. Emma felt her eyes fill with tears.

Thane released her so suddenly that she stumbled forward. Then he was gone. Emma was alone in the woods. She was alone in life again.

Tears blinded her as she made her way up the path to the house. She crossed through the kitchen to the stairs. Making her way up to her room, she sat on her bed. Picking up her Mama's Bible to find comfort, Emma opened it to see the little purple flowers she had pressed there. She ran her finger down the stem. The hopelessness, of it all, overwhelmed her and the first sob escaped her throat. A burning pain filled her chest. The pain was too intense for her. Emma curled into a ball. Pulling her pillow to her face to muffle her sobs, she cried. And she cried. She cried until all her emotions were spent. Then exhaustion took over and Emma fell asleep.

~Eighteen~

The cheerful whistling at the door informed Emma that she was about to be intruded upon. She turned her thoughts back to the bacon and eggs frying on the stove.

"Mornin' Em'," Seth called as he headed to the wash tub in the corner of the kitchen.

"Mornin'," she replied, not turning around. Emma set about scooping food onto plates. She was almost finished when the door opened. Mark came in and it was apparent that he was laughing at James.

James crossed the room, stopping a few steps from Emma. He waited patiently for her to finish filling the plate she held. When she looked up, the joy in his eyes overflowed into his smile. "Good Morning, Emma." He took a small step closer to her. A sudden thought that he would embrace her made Emma's heart freeze. Before she could react, a deep cough let them know her father had entered the kitchen. With a sheepish smile, James turned to join the other men at the wash tub.

Emma released a slow sigh of relief. Glancing toward the corner, she saw her Da eyeing her with a cocked eyebrow. Looking away, she caught Mark's laughter with a wink in her direction. James turned to her with a happy smile. She quickly turned back to the table and finished serving the food. She put the pot on the back of the stove to cool. Bracing herself with a deep breath, Emma turned to join her already seated family.

Da blessed the food and the weather. "Lord, we sure could use some rain if it's in Yer Will, and Bless my lil' girl with happiness. In yer name, Amen."

A chorus of "Amen's" followed. Emma's came out as a whisper. "Happiness?" she thought. Looking at her father, she saw that he was watching for her reaction. She forced a smile for him. Looking down at her plate, she took a bite of food and turned to her brother. She watched Mark talk for a minute before glancing back toward her Da. Her small show of life seemed to be enough for him, he was deep in conversation with James. She tried to swallow her bite of food, but it got stuck in her throat. She reached for her glass of milk to help it down.

Remembering her Da's prayer, Emma sent up one of her own. "Lord, please send the rain." The last few days had been almost unbearable. The sun shone beautifully, the birds sang, and everything seemed to live in harmony. Her family was especially happy. She took a deep breath and looked out the window. The ache in her chest was slowly turning to numbness. She preferred the numbness. Preferred not having to brace herself against each new emotion. "It sure would be easier without the whistling and the laughter," she admitted silently. "Don't know how everythin' goes on as before, like nothin' has changed. They're so full of joy when I feel so empty inside." Emma turned back to her plate. Preparing herself for another bite, her father's question stopped her.

"What time were ya plannin' yer trip ta town, Emma girl?" Da had already informed her he would be taking her to town this morning.

"As soon as I clean up after breakfast," she replied softly.

"Well Seth if yer plannin' on riding along, you'd best be finishin' the stalls before yer sister finishes the dishes," Da stated.

"Yes sir," Seth answered. Concentrating on finishing his food. Emma's heart sank, "Yer goin' ta town too?" she asked Seth.

"We're all goin'," came the answer from James.

"All?" she repeated slowly, changing her attention to James.

Seth laughed, "We don't wanna miss the talk in town. Our sister's marryin' the best man in the area.. there's bound ta be talk." He pounded James on the back as he headed out the door. His whistling echoing in through the windows.

"Everyone knows?" Emma asked James. He turned to her, with a sheepish smile.

"I was gonna let you tell the news, but my Pa's a mite proud of how it all turned out. –And it's a small town," James cleared his throat with a laugh. "When Ms. Phelps asked me if there was truth ta it.. I saw no reason ta deny it then."

No one noticed Emma's lack of response. Mark laughed at James's words, "Yer Pa is proud? It seems yer buttons are fair ta burstin' yerself. That ridiculous smile hasn't left yer face this week."

James's cheeks flamed red as the laughter and teasing continued. Even her father's laughter was heard blending in. Emma started gathering up the dishes. While she cleaned up the kitchen, her thoughts turned in dread to what she would hear when she got to town. Emma had hoped to keep the news quiet until she could find happiness in it herself. Keep it to herself until she could at least accept it. She left the skillet to soaking while she went back to wash the table. She was startled when James put his hand on top of hers. Mark laughed again as she pulled her hand quickly away. Her eyes lifted in question to James.

"Sorry Emma - - Was jest gonna remind ya that ya already washed the table," James explained. Laughter rang out from the men.

"I did?" Emma asked confused. She looked around to see the evidence of dampness. "Oh. Sorry."

"If ya wanted ta be close ta James, ya can jest sit in the chair next ta him," Mark said between laughs.

Emma felt her color drain from her face. "Is that what it looks like?"

"Mark be easy on yer sister. Yer Mama always taught her ta be proper like," Da chuckled. "She'd be right proud of ya, Emma girl."

Emma hurried back to the washtub. She finished scrubbing the skillet and hurried up to her room to freshen up. Once she had her bonnet tied on, she headed out the front door. Rounded the corner of the house, Emma saw that the wagon was hitched and ready to go.

"We're takin' the wagon? I usually jest walk, Da," she stated as she came to his side.

"I know Emma girl, but the team could use the exercise," he answered with a smile. "And we'll have a full wagon today. 'Sides - - James bought some of our livestock, so I could get ya started with some purchases," Da put a finger under her chin. "You've a dress ta make." He placed a kiss in her hair and then moved to check the next horse.

The ache in her chest flared up suddenly. She took a deep shaky breath to get it under control. A hand appeared at her side. She followed it to James's smiling face. "Here, let me help ya up, Emma." Her heart wanted to deny his help. But she felt herself force a smile and a "thank ya". Accepting his hand, she climbed onto the bench, then quickly released it once she was settled. He flashed her a happy smile, before jumping in the back with Mark and Seth. Da climbed up next to her, clicked to the horses and the wagon lurched forward.

Pretending to go carefully over her list again, Emma avoided any conversation. They arrived in town before she realized it. She sent up a prayer of thankfulness. "This'll be over soon," she sighed to herself.

Seth jumped down as they came to a stop. He reached up to help his sister down. "Was wonderin'?" he leaned in secretively. "Are you buying ginger today?"

Emma smiled in spite of herself. "Seth Wells are ya beggin' fer cookies again?"

"Those ginger ones?" he nodded hopefully.

In response, Emma held up her list. Seth scanned the list and let out a "whoop" of satisfaction. He ran into the store before she had even climbed the steps. Stepping ahead, James held the door open for her.

The atmosphere changed when Emma stepped into the mercantile. Abigail was instantly by her side, giving her an excited hug. She saw over her friend's shoulder that David was shaking James's hand. James was receiving the attention with a genuine smile. Mrs. Phelps rushed over to greet them. "Well Joseph Wells. I heard yer good news. Must be a relief ta finally have one of yer young'ns marryin' off?"

"Had hoped ta keep her forever, but doesn't look like I'll be that lucky," Da responded with a wink in Emma's direction.

"Of course not. A sweet girl like our Emma was bound ta be noticed eventually," Mrs. Phelps said with a smile.

"Oh, I've been noticing Emma Fern since that first day she came ta school, trailing behind Mark," James commented above all the talking. "It jest took her awhile ta notice me back."

Emma turned in James's direction. She found his gaze already on her. The pride and joy shining from his eyes, made her throat ache with guilt. "I was six," she responded astonished.

James laughed, "Mark told me I'd have ta wait awhile fer ya. He jest didn't say it'd be 12 years." Laughter echoed around the store.

Mrs. Phelps stepped forward to embrace Emma before heading back to her customers at the counter.

Emma thought back to her childhood. She couldn't remember James ever treating her special. He had just acted protective of her. Just like Mark always had. James had brought Emma her homework for awhile after Mama had gotten sick. Then he had sat with her until she understood it all. Mark had been too busy to explain it all to her. Eventually, Mark and Emma had both given up on their studies. In the end, only Seth had continued with school. She glanced back to James. He was still watching her as Abigail led her away.

"I told David how mad I was that I found out from someone else. But he insisted that you were plannin' on visiting me when ya came ta town ta tell me the news. Guess it's not yer fault gossip got ta me first," Abigail reasoned, as she was steering Emma toward the bolts of fabric. Lowering her voice, she continued, "I understand yer reluctance at meetin' Mr. Nash now. I told David that ya turned him down flat. He said was glad ya had the good sense. Heard he was out ta the Moore place. He asked ta court their oldest girl. I guess David is right. Ya made a good choice." Suddenly Abigail turned Emma toward her. "Tell me ya're gonna live in town now? Close so we can visit every day?"

Emma was surprised by the question. She never considered living in town, but it was true that James worked with his Pa. "I'm not sure –," Emma started to say but was interrupted.

"We haven't decided where we're ta live. Still figurin' out the details," James explained to Abigail as he stepped up beside Emma. He smiled down into her eyes, letting his hand settle on her back. She smiled her thanks for him stepping in. "I'm not sure I'll get her far from her Da and brothers though."

"But ya'll have more time ta visit! Only carin' fer one man instead of three..," Abigail went on. "Are ya pickin' out fabric today?"

"Main reason we're here," James answered happily.

Emma felt herself nod. She turned to face the shelves and easily found the soft purple bolt on the table closest to her. Reaching out to run her fingers along it, she recalled the way Thane's eyes had lit up when he saw it. Her chest started to ache with the memory. She closed her eyes and concentrated on breathing. Only to open them to a bolt being slammed down on her fingers.

"Here's a white one," Seth announced proudly.

"This one's pretty. It has lace," James offered her the bolt for her approval.

Both bolts were for underclothes. Emma's thoughts turned to the day she had been embarrassed by Thane helping her hang clothes on the line. Again, she found herself closing her eyes against the ache in her chest.

"Oh BOYS!" reprimanded Abigail. "How could you embarrass her so? Those aren't dress bolts. They need ta be thicker. An' it hasta have a shine." Emma turned to see Abigail searching the shelves. For once, Emma was happy for her friend's bossiness.

"Em, ya alright?" Mark asked softly.

"Yeah," she nodded slowly, "jest tired and a mite overwhelmed."

He nodded back in understanding, "Come on James and Seth. This is women's work. Let's leave 'em ta it." Shooing the boys out of the crowded corner and back toward Da.

When she turned back to Abigail, her friend had arranged three bolts in front of her. All three looked heavy and hot. All three were pale white colors. So pale that she would only wear this dress once.

Emma reached out to feel one of the bolts, "They're so white.. I'll never be able ta wear it again," she stated softly.

Abigail laughed at her. "Ya won't be able ta wear it again iffen ya wanted. Soon after yer weddin' you'll look like me," indicating her expanding waistline.

Emma had a flash of a little boy running along side his father. As the image turned to wave to her, she gazed into his deep gray eyes. She closed her eyes again. Closed them against the color, trying to close her heart from the hurt. But a tear escaped. She quickly wiped it away.

Opening her eyes to tell Abigail she would return later, she instead opened them to see those same deep gray eyes. Surprised, Emma couldn't look away. She could not take her eyes from Thane. But as she stared into his stormy eyes, she gradually came to realize they were angry. She searched the rest of his face for a clue for his anger.

"She'll need a dress length of this," Abigail told the store keeper. "Oh and let's see," Emma turned to see her friend picking up the fabric and placing it on the cut counter. Abigail was not waiting for Emma to answer.

Emma turned back to Thane. Her throat hurt just looking at him. She wanted to rest her head against his chest and block out everyone. But she couldn't and she had no one to blame except herself. So she kept her feet where they were. She looked back down at the material in front of her. The purple was still there. She reached her hand out to feel it between her fingers.

"Ya would've been beautiful in the purple, but I'm glad ya won't wear it fer him," Thane said softly. "You were right. When ya're with them, they make ya more plain. They don't see ya at all, do they?" he asked, anger burning in his eyes.

Emma wrapped her arm around her ribs to hold against the ache. He stepped back, tipped his hat to her and walked out the door. It hurt to breathe. Emma wanted to run out the door, whether to follow Thane or run home she didn't know.

"Well Emma," Abigail said drawing her back." I think this'll get ya through all yer weddin' clothes." She handed the bundles to Emma, piling them into her arms.

Da stepped forward to hand Mrs. Phelps the list of other items they needed.

Emma tried concentrating on what was going on around her, but could not follow the conversation. Knowing her father would pay for her packages along with the other items the store keeper was wrapping up, she excused herself to get some air. Forcing herself to smile, Emma wished Mrs. Phelps and Abigail each a good day.

She walked through the door, gently pulling it closed behind her. Not seeing her brothers or James, she headed for the wagon.

Putting her packages under the seat, Emma gathered her skirts to step up. Suddenly, she felt herself being lifted up. She sat back and lifted her eyes to see Thane standing there. She smiled weakly as he tipped his hat before walking away. She didn't bother checking to see if anyone saw the exchange, because she knew no one would have. The only person who ever noticed what she did was walking quickly out of her sight.

~Nineteen~

The silence around Emma was broken as the men opened the kitchen door and flooded the kitchen with talk. She jumped up to take the food off the stove.

"I apologize fer us bein' so late Emma girl," Da stated. "We found a section of fence that needed repairin' before we came in fer the night."

"It's fine. Supper kept warm on the stove," Emma assured him.

James stepped in front of her and stopped. "How are ya today?" he asked softly.

Emma smiled weakly, but was spared from replying.

"James has asked ta go walkin' with ya," her father informed her. Emma looked up at James. He was watching for her reaction. "Told him it was too late tonight, but might be tomorrow. Iffen we finish up earlier." She simply nodded her head as she finished dishing the food out. "Since ya won't want yer brothers taggin' along with ya, ya'll stay in sight of the house. I'll be watchin' ta keep it proper," Da instructed.

"Yes sir," James answered as he sat in his chair. He looked up at Emma as she walked past him and smiled.

"I can do this," she told herself. She had walked with James before, it would be easy. "Yes Da," she repeated aloud.

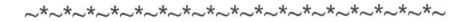

~*~*~*~*~*~*~*~*~*~*~*~*~

The hoot of an owl made Emma start. She was confused at why she was awake until she heard another call from the bird. She let out a deep sigh into her pillow. The exhaustion, from her hard work, had helped her fall asleep easier the night before, but it had not kept her asleep. It was well before dawn and she found herself awake again.

Her thoughts turned to another morning, weeks before, when she had woke up before the sun. Emma had been so excited at the thought of Thane stopping by, she had gladly gotten up to start her day. Breakfast had been cooked and ready as the sun came up that day. Emma smiled at the memory. But the smile died on her lips as the last couple weeks came rushing back. The ache in her chest grew until she could hardly breathe.

Pushing back the covers, Emma forced herself to get up. Reaching for her dress that hung on the peg of her wall, she pulled it down over her shoulders and headed for the kitchen. As she started some oatmeal to boiling, she began making a list of all the chores she would do to keep busy that day.

~*~*~*~*~*~*~*~*~*~*~*~*~

"Will ya be needin' a new dress, Emma girl?" Da's question broke through her thoughts.

"New dress?" Emma repeated. "Fer what?"

Mark chuckled, "Our Emma'll be the only girl in town not beggin' fer a new dress!"

Emma turned toward her family. They sat around the table enjoying one last cup of coffee before heading out to the field. "I jest made two dresses. Why would I be needin' another one?" she repeated, confused.

Da took his last swallow of coffee before answering, "Jest thought ya'd want ta look `specially nice when James shows ya off at the church social."

Emma forgot for a moment that she was holding the oatmeal pot. It slipped from her fingers, dropping into the dishpan. Hot soapy water splashed wildly and Emma felt it soak through her apron to her dress front.

Seth erupted with laughter. "Ever since ya fell fer James, Em, ya're so much more fun."

"Let's get outta her hair, so she can clean up her mess," Mark remarked with amusement.

She heard chairs scrape the floor and the door slam.

"Ya wantin' a new dress, Emma Fern?" Da asked again before he followed.

"I've only worn my church dress a handful of times, Da. It'll do fer the social," Emma replied. "Too much ta do without addin' the makin' of another dress."

"Sounds about right," Da nodded as he approached her. He kissed the top of her head. "Imagine ya'd find the time if ya needed ta."

Emma heard the door slam as her Da left the house. Her shoulders slumped forward. The thought of going to the church dance with James, made her lip quiver. A whole night of pretending to be happily in love. Wiping her tears away, she straightened her back, determined not to fall apart. "First, I need ta get out of these wet clothes." And she went in search of her patched up work dress.

~*~*~*~*~*~*~*~*~*~*~*~*~*~*~

Emma wiped the sweat from her eyes before she continued brushing down the walls of the sitting room. Her arms ached from the strenuous work, but the walls were looking better. The cobwebs were disappearing and the chinking was looking whiter. Her whole body ached from the exhaustion, but Emma didn't stop. With the exhaustion, came a peace from thinking too much about her future.

Stopping to get a drink of water, Emma leaned against the table. With a deep breath, she stood to her feet and began to brush down the walls in the kitchen. She would have just enough time to clean up the floors before needing to start supper.

~*~*~*~*~*~*~*~*~*~*~*~*~*~*~

Emma pushed her food around the plate. As supper came to a close, the talk stumbled to a stop. She waited, in dread, for James to ask her to walk out with him. Looking closely at her food, she couldn't remember if she had eaten anything. Spearing a carrot, she lifted it to her mouth.

"Would ya hurry up already, Em'? Put James outta his misery," Seth said with a laugh. Emma looked up at him and then over at James.

"Sorry," Emma said guiltily. Smiling weakly at James, she added, "I'm not really hungry today."

Seth made mooning eyes and batted his eyelashes. "One cannot live on love alone," he declared mockingly, followed by a deep sigh. He ducked his head just in time to escape Mark's hand aiming for the back of his head.

"Why don't ya go change inta something pretty, Emma girl. Seth will see ta yer dishes," Da suggested.

Emma forgot that she was wearing her work dress. Using the excuse of changing, she fled the room.

"Why do I hafta do her dishes? James wants ta walk with her, not me?" Seth's muffled complaint drifted up the stairs behind her.

Taking her time, Emma slipped into her church dress. She splashed cool water on her face and neck, before going to sit in front of her small mirror. The soft blue dress looked nice against her pale brown hair. Her eyes absorbed some of the color and almost looked blue. Her hair look frayed and was sliding down from her day of hard work. "I'll hafta redo my hair," she realized. Taking her hair down, she brushed it out. Carefully, she pulled it back up, trying to keep the knot looser and less severe, like her Mama had showed her years before. Thoughts of her Mama brought tears to her eyes. "No!" Emma insisted. "No tears." Forcing herself to think of nothing but her hair, she managed to do an acceptable job of it.

When she could put it off no longer, Emma slowly made her way down the stairs. She could hear the boys talking and teasing as they put the dishes away. Taking a deep breath, she walked through the entrance to the kitchen.

James turned to her as soon as she entered. Admiration softened his gaze and Emma had to look away. "Ya look beautiful!" he declared.

Emma's stomach fell. She put a smile on her face, but she felt like an imposter trying to impress him. She suddenly wished she hadn't bothered fixing her hair. She didn't want James to think her lovely.

"More beautiful than usual, he means!" Seth added with a wink.

"Rotten kid," Mark muttered as he grabbed his brother by the shoulder and shoved him out the door.

"Shall we?" James asked, offering her his elbow.

Da kept his gaze diverted when Emma glanced at him. She stepped forward with a determined nod of her head, and slipped her hand through James's elbow. They stepped through the door and down the porch steps together. Heading toward the garden, Emma felt him sigh contentedly. They walked for a few minutes in silence.

"I found a house fer us. It's close by. Yer Da said he'd help us get it ready so we can get married sooner," James stated, finally breaking the awkward silence. Emma forced herself to smile, but could not bring herself to look at him. "The fields will need ta be cleared, but I'll have all winter, after the weddin', ta do that." He smiled down at her. "Mark said he'd help me run crops next year, `til I get the hang of it. It bein' my first growing season and all. With Seth bein' done with school, yer Da said he has plenty of help."

As he continued to talk to her of his plans, Emma grew more uncomfortable. "If only I was washin' dishes or pickin' beans," she thought, "At least then I'd know where ta look and what ta do with my hands." She took a deep breath and tried to focus on what James was saying.

James put his hand over the one tucked in his elbow. "We'll have a good life, Emma. I know we're gonna be happy together," he whispered. Emma felt tears fill her eyes, wishing she shared his joy. "Makin' ya happy's been my plan fer as long as I can remember. I was always lookin' fer ways ta make ya happy. Whenever I could make ya smile, my heart would start ta overflowin'." He turned toward her and she looked up surprised by his stopping. "Now my heart is so full, it's pert near ta burstin'." He pulled her into his arms, and crushed her to his chest. He pressed his lips to her forehead. Tears slipped from Emma's eyelids and ran freely down her cheeks. Thoughts of Thane filled her mind and she longed to push away from James. Her hands gripped his shirt front as she forced herself to breathe.

A throat cleared itself loudly and James released her. She looked toward the house and saw her Da sitting in her rocker. James laughed uncomfortably, "Sorry sir."

Emma wiped the tears from her face. Determined to find a safe subject, she forced herself to smile. "How is yer Pa? Ya been busy at the shop?"

James took her by the hand and began to fill her in on the happenings at the blacksmith shop. Emma felt the world around her slip away and a comfortable numbness surrounded her.

~*Twenty*~

"Poor things," Emma thought. She watched the hen in the corner sitting on her eggs. "Ya eat, lay eggs and raise yer babies. The whole time yer stuck in a fence ya care nothin' fer, until someone decides ta let ya out." She started to wonder if that's how she'd feel soon. "Not much of a life."

"Emma?"

Emma was startled by the voice being so close suddenly. Her heart hammered as she turned to face the speaker. When she saw that it wasn't Thane, her heart sank. She blinked to keep the tears away.

"Didna mean ta make ya jump," James apologized.

Emma smiled weakly. She looked around her. She stood in the chicken yard with an empty bucket. Trying to remember if she had brought food with her, she looked at the ground around her. The chickens were scratching at food sprinkled around her feet, so she suspected she had.

"Do ya ever wonder what it's like for chickens? Locked in here, relyin' on someone ta feed `em, ta let `em out? No freedom ta come and go as they want ta?" Emma asked softly.

James cleared his throat. "The fence is ta protect `em Emma. It's ta keep them safe from the hawks and fox and coyotes. Ya feed `em and give `em shelter. That's all they need," he assured her.

His words made sense, but she didn't feel any more certain. They just looked trapped t o her.

Stepping closer, James cleared his throat again. "I found these flowers and I thought of ya. Mark said purple flowers were yer favorite."

Her breath caught as he held the small purple flowers out to her. They were similar to her mama's flowers but darker. "Thank ya," she said with a shaky voice. She reached for them, remembering another time when someone held small purple flowers out to her. Different flowers, smaller hands, and the eyes she looked up into then weren't blue. Emma gave James a watery smile. He stood there for a moment longer before he turned and went back to the field. As she watched him walk away, her heart broke. "He's such a wonderful man," her heart cried. "He deserves better than me Lord. He deserves someone ta love him."

"He wants you," a voice reminded her. Emma agreed with the voice, but her heart still yearned for someone else.

~*~*~*~*~*~*~*~*~*~*~*~*~*~

Another flash of lightning lit up the sky. The answering crack of thunder shook the cabin. Emma watched through the open door. She closed her eyes and relaxed with the storm. Stepping through the doorway, she lowered herself into her rocker. Watching the dark clouds roll and churn, she felt it mirrored her warring emotions.

After awhile, Mark joined her on the porch. He leaned against the post watching the storm in silence. Turning to her, he studied his sister's face. "What're ya so worried 'bout, Em?" he asked softly.

Emma turned her eyes toward Mark. The caring that she saw there broke through the numbness surrounding her. She felt a swell of emotion rise up into her throat. "I'm worryin' about all this. Worryin' that we're not doing this right? What if we're wrong?"

"Wrong about what?" Mark asked confused.

"What if I'm not supposed ta marry James? What if it's not God's plan fer me? What if this isn't good fer James?" Emma asked, her voice pleading with uncertainty. Her emotions making her voice thick.

"What are ya talkin' about Emma?" Mark exploded. "Of course yer good fer James! Yer the only girl he's ever wanted," her brother stopped himself and rubbed his forehead. Taking a deep breath, he knelt in front of her. "Look Emma," Mark urged her. "Ya've been

James's whole world since we were kids. Yer all he's ever thought of. All he's ever talked about. Yer the only girl he's ever wanted in this life. He's been content waitin' fer ya, knowin' ya'd make him happy in the end," he paused for a second before continuing. "But since ya've agreed ta marry him? Since ya've noticed him as a man and not jest my friend? He has this new life in him. He's workin' so hard ta provide fer ya, and yet still hopin' ta spend every moment he can with ya. I've never seen him this happy."

An ache filled her chest at the thought of hurting James. Feeling frustrated and completely alone, Emma let the numbness settle back around her. Not bothering to wipe the tear that slid down her cheek, "That's what I want. I jest want everyone ta be happy." Her eyes blurred out of focus as she turned back to the clouds above.

Mark rubbed his hands over his face again. When he spoke, it was much softer. "I know that, Em. I know. Yer jest nervous is all. I understand." When Emma didn't respond, Mark watched her rock for a few minutes more, while the storm carried on. Then he gently squeezed her shoulder before going back into the cabin, leaving her to herself.

The storm raged on. The clouds grew darker and the thunder rumbled close enough to rattle the windows. Emma continued to rock, feeling comforted by the anger of the storm. She rocked well into the night.

~Twenty One~

Emma felt her world sway. She set the washtub back down with a loud "thud" and leaned on it. Taking a deep breath to try again, she felt strong arms reach around her to lift the heavy tub out of her grasp.

Surprised, she turned to see her father walking away from her. Embarrassed that she needed help, Emma followed him through the back door as he dumped the water. "Sorry Da, I-," but the look on her Da's face stopped her.

"Enough Emma!" The anger in his voice made her breath catch. "Enough," he repeated softer. "You don't eat, you don't laugh. I know you aren't sleeping. Ya don't answer when people talk ta ya. Yer workin' non-stop in this heat. What is goin' on?"

"I'm fine Da," she lied. She gripped the railing to keep upright.

"No," he disagreed, "Ya aren't fine. I've seen ya almost fall over more'n once. Ya yawn from mornin' `til night. An' yer dresses look like sacks hangin' on ya. Ya were already a thin girl and now-," he stepped closer to her, handing her the empty washtub. "Are ya jest upset about postponin' the wedding?"

"Postponin'?" she repeated confused. She hadn't realized there was a date set.

"Emma girl," her father said with concern, "Ya know we're hurryin' fer ya. We're workin' on gettin' ya a home. We're gonna work on it around harvestin' the crops."

She nodded numbly in agreement. Not understanding what he meant, but she knew he wanted to see that she heard him.

Her Da stepped closer, putting his hands on her shoulders, he studied her face. "Maybe we shouldna put off the weddin'. Ya can marry James now and jest live here until we finalize the house. Maybe ya'd be happier. This waitin' seems ta be wearin' on ya."

"No Da," Emma insisted shaking her head. "We need ta wait. I need the time ta be ready." She tried to smile to convince him.

He studied her face again before releasing her. "Then eat! And get some sleep. Ya aren't ta clean anything else today."

"Da- it's Monday. I have ta get ta the wash," Emma explained.

"No Emma," Da said firmly. "Ya need ta rest." He kissed the top of her hair and strode off toward the barn.

Emma sat down on the step behind her. She covered her face against the dizziness that threatened to overcame her. "Maybe Da's right," she admittted to herself. Rubbing her eyes, she looked toward Mama's hill. Sitting up straighter, she blinked her eyes. It looked like Thane was standing down the path. She stood and walked toward him. Halfway down, the path straightened and Emma could clearly see Thane standing there watching her. She stopped in surprise and felt her world sway again.

Thane moved quickly to her side. Tucking a package under his arm, he grasped her under her elbows to steady her. His stormy eyes narrowed with concern. "Emma-," he started.

"I can't believe yer really here," Emma interrupted, refusing to take her eyes off him.

"Can you walk?" Thane asked.

"Yeah, I'm fine," she insisted. She stepped carefully around him toward her mama's rock. Thane's face told her he didn't believe her. He walked close to her side, just in case she got lightheaded again.

As Emma sat on her Mama's giant rock, Thane hovered close by until he saw she would not fall over. Then he stepped back. "Ya've not been sleepin'?" he asked.

Emma looked at Thane, surprised that he could tell.

"Yer Da seems worried about ya," he stated quietly.

She looked toward the house. "Ya heard him?"

"Tough not ta," Thane said. "Why aren't ya sleepin'?"

Emma looked down at her hands. "As soon as I lay down, all these thoughts go through my mind. I think if I could jest go back ta the beginnin', I could do it all differently. I wonder if that woulda fixed this. But I can't go back. So I lay there thinkin' what I could say ta change everyone's minds. But it always ends with someone I love gettin' hurt. And then I remember-," she turns to look at him. "I remember that this way everyone's happy."

"`Cept you?" Thane added sadly.

Emma nodded slowly, "Everyone `cept me." She looked upstream toward his hills. "I canna stop thinkin' about ya. I wonder if ya'll have someone ta talk ta. If ya'll find someone ta marry. Someone ta keep yer sadness from comin' back." The thought of someone else taking care of Thane made her throat hurt again. She coughed softly.

"When did ya eat last?" Thane asked softly.

She blinked in confusion. "I jest finished breakfast."

"How much did ya eat?"

Emma blinked again. She couldn't remember if she had actually put anything in her mouth today. "I drank my milk," she muttered to herself. "I think."

Thane strode over to the path by the creek and grabbed his sack hidden there. He pulled out a piece of salted pork and put it in her hand. Emma just stared at it. "We'll have a lil' picnic," he said softly. He sat down on the grass near her.

Her eyes filled with tears. "The food jest sticks in my throat." Thane pulled out a canteen and set it gently next to her. He sat on the ground to watch her. With a sigh, Emma tore off a small piece and put it in her mouth. After chewing, she took a swallow of water to wash it down. "I feel like a terrible person. Feel like I'm tryin' ta fool everyone. Like I'm being someone I'm not. Like I'm lyin' ta everyone." Emma took another bite before she continued. "I try ta stay busy. Try ta stay by myself. Thane, I feel so empty. Do ya think I'll always feel this way? Do ya think it'll go away?" she asked as she pulled off another small piece and ate it. As Emma spoke, she gazed off into the hills. Her eyes not focusing on anything.

"Ya know. I was there jest before Mama died. She told me that when you feel the most alone in this world is when you'll see God around the most – It's not true. I don't see God at all..," Emma said softly.

Thane looked away from her, swallowing hard. "Did ya ask yer Mama about it?" he suggested.

Emma looked at her mother's gravestone. "I tried talkin' ta her last week. It doesn't help anymore. I can't talk ta her. She doesn't answer. So I jest sat there, wishin' she was alive. Wishin' she could help me." Looking toward Thane, she felt her lip quiver. "What is the reason fer all this?"

"Emma -," Thane started but her huge yawn stopped him. "Ya need sleep," he finished instead.

"My Da told me ta rest," she stated with another yawn.

Thane looked up at her. "Ya need ta take care of yerself."

She nodded, "I try. I jest ferget sometimes." Tearing off another chunk of the pork, she chewed it slowly. They sat in silence until Emma had eaten the last small chunk and washed it down with one last drink of water.

Thane held out his hand for the canteen. "I came ta apologize fer my words in the mercantile last week. I can't get mad when things are turnin' out different-," he cleared his throat, "- different than I hoped they'd be fer ya. Getting' mad doesn't help ya none." Thane stood to his feet. "So I'm goin' away." He looked down at the brown package in his hand. He tapped it against his leg a couple times before tucking it inside his sack with the canteen.

"Where will ya go?" Emma asked softly.

"Trappin' fer awhile I suspect." Thane looked into the hills. "I jest can't stay here. I can't stay and watch."

Maybe that was best, she told herself. If she didn't see him, she would not miss him. She found herself nodding. "Thane," Emma called out softly, looking into his stormy gray eyes one last time. "Take care of yerself."

Thane was quiet for a minute, struggling with something. Then he nodded once and disappeared along the creek path.

Emma wrapped her arms around her ribs as she watched him go. Lowering herself down onto the ground, she leaned back against the cool rock. Tears streamed down her cheeks, but she made no effort to wipe them away. She repeated to herself that with Thane leaving, she could start anew. Having no reminders of him would help her to move on. But only two words echoed in her mind, "Thane's leavin'."

~Twenty Two~

"Not sure ya should be carryin' my sister until yer married," Seth's voice quietly pointed out. "Why don't ya let me take her?"

Emma felt warmth seep into her.

"I wouldna want ya ta drop my soon-ta-be bride," laughter rumbled in her ear. Confused as to why it seemed so close, she tried to open her eyes, but sleep still clung to them.

"I dunno," came Seth's reply. "Maybe we shoulda got Mark."

"Got me fer what?" asked a voice further away.

Emma felt her floating come to a stop. "When we realized Emma wasn't in the house, we went lookin' fer her," rumbled the voice in her ear.

"We found her on Mama's hill sleepin'," Seth went on. "Lover boy here insisted on carryin' her back. Jest not sure Emma'd permit it were she awake," he added uncomfortably.

"Carryin'?" Emma thought. "Am I bein' carried?" She again tried to open her eyes, unsuccessfully. But she could now recognize the voice carrying her. She could feel the strength in his blacksmith arms. "James?" she asked, sleep making her voice hoarse.

"Yes Em', I got ya," James answered, tightening his arms around her.

She cleared her throat, to speak louder. "Seth's right. Isn't proper fer ya ta carry me before we're married," Emma managed to open her eyes a crack. "Ya can set me down now."

"Ya sure," James asked reluctantly. "Ya're sleepin' pretty sound." His arms pulled her closer to his chest. She felt her resolve slip. It did feel effortless to be carried.

Emma nodded slowly. "I'm fine now. I'm too heavy fer ya ta be carryin' me."

A chuckle was his response. "Ya don't weigh nothing. Less than a newborn calf."

Mark snorted. "Only cuz you don't enjoy carryin' the calf around."

Seth laughed loudly to that.

"James," Emma repeated, squeezing his hand gently.

James let out a sigh, and slowly lowered her to the ground. Emma's world swayed for a moment before it righted itself. She kept a hold of his arm for support. Looking up to thank him, she saw concern flash across his handsome face. She made herself smile in response. She tucked her hand through his elbow, partly to keep from hurting his feelings again. But mostly because Emma needed his strength to keep upright.

"Mornin' kid," Mark laughed when she looked his way. "Ya look terrible!"

James patted the hand held at his elbow. "She looks fine," he insisted as he smiled down at her.

Emma raised her hand to her hair to check for herself. Immediately, her fingers found a twig. "I guess I better straighten up before dinner."

Seth laughed loudly again, "Dinner? Try supper Emma."

"Supper?" she repeated again, shocked she had slept so long. She turned to Mark in question.

He smiled. "Da said ya weren't feelin' well and were takin' a nap. Guess we all figured ya was in the house though."

"Ya feelin' any better?" James asked softly.

Nodding, she looked into James's face. Seeing the kindness there, she forced herself to smile. "Much better." She gently squeezed his hand before releasing his arm to walk into the house.

James caught her hand. "Do ya need some help cookin'?" he asked hopefully.

Emma smiled at him. "I'm jest gonna fry up some ham. The fried chicken will have to wait until tomorrow it seems." Turning away, she added, "Ya could see if there's enough beans hangin' fer dinner."

"Sure," James readily agreed.

"Fried chicken?" Seth repeated horrified. "We should've went lookin' fer her earlier."

As the door swung closed behind her, she heard Mark mutter, "Rotten kid." Emma smiled to herself. Taking her hair down, she quickly brushed it out. Once she was convinced there were no more leaves in her hair and it was tangle free, she gathered her hair together. To save time, she simply braided it and went to start dinner.

James met her in the kitchen with his pickings from the garden. He dumped his shirt front into her waiting basket and tucked his shirt back in. "I fergot ta grab the basket," he explained sheepishly.

"Thank ya," Emma said softly.

She watched him turn and walk out the door. "He is handsome," she admitted to herself, "and thoughtful." If she hadn't met Thane she would have been honored that James had asked her to marry him. "But ya did meet Thane," her heart whispered. Pushing back that thought, she tried to remember spending time with James. He seemed to always be around. Since they lived so close to town, he would always be at the farm when his chores were done. He was in so many of her memories. And James had always been so patient with her when he brought her lessons to her so long ago. "Could he really have been carin' fer me back then?" she wondered. Emma had been so consumed with the heartache of losing her Mama, that she had just included James in her life. Without a thought of how appropriate it was.

Turning to the beans, she started snapping them and dropped them into the waiting pot of boiling water.

By the time Emma rang the bell for supper, she had made up her mind that she would concentrate more on James. Listen to what he said to her and ask him questions of her own. Maybe if she tried to act interested, she thought eventually she really would be. Taking a deep breath, she steeled herself to stay strong.

"Ya look rested," her Da noticed as he entered the kitchen.

Emma nodded as she brought the food around. The boys all came in together and stood around the washtub scrubbing their hands.

"Which girl are ya takin' then?" Mark teased Seth. "Lil' Rachel Moore?"

Seth pretended to look thoughtful. "Not sure. Not Rachel though. She's going with that Mr. Nash." His playfulness faded for a second, letting his irritation shine through.

James turned at the mention of Mr. Nash and caught Emma's attention. He gave her a soft smile before she turned away to finish setting the meal.

"But Ellen and Isabella are both waitin' fer me ta ask 'em," Seth continued, his face breaking into a huge smile. "I jest have ta pick."

"Ya've only a few days before the social," Da reminded him.

"I know," Seth sighed. "I can only take one but it's hard ta choose."

Mark laughed, "Tough choices lil' brother," hitting him in the arm.

Da looked thoughtful, "Lucy Eaton seems nice enough. Ya thinkin' on her?"

Seth looked appalled. "I'd prefer ta be smarter than the girl I escort."

"Yer rotten Seth!" James retorted as Mark laughed loudly again.

Da smiled at the boys. "Church socials are one thing, son, but when yer lookin' ta take a wife, look fer one quick minded and lively. One ya can respect. Someone ya can talk easily with. Pretty faces ain't always the best company."

"Yes sir," replied Seth as he slid into the chair next to Emma. They all joined hands to pray.

Emma thought about her Da's advice. "Could be that's why Thane enjoyed my company," she thought to herself. "Without a pretty face, he could always hear what I was sayin'."

The "Amens" echoed around the table, and Emma started guiltily. "A fine start I've made.. I already missed the prayer," she reprimanded herself. Squaring her shoulders, she focused once again on those around her.

"I spoke ta Sheriff Granger this mornin'. He said he didna see any harm clearin' some brush while we wait fer a response ta our letter. Should speed things along a bit," James shared with her. Sitting directly across from him, Emma could easily concentrate on him.

"Which property is this?" Emma asked, trying to be curious. She focused on taking small bites that could be easily washed down.

"The Preston place. Needs a lot of work, but we should be able ta get it cheap," James replied quietly.

Having no idea where the property was, she simply nodded.

James continued. "Was thinking we could look for a shallow place 'cross the crick. We could make a foot bridge there and clear a path ta it. Since we'll border each other, no reason ta go so far around by the road, unless we hafta."

Her Da agreed, and they discussed different areas of the creek that would be the best place to build the foot bridge.

As Emma listened, her heart turned cold. "Where exactly is the Preston place?" she asked softly. "Ta the East?"

James looked at her thoughtfully, but Emma's father was the one who answered. "'Tis ta the West of us along the road. The turn off is jest before the Williams farm."

"It's not the Williams farm anymore. That's the Nash place now," James reminded him, before he took another bite.

"So he's settled in then," Mark asked.

"Wait!" Emma demanded. "The Preston place is the abandoned farm?" Horror added an edge to her voice. "This is what we're buyin'?"

Everyone turned to look at her. They were all surprised by her outburst.

"That's the one, Emma," James replied softly. He looked to her father before finishing. "We'll fix it up real nice, I promise ya."

Emma closed her eyes. Panic threatened to overwhelm her. She had hoped to start fresh, where there were no memories of Thane. Somewhere she could pretend she could be happy without him. But James and her father had picked the one place that she could never forget spending time with Thane.

Feeling pressure on her hand, she turned to Da. The concern was back in his face. Emma forced herself to smile. "Jest seems like a lot of work is all. Could take quite awhile," she managed to say, pushing passed the lump in her throat. Concentrating on putting another bite into her mouth, she hoped no one saw her hands shake.

"It'll be a lot of work. And we'll have ta wait ta hear from the family first. They went back East years ago. Hafta see iffen they're interested in sellin'," James explained. She gave him an understanding nod and turned her full attention to her plate. Emma sent up a plea to God, praying the family would not sell to them.

Emma let the familiar numbness surround her. When she had swallowed her last bite, she rose to clear the dishes. James rose with her. "Well, I think I'll head home. Get a head start on anything my Pa has fer me, so I'll have more time tomorrow. Maybe we can go walkin' again?" he asked hopefully. When Emma nodded in agreement, he flashed her a happy smile, "See ya tomorrow."

"Yeah, tomorrow," Emma repeated. Luckily, everyone called farewells and it drowned hers out. No one heard the numb tone to her words.

Soon after, her father and brothers finished eating and headed back to the barn. They aimed to finish unloading the last hay wagon into the loft before dark.

When the last dish was being dried, Emma looked out the window. Her eyes settled on the path to the hill. Placing the plate in its stack, she laid her towel on the counter. She walked slowly to her Mama's hill. Once again, she sat on the giant rock. "Oh Mama," she whispered, "It's so hard, I don't know what ta do. Every time I try ta forget about Thane, somethin' brings him fresh ta my mind. The pain comes floodin' right back. I can barely breathe it hurts so."

Taking a deep breath, she looked toward the hills. The sun was peeking through the trees. It was a beautiful sight to behold. Like the sunshine was hope shining through the darkness and shadows of the trees. Emma sat up a little straighter. The sunlight was illuminating the path that ran next to the creek. Before she even realized what she was doing, Emma had started down the little path. Stepping over rocks, she crossed the creek. Moving quickly down the familiar path, it wasn't long before she spotted the fallen tree that guarded the way to the abandoned farm. As she stepped into the clearing, the sunlight poured through the trees and lit up the little house. She lowered herself slowly to the ground in front of the abandoned building. The building with such a sad past, but that brought back such happy memories for her and Thane. She tried to picture James bringing her here and her chest tightened. Wrapping her arms around her ribs, she whispered, "But if it's God's plan?"

She dropped her face into her hands and found herself praying, "Here I am Lord, I'm broken ta yer Will. I don't know what yer plan is fer me, but I know yer plan is ta give me hope and a good future. Since yer word is promisin' ta not harm me, I want ta go where ya lead me. But I'm weak – I'm askin' ya ta lend yer strength ta me. Lord, if James is yer plan fer me, fill me with love fer him, so that he has a wife that he deserves. Make me strong through you, so that I might do you honor," Emma felt her voice crack. "And Lord, I am askin' ya ta check in on Thane from time ta time. Make sure he's doing ok. And could ya bring him happiness? He needs it.. -Iffen it's yer will?" Tears fell through her fingers, as peace filled her heart. For the first time in weeks, she felt the fight go out of her. "Amen."

She continued to sit with her hands holding her face, breathing easily. Breathing without pain.

The silence around her was suddenly filled with the calling of coyotes. The sound brought Emma's head up. The sun had fallen behind the abandoned house and the shadows were growing. She quickly got to her feet, walking toward the creek to head home. Another coyote called, sending a chill down Emma's spine. "It sounds so close," she thought.

Out of the corner of her eye, Emma saw a dark shadow move. Turning toward it, two shapes emerged.

"Fancy meetin' ya here," an amused voice declared.

Then Emma's world went black.

Shadows

~Twenty Three~

Everything was dark.

There was something very peaceful about the darkness. Emma wished she could stay there, surrounded by the dark. But the edges of the black were starting to crumble, letting in flashes of light. With them came bursts of sound. She turned her head away and tried to return to the peaceful darkness.

As the cry of a coyote cut through the peaceful silence, she shivered. Emma realized she needed to break free from the darkness. She became aware of a pain in her side and she focused her attention on that.

Sounds of footsteps echoed softly back to her. Emma listened closely, but waves of dizziness overwhelmed her -- forcing her to relax back into the darkness.

Coyotes called to each other, howling into the night.

Pushing at the edges of the darkness, Emma tried to focus on the sound. She struggled to sit up, pressing her hands against the ground. The ground moved and Emma slammed back onto her chest.

A deep chuckle echoed through her dizziness.

Holding still, Emma tried to focus on her surroundings again. Other sounds filtered through the darkness. Breathing. Loud breathing. Footsteps splashed along at a slow pace. Suddenly her world jolted, causing the pain in her side to increase. Inhaling deeply to calm the pain, the scent of a horse filled her senses. "A horse?" she wondered. Becoming aware of her head hanging down, Emma realized she was draped over a horse's back. "Why am I on a horse?" she wondered, putting her hands down again. This time, she felt the warmth of the horse's side against her palms.

Howling broke the silence again.

Emma reached her hand up by her side, grabbing what felt like a saddle horn. She tried to pull herself up to sit, but she felt strangely weak. She did manage to shift sideways and the pain in her side disappeared. Emma tried to pull herself up one more time before giving up. Relaxing back against the horse, she kept hold of the saddle horn so that it wouldn't press into her sore side again.

Hands gripped her body, "Be a good girl now." Her body was flipped upright so quickly that the darkness threatened to return. Her hands reached for something to hold onto as her knee hooked around the saddle horn. Her fingers latched onto the horse's mane and she leaned into it, holding on tightly.

As the dizziness lessened, Emma forced her eyes open. The darkness remained. She let her eyes close and opened them again. Still black. Confused, she stared forward into the darkness.

Coyotes called again, louder and closer this time. Emma shivered again.

As her eyes slowly adjusted, Emma could see shadows. Shadows of the horse. The shadow of a man. Shadows of trees. "Nighttime?" Emma thought. "What am I doin' out at night? Where am I goin'?"

The horse snorted and tossed its head, shaking Emma from her confusing thoughts. She held on tightly as the horse changed directions suddenly. The sudden direction change caught Emma off guard and she let out a gasp.

"Steady girl," the voice from the shadow laughed.

Emma felt a slight recognition at the sound - and then it was gone. She shook her head, trying to clear away the foggy feeling, but the movement made her dizzy again. Taking a deep breath, she kept the darkness from returning. The horse lurched forward, going up an incline. Emma leaned forward instinctively to balance and realized there was no longer a reflection under the horse. The sound of hooves splashing was replaced with the sound of brush under foot. But the study of her surroundings was short lived as the path became more bumpy. Emma's dizziness returned. She closed her eyes and concentrated on keeping her grip tight.

"BOY," the shadow suddenly bellowed. Emma winced in pain from the noise.

Light flooded around her as the horse stopped moving.

"I brought ya a little somethin'," the shadow announced.

Light bursts filled Emma's vision with every loud word the man spoke. She winced away from the voice.

"Emma?"

She turned her head toward the light, but it was too bright for Emma to open her eyes.

"Emma?" the voice came again softer, close by her side.

She carefully opened her eyes a crack, to see Thane standing at her knee. Relief filled her. Something familiar in this strange world.

"Oh Thane. There ya are. I was lookin' fer ya.."

"Lookin' fer me?" he asked as he tried to loosen her grip from the mane.

"Was I lookin' fer him?" she wondered. Emma nodded her head in answer but stopped when the dizziness overwhelmed her. She swayed forward. Strong arms caught her. She burrowed into the warmth she found there.

"Oh.. Yer chilled through," Thane exclaimed quietly.

A coyote called from a distance and Emma shivered. She felt herself talking to Thane but could only concentrate on the warmth and trying to stay awake. Exhaustion started to pull at the edge of her focus.

A booming voice laughed and Emma flinched away from the sound. She pressed her free hand over her uncovered ear. "I see ya like what I stole fer ya," he chuckled. "I guess I coulda jest told her I was takin' her ta see ya. I coulda spared her the lump on her head." Another chuckle.

"What have ya done, Pa?"

Emma felt herself set on her feet. The sudden motion brought on a wave of dizziness. She fought to stay standing. Hands felt her head, gently searching through her hair.

"I done some convincin'," was the amused reply.

When the hand touched behind her ear, Emma's knees buckled. Thane caught her and lifted her again. He pulled her in tight to his chest.

Emma smiled contentedly. She realized God had answered her prayers. Relief washed over her. "I'm not gonna marry James, am I?" she stated softly.

"No Emma, ya won't be marryin' James," Thane assured her.

Darkness surrounded Emma again and her world was again peaceful.

~Twenty Four~

"An iffen she's hurt worse than that?" Thane's worried voice filled Emma's head.

"I checked boy. She's fine," an annoyed voice snapped.

"Ya checked?" Thane's voice shook with anger. "Ya touched her?"

"Yeah I touched her - I had ta put her up on Black, didn't I? Isn't much ta her but I still had ta have my hand on her," the man jeered. "Made sure she weren't bleedin' before we set out."

A door slammed and Emma jumped. The movement hurt and the darkness started to settle again. "Where am I?" she wondered before she slipped back into sleep.

~*~*~*~*~*~*~*~*~*~*~*~*~*~

Emma opened her eyes. Light was shining through a crack in the wall she faced. Trees danced in the breeze and birds were singing.

Confused, Emma tried to figure out where she was. She remembered praying down by the abandoned farm. She remembered telling God she was putting her life in his hands. But how did she get here? Where was she?

Rolling over, she saw Thane sitting in a chair near her. She smiled. He smiled back, but there was a sadness about him as he leaned toward her. "Rest Emma."

Emma nodded as her eyes closed again.

~*~*~*~*~*~*~*~*~*~*~*~*~*~

The flame danced and swayed before her eyes. It was a peaceful sight to open your eyes to. But the throbbing pain in her head made her look away. When the movement didn't help the pain, Emma raised her hand to her head. Feeling behind her ear, she found a raised knob.

Thane stepped closer and moved her hand away from the bump. "Best ta not touch it," he said softly. Taking a cool wet cloth, he tucked it behind her ear.

"Where are we?" Emma asked just as softly.

Thane paused before he answered. "We're at my cabin.. up in the hills."

Emma's thoughts swam, "How did I get here?"

He stopped fussing with the cloth then. Thane turned his gray eyes toward her and they filled with sadness. "My Pa brought ya here ta me."

She nodded in understanding. The movement caused the throbbing to return. "Why does my head hurt so bad?"

"Ya have quite a bump," Thane stated sadly. "Ya need ta rest Emma." He rewet the cloth and put it back behind her ear.

"Rest," she repeated. Leaning her head into the cool cloth he held, Emma felt herself falling back to sleep.

~*~*~*~*~*~*~*~*~*~*~*~*~

"Fancy meetin' ya here."

Emma sat straight up in bed, knocking the blankets on the floor. "Thane?" she called frantically.

"I'm here," replied a voice in the darkness.

Thane stepped into the light of the oil lamp, sitting on the edge of her bed. Emma leaned into his chest relieved. "I had the worst dream. My heart's still racin'."

Thane placed his arms gently around Emma, rubbing her back soothingly. As the pounding of her heart slowed, she leaned back to look up at him. "Oh.. ya still look sad.. jest like in my dream," She reached up to touch his face and froze. "Why are ya in my room? My Da --," Emma stopped talking and looked around her. Thane lowered his arms as she stiffened. "It wasn't a dream was it?" The words came out barely louder than a whisper.

"No," Thane whispered back.

Tears began to stream down Emma's cheeks. She allowed Thane to pull her back against his chest for a while. Then she pulled away. "Please let go," she sobbed. He dropped his arms immediately. She laid back down, curling onto her side away from him. She felt him cover her with blankets and tuck them close.

Emma heard Thane sit on the floor and settle in. From the sounds, he seemed close. She rolled over and with the little bit of light from the lamp, she saw that he had a bedroll on the floor. He was within an arm length of her bed. "Why are ya here?" she asked, her voice still quivering.

"This is my cabin -- my Pa's cabin," Thane answered slowly. His words were spoken cautiously, like he assumed Emma was confused.

"No," Emma interuppted. "Why are ya in my room? --in THIS room?" Closing her eyes to the dizziness she caused by correcting herself.

"So I can hear ya iffen ya call out again," he stated.

"I'll be fine," Emma assured him. "Ya can go."

Thane sat up and looked at her. He was closer than she felt comfortable with, but she did not allow herself to back away. When she looked into his eyes, she saw the sadness there. "I need ta be here.. so I know that my Pa'll leave ya be while I sleep," he held her gaze to make sure she understood what he was saying.

Emma nodded. No words were possible. Her throat burned with the knot that was growing there. She managed to not start crying again.

Thane lay back down but it looked like he still watched her. Her friend - now her betrayer. She had felt safe from the shadows while he was here with her. But now she didn't feel safe from the hurt.

Emma rolled back over to face the wall. Exhausted, she soon fell back asleep.

~*~*~*~*~*~*~*~*~*~*~*~*~*~

When Emma woke again, she startled awake with a gasp. Thane was next to her in a moment, feeling her forehead, checking her eyes. She lay back down and closed her eyes. Shutting out the throbbing pain in her head, she was hurt that he was really there. That he was a part of all this.

Someone moving in the next room reminded Emma that they weren't alone. Thane's Pa was there as well. Emma thoughts immediately turned to her father. She knew he would be sick with worry. A tear escaped her eye. "Why did I have ta turn inta such a crier?" she wondered bitterly.

A hand wiped her tears away. "Where are ya hurtin'? Is it yer head?" A cold cloth was again pressed against the lump behind her ear. The pressure was uncomfortable but the coolness felt good.

Finally, Emma pulled away from the cool cloth. She turned and faced her friend. "How could ya?" her voice cracked. Clearing her throat, she started again. "How could ya be a part of this? Couldna ya see how worried this'll make my family?" Tears streamed down her cheeks unchecked. "That's what hurts!" Rolling away from him, her sobs came in full force. Her only friend - the only one who had truly listened to her - the one who always knew what she needed - had betrayed her. Emma felt alone.

Thane stood and quietly left the room.

~*~*~*~*~*~*~*~*~*~*~*~*~*~

Emma opened her eyes to the click of the door latch. Keeping her breathing even, she hoped he would believe she was still asleep. She heard a chair pulled closer to the bed. When she heard Thane clear his throat, she knew she hadn't fooled him.

"I know yer hurtin' Emma, an don't want ta see me none. An' I don't blame ya." Coughing to clear his voice, he continued, "I had a part in this, but it's not whatcha think. I never should've told my Pa about ya." She heard him stand and walk away. Emma rolled over to watch him. "But I won't refuse the blame." He turned to meet her gaze. Slowly, he walked back over to take a seat in the chair. "My Pa says if I don't want ta claim ya fer my own then he will,"

Thane looked down as she gasped. The room was quiet for a long pause. "I do want ya fer my own," Thane said quietly as he stood and walked back to the small window. "Or I did before ya found someone better'n me. But not like this," his voice grew thick with emotion and quivered. His hands raked through his hair and balled into fists. "NEVER like this!"

Emma felt tears slip from her eyes. Slowly, Thane turned back to her. He looked defeated. The emotions she saw in his face added to her confusion. She felt so conflicted. So angry. So hurt and confused by his words. The throbbing in her ear was not helping her to think clearly.

"Emma, I-," Thane's whispered words were barely loud enough to be heard.

But Emma did not think she could handle much more. She turned her back to him and curled into a ball. Breathing deeply, she fought through the emotions that tightened her chest. She stared through the crack in the logs and tried to clear her thoughts. Staring out at the trees, she wouldn't let her mind wonder back to what was happening to her.

She heard the bedroom door open and close.

A short time later, the outer door burst open. "Well boy? Have ya made up yer mind if ya want her?"

The loud voice must belong to his pa, Emma reasoned.

"Course I want her," Thane answered softly. Emma put her hand over her mouth, as sobs threatened to overwhelm her.

"Now yer startin' ta talk like a man," his Pa bellowed with a loud laugh.

"But she'll never accept me - not like THIS," Thane answered. His misery making his voice thick.

An awful laugh followed, "Ya don't ask a woman - ya tell her! Need me ta show ya how?"

Emma pulled the blanket up to her neck.

"Don't go near her! Do ya hear me?" Thane's voice was deep and threatening. She almost didn't recognize it. "Don't talk ta her. Don't touch her. Ya have done enough. Just stay away." The last words came out as a growl. Emma held her breath.

The old man laughed loud, amused by Thane's protectiveness. "Guess it took a woman ta make a man outta ya boy!" He laughed again, making Emma's skin crawl. "Well I'm goin' out huntin'. Give ya two some time ta yerself." The amused old man left the cabin and silence once again settled in.

Emma heard Thane come into the room and heard the floor boards creak near the bed. But she never turned to face him. "Lord, what could be the reason fer all this?" Emma cried out silently as tears rolled down her cheek.

Eventually, she fell back asleep.

~*~*~*~*~*~*~*~*~*~*~*~*~*~*~

When Emma opened her eyes again, there was a bowl of stew next to her bed. Realizing how hungry she was, she started to sit up. But she froze when she heard a sound outside the wall.

"Lord? It's me Thane. I don't know what ta do," hearing his voice crack, made Emma's throat hurt. "I can't take her back. If they woulda thought I ruined her jest talkin'? Then this-," his voice cracked again. Clearing his throat, his voice continued, "She won't want ta marry me now - She CAN'T want that now. There wasn't much ta love before an' now? But Lord, what choice do we have? This -- Oh-- What have I done ta her? What do I do now?" The anguish, in his voice, shot through Emma and it took her breath away. Tears flowed down her face as she turned back toward the wall.

The stew was forgotten.

~*~*~*~*~*~*~*~*~*~*~*~*~*~*~

Emma woke to darkness. There was a painful pounding ringing in her ears. Carefully, she felt the side of her head, behind her ear. She pulled her fingers away quickly, wincing away from the pain.

"The word in town is that they look all through the day and inta the nights. As I was leavin', a couple young fellas came inta the hotel. Started threatenin' a man who goes by Nash?"

Emma's eyes flew open to look around her, into the darkness. When she realized the voices were coming from the next room, she relaxed back into her bed.

Someone laughed on the other side of the door, amused, "They'd really no idea ya knew her. They think it was the coyotes or this Nash. Fools won't stop lookin' fer her. Sounds like they'll let their crops rot in the fields while they keep lookin'."

Emma's felt an ache fill her chest. Her father and brothers must be so worried. She imagined them searching until they were exhausted. James was probably with them too, she guessed. "Oh James," she thought, "Oh - -." Her chest tightened so hard, she couldn't breathe. She struggled to keep from crying. Trying to breathe through the pain until it loosened.

"Where are ya goin'?" Thane's voice asked suddenly.

"Gonna make sure the girl's still in there? Wanna make sure ya didn't go soft an' take her back," his pa stated.

"She's in there. Wouldn't do any good ta take her back till I figure it all out," Thane reassured his Pa.

"I'd like ta see with me own eyes," came the eery request. Silence followed.

Emma lay frozen in terror, the drumming in her ears grew louder.

"Ya ain't goin' in there. She's scared enough without ya makin' it worse," Thane's voice rang out with a clear warning in it.

Suddenly laughter rang out, echoing off the walls. "Ya have yer Mama in ya, ya do. I see her eyes in yers.. flashin' with danger when protectin' the one ya love."

Emma covered her head with the blanket, covering her ears with her fists to block out his laughter. It was awhile before her silent sobs ended. The darkness finally came.

~Twenty Five~

"Emma?" a soft voice called through the darkness. "Emma? Ya need ta wake up Emma," the voice pleaded. "Please Emma..?"

Emma struggled against the sleepiness, but the darkness once again pulled her in.

~*~*~*~*~*~*~*~*~*~*~*~*~*~

The darkness surrounding Emma was filled with a loud constant noise. The noise sounded like someone was knocking on the door. Emma tried to ask someone to stop the noise but her mouth would not move. Listening more carefully, she could tell the pounding was coming from inside her head. And it would not stop.

Something moved in the darkness. A coolness was pressed to her head. After a moment, a coolness spread inside her mouth and she swallowed.

"Lord, I'll do anythin' yer askin'. Jest let her wake soon. Jest let her wake please," Emma heard the exhaustion in Thane's voice. "Please..."

The sounds grew more distant and Emma was once again alone in the darkness. With only the pounding.

~Twenty Six~

Emma woke to the sun shining on her face. She turned away from the light and saw Thane sitting in a chair. His head leaned forward, resting in his hands. He looked up when he heard her move. A look of relief passed over his face, "Yer awake!"

His relief made Emma wonder how long she had been sleeping but refused to ask. Trying to sit up, Emma said, "I think ya should show me where the outhouse stands."

Thane stood up so quickly, he almost knocked the chair over. "Of course. Can ya walk?"

"Of course I can!" Emma answered abruptly, even though the room started to sway. He reached for her, but she put her hand up to stop him.

"Least let me help ya," he implored.

Finally, Emma allowed him to hold her elbow and help her stand. It was slow but they finally made it. When she shut the door to the outhouse, Emma realized it didn't close tight. The cracks in the boards were wide enough to put her fingers through. She gasped!

Thane was immediately at the door. "Are ya alright?" He stood close to the outhouse, but did not look at it or touch it.

"Go away!" Emma yelled. Thane backed away. "Turn around - away from here! The door doesn't shut." Horrified at her emotions being so frantic. And horrified at her predictament.

Thane hesitated, "Do ya want me ta hold it?" he asked softly.

"NO!"

He blushed and reached up to rub his hand on the back of his neck nervously. "How about a rock?"

Her eyes filled with tears. "All right." Thane ran away and was back almost immediately. He pushed a rock against the door and ran a good distance away before he stopped.

The excitement had exhausted her. By the time she called to Thane to remove the rock, she could barely hold her head up. He reached for her elbow when she stumbled. When she didn't take another step, he hesitated a moment, then reached down behind her knees and lifted her.

"I don't want ta be carried," she stated weakly. "I canna bear fer ya ta touch me."

He sighed, "I know Emma." She could hear the hurt in his voice and it made her throat tighten.

Thane carried her into the house and laid her on the bed, covering her with the quilt. He kneeled next to the bed. "Ya need ta eat. Tell me what ya'll eat and I'll make it. Ya need ta get yer strength back. Ya already lost too much weight from -- before."

Emma knew he was referring to her worry filled weeks at home. She closed her eyes. "Maybe it's best this way."

"Please don't say that," he insisted. "We'll figure this out."

A tear slid out of the corner of her eye, "I keep thinkin' I'll wake up soon and realize it was jest a bad dream. That I'll wake up and no one'll be hurt by all this. That none of this is real. But then I realize that I couldna dream this sadness. I couldna imagine the holes and darkness of everythin' here."

"No.. ya couldn't," Thane rubbed his hands across his face slowly, "I'll figure somethin' out. Jest eat somethin' please," he urged in a whisper.

She sighed, "Do ya have bread?"

"How about a biscuit?" Thane offered.

Emma nodded once.

He was back before she realized he had gone. He put a small chunk of biscuit, with something sweet, in Emma's mouth. She forced herself to chew. When she managed to swallow, she asked for water. She felt her back lifted and drank from the tin cup pressed against her lip.

As soon as she lay back against the pillow, Emma fell asleep.

~*~*~*~*~*~*~*~*~*~*~*~*~*~*~

Voices were everywhere. Her Da, Mark, Seth and James were wondering through the woods calling for her. She tried to call out to them. To let them know she was safe. She wanted to ease the worry she heard in their voices. Voices that were so near. But she simply lay there, too weak to answer them.

Emma woke with a gasp.

Voices were coming from the next room.

Thirsty, Emma looked on the table next to her bed. She found a cup there and the remains of her biscuit. After taking a few sips of water, she broke off a small chunk of biscuit and began chewing it slowly.

"I think I'll head north fer a spell. Been wantin' ta do my trappin' up there this winter." The laugh sent chills down Emma's spine and she put the rest of the biscuit back on the plate. "Since ya's gettin' real cozy, I'm not needed no how."

Emma's eyes rested on the empty floor and realized the bed roll was gone. Looking around, she found it rolled up at the foot of her bed. Realizing what the man thought, she felt her color rising.

"Ya think this is laughable?" Thane asked astonished. "We ruined her and ya laugh?"

"Well it brought ya back ta life. When ya've a chance ta think on it, ya'll thank me!"

"I'll not be thankin' ya," Thane growled. "My comin' ta life isn't worth ruinin' hers."

The older man laughed again. "See ya in the spring boy." And the voice left.

Emma felt herself sigh with relief.

~Twenty Seven~

The sun shone through the crack in the wall. It's warmth felt so wonderful on her face. Blinking a couple times, Emma realized that the pain was starting to fade. She tried to feel the lump on her head, but her hand would not move. It stayed where it was on the floor. She turned her head toward her hand curiously and saw her fingers were entwined with Thane's near his pillow on the floor. She marveled at how her hand could be so comfortable when he was such a man. But the look on his face made her pause. In sleep, his face was relaxed and yet still touched with sadness. The same sadness she had first noticed there, the day he had so casually saved her. How could he have been so worried about her then - and be a part of this now? "He couldn't," her heart whispered.

She tugged gently, trying to free her fingers. Thane's eyes blinked open to focus on their entwined fingers and then up at her. Suddenly, he pulled his hand away from hers. He jumped to his feet and ran his fingers through his hair to make it lay down better. Then he fidgeted with his shirt to tuck it in.

When Thane finally looked at Emma, surprise crossed his face and then he relaxed a little. "Ya look like yer head feels better?" He almost sat on the bed next to her, but changed his mind to kneel beside the bed. "Yer eyes look better. The black circles are much smaller."

"The poundin' in my ear's gone as well," Emma commented.

A smile of relief touched his lips for a moment before it slowly disappeared again.

Emma looked into Thane's eyes. Those same smoky gray eyes that she had come to love. Those gray eyes that she could tell anything to, just days before. She felt herself ask, "Did ya ask yer Pa ta bring me here?"

Thane took a deep breath before answering, "No ma'am."

"Did ya know he was comin' fer me?"

He shook his head, "No, I would've stopped him."

"Why should I believe ya?" Emma asked quietly.

"Ya shouldn't! I wouldn't," Thane paused for a moment. "My Pa thought I was weak fer lettin' ya go. He thought I needed his help. So he went-," he swallowed hard. Silence filled the room as Thane studied the floor. Finally, he turned toward her, not meeting her eyes, "I'm so sorry, Emma."

Studying his face, Emma saw truth. The same truth that had been there all along. She smiled weakly, "I do believe ya."

Thane looked up surprised. Then embarrassed he looked down again. "My Pa said I shouldn't have stood by and gave ya ta another. But I've nothin' ta offer ya. I knew that I could never bring ya here. Bring ya ta where my Ma died? Ta a cabin that leaks? With no well fer fresh water? Where the sun's blocked by the trees? What kind of a life is that fer ya?" his voice was thick with misery.

"Not ta mention, an outhouse with holes ya could ride a horse through," she teased softly.

Thane's lip curled up into a lopsided smile at that. But the sadness in his eyes made her throat hurt. "I don't know what ta do," he finished in defeat.

Emma watched him in silence. Reaching over, she rested her hand on his, giving it a gentle squeeze. "Well," she suggested. "First ya can fix that outhouse. That way yer away from the cabin while I wash."

Putting his hand over Emma's, Thane held her hand between his for a full minute. Then reluctantly he stood up. "Yes ma'am. Would ya like me ta fill a tub or jest a bucket?"

Emma looked around. "A bucket," she replied. Thane left to do as she asked. Seeing the light peaking through the logs made her shy away from the thought of a bath. Besides, she had nothing clean to change into.

When Thane returned, he set a full bucket of water on the floor. Stepping up to the trunk at the foot of the bed, he opened it and pulled out a porcelain bowl. He crossed the room and set it carefully on the table by the bed. He poured water from the bucket into the bowl, then set the bucket back down. Returning to the trunk, he pulled out a stack of white fabric. "These belonged ta my Ma. If ya'd like ta wear them, we can wash yer other clothes."

Emma smiled weakly at him. "Thank ya."

~Twenty Eight~

Emma sat close to the fire, rocking. Occasionally, she would move to separate her curls so that her hair dried evenly. When Thane came inside, he went into the bedroom without a word to her. Emma leaned her head back against the chair, letting her eyes close. Her sponge bath and the trip to the finished outhouse had worn her out.

A slight pressure on her knees startled her. With a gasp, she sat up quickly.

"Shhh," Thane soothed. "I didn't mean ta scare ya." He tucked a small quilt around her legs and stepped back. Picking up an object from the table, he handed it to Emma. "Thought ya could use this."

Emma reached out and took what he offered. "A brush?" she gasped. "Where did ya find a brush?"

Sitting down in the other chair, Thane smiled softly. "It was my Ma's. When she died, my Pa gathered everything that reminded him of my Ma and put it in that trunk," Thane gave a low chuckle. Leaning his elbows on his knees, he stared into the fire. "It's pert near full. Some of it doesn't make any sense ta me, but I still use some of it. Like the brush. And her sewing basket."

Excitement filled Emma's face, "Ya have a sewing basket?"

Thane nodded. "Ya be needin' it?"

"My dress has an awful tear in the back. I didna know how I was ta fix it," she leaned back, with a sigh.

"Do ya want it now?" Thane asked helpfully.

"A little later please. I'm very tired jest now." Emma reached up and started brushing the ends of her hair. "When did it get so cold? It's been such a hot summer."

Thane looked thoughtfully at Emma then. "The heat broke that day ya came... the day my Pa took ya," looking down at his hands, he continued, "but I think the rest has ta do with that bump ya have. Ya were shiverin' the night ya came here and I haven't been able ta keep ya warm enough since."

Emma nodded. After one small section of her hair, her arms were too tired to continue. Laying the brush in her lap, she leaned her head back to rest.

"Would ya like my help?" Thane asked uncertainly.

Emma opened her eyes to see the concern in Thane's face. Embarrassment flooded her own. "I'm not sure-, I mean-," she stopped talking, searching for the words to explain that it wasn't proper for him to brush her hair.

"Emma," Thane whispered, "It's alright, I understand. I shouldn't have asked."

He turned back to stare at the fire. Emma watched him. "It's jest hair, Emma," Mark's words echoed through her mind. She smiled. "It's jest hair," Emma repeated softly.

Thane looked up at her words, surprised. He reached out slowly to accept the hair brush she offered him. Cautiously, he came and kneeled next to her chair. Almost like he expected her to change her mind. Mimicking what he had saw her do, he brushed the bottom of her long curls first, going higher and higher when each tangle was conquered. When her hair slipped from his grasp, letting the brush pull the hair above her ear, Emma let out a sharp gasp. She felt a tear slip from her tightly closed eyes. She knew she should wipe it away, but she needed to keep breathing through the pain.

"I'm so sorry Emma," Thane whispered hoarsely.

Emma opened her eyes to see his horror stricken face. She tried to smile. "Perhaps ya could brush the other side fer awhile," she suggested.

Moving to the other side of her chair, Thane sat on the hearth. Starting slowly, he began brushing her hair again. The whole time he brushed, he was very careful not to touch her. Emma found herself thinking back throughout their friendship.

"Thane?" she asked thoughtfully, as she watched the fire crackle. She could feel him turn his face toward her as his hands paused. "The first day ya met me down by the creek, ya kneeled next ta me.. Why? When ya've always been so careful ta keep yer distance from me proper? Why so close that day and no other?" A smile crept onto her face, "Except fer the day ya were persuading Nash that we were getting married, that is.."

When he didn't respond she turned her head to lean it against the back of the rocking chair. Thane continued brushing her hair in silence. Finally, he cleared his throat. "Ya were leaning back against that rock, right next ta yer Mama's grave. Ya looked so peaceful, looked like an angel. But ya were so still. I started ta worry. I didn't even know I was close ta ya until I felt relief ta see ya breathin'. Before I could move away - ya reached out ta me."

She chuckled then, "Ya looked like ya saw a ghost."

"I thought I might've," he admitted with a lopsided smile.

A log split in the fire, showering sparks out near her feet. Thane swept them back with his hat. Reassured that she was safe, he picked up the brush again. After a few strokes, he cleared his throat. "Ya do know we're goin' ta have ta."

The soft spoken words confused Emma. "Have ta?" she repeated, trying to figure out what he was referring to.

"Have ta get married," Thane clarified as he slowly kept brushing her hair. "If I return ya ta yer family not yet married, I'll hang. But you.. ya'd be disgraced and possibly shunned fer the rest of yer life. Dependin' on if I can convince them that you'd no choice." Turning away from her, Thane rubbed his face with his hands. "Maybe this's my punishment fer my behavior that day. Talkin' so familiarly ta a lady with no connection ta me."

"God won't be punishin' ya Thane. Yer a good man," Emma insisted.

"No I'm not," he growled in frustration.

"Thane - I see it," she continued. "Ya've always treated me proper. Yer always thinkin' of my safety. Always thinkin' of my needs before yer own. God sees that."

"He can see inta my heart too. He can see the blackness there. He knows a small part of me is so glad ya aren't marryin' James Abernathy. That's the truth of it. Even though my mind knows ya'd be better provided fer." After a pause, he cleared his throat. His voice sounded raw as he went on, "God saw how happy I was when ya fell off the horse inta my arms that night. Foolish man. If I woulda taken ya back then..," his voice broke then, "I thought ya'd come ta see me. Ta tell me-," Thane stopped and sat in silence.

"Thane?"

"I didn't know what he'd done - But my Pa was right. I was foolishly happy at first. I'm jest as guilty as he is. When he told me his actions, I was angry then, but it was too late. God saw my selfish heart." The shame Thane felt could be heard in his voice.

Emma's throat felt thick with the emotions she heard in his words. "Thane, ya couldna have taken me back unconscious anyway. They wouldna have believed ya," she insisted gently.

He looked up at her then. "Unconscious?" She saw the question in his eyes. "Emma, ya were jest as awake as ya are now. A little more confused but..."

"No," she said, pointing to the bedroom, "I woke up in there, when I heard ya arguin' with yer Pa."

"Ya don't remember comin' here?" Thane asked slowly.

She shook her head, "I went down ta Mama's hill ta pray and I decided ta walk ta the abandoned farm." Not sure she wanted to share the experience she had there, Emma skipped over it. "I heard coyotes, like they were close. So close. I decided I needed ta leave. And then a man stepped outta the trees. The next thing I knew, I woke in that room."

Thane stood suddenly and walked across the room. "Ya were talkin' ta me. I thought-," he stopped talking as he continued to pace. "Ya kept sayin' coyotes - they called that whole night. Ya were shakin' so bad ya couldn't walk. I had ta carry ya." His hands balled in fists as they gripped his hair. Abruptly, he turned and strode toward her. Kneeling in front of her, he explained, "I knew ya were confused but I thought ya were jest a lil scared. Ya - Ya don't remember it?"

Emma slowly shook her head again, "Ya said I was talkin'? What did I say?"

He closed his eyes and took a deep breath. "Mostly didn't make sense, I guess. Ya said ya were lookin' fer me -," he paused, "I should've taken ya ta the doc." He stood and walked away then. This time, he walked out the door and latched it behind him.

Turning back toward the fire, Emma started to rock again. She reached for the brush on the hearth to finish her hair. "What did I say that night that was so terrible?" she wondered. But as hard as she tried, that night was a blank.

She felt sleep tugging at the edges of her thoughts. Her brush strokes slowed as her rocking did.

~*~*~*~*~*~*~*~*~*~*~*~*~*~*~*~

Emma felt herself being lifted and then placed somewhere soft. Her nightgown was tucked by her ankles. She felt her back lifted, as all her hair was gathered to one side and draped across her shoulder. The blankets were pulled up and tucked under her chin.

"No wonder ya woke up angry and hurt. I never blamed ya fer changin' yer mind... Knew I deserved it. Deserved all yer anger," his voice quivered. "I'm so sorry Emma." He tucked a hair behind her ear and stood to leave.

As he reached behind him to pull the door closed, Emma's voice stopped him. "Thane?" she called out uncertainly.

"I'm here," he reassured her without turning around.

Rolling to her side to face him, she asked tentatively, "What did I say ta ya that night? What was so bad that I don't remember?"

Thane stood still so long, that Emma feared he wouldn't tell her. Finally, his soft voice explained from across the room. "Ya told me that ya had put yer life in God's hands and asked him ta show ya the right path. Ya insisted," a long moment passed before he continued, "Ya insisted that God had sent an angel ta bring ya ta me then. Ya were so happy that God had chosen me fer ya. That joy ya had.. that's why I didn't think ta take ya back ta yer family that night.. and then.. Then it was too late," Thane cleared his throat again, but his voice was still thick with emotions. "Maybe I jest imagined it. If ya don't remember it, it means it wasn't ya talkin' anyhow."

Emma felt her chest tighten. "It was me talkin'. The part of my heart that didn't need ta worry about what anyone else thought or who would be hurt from my choice." Trying to decide if she wanted to share the next part, she realized it might help him in his despair. "Ya know I did put my life in God's hands that night. I knew what I wanted, and I knew what my family expected. The pull was too hard fer me ta live with. The peace that filled me that night in front of that abandoned house, -it was amazing. I told God I would follow where he led me." Studying Thane's immobile back, she went on. "And then yer Pa stepped out of the shadows. I know he's hardly my idea of an angel, but maybe God's used him ta do His work that night?"

"Maybe," Thane agreed quietly. "Or maybe my Pa hit ya harder than I thought." The door closed gently as he left the room.

"Oh Lord. I'm still willin' ta follow where ya lead me. Please be givin' us the strength ta stay true ta yer plan," Emma prayed softly. "And please heal all the hurt that's been caused. Amen."

~Twenty Nine~

"Sit ya down there," Thane's voice reprimanded softly. Emma opened her eyes and pushed away from the hearth. She still felt weak when she tried to do too much. And starting a fire for breakfast had definitely been too much. Relieved at his gentle command, she sank into the rocking chair he held out for her.

"Sorry," she apologized. "I was hopin' ta help make breakfast taday."

Thane didn't reply as he set in to finish the breakfast preparations. The flapjack batter was all mixed together and set by the hearth. Emma hadn't been able to find any maple syrup, but she thought they could do without.

"When I woke this morning, ya were already up and gone. I wasn't sure when ya'd be back," she explained. "I didna want ya ta be cookin' after that. I jest wanted ta feel useful," she finished weakly, barely above a whisper. Leaning her head against the chair back, she closed her eyes to rest.

Emma could hear the flapjacks sizzling in the skillet, before Thane spoke. "I hadn't been up long. Jest workin' in the barn until I heard ya up."

"Ya were up early workin'. Yer bed was all rolled up before sunrise. That was hours ago," Emma said. She started to rock slowly, as she watched Thane flip the flapjacks.

"I slept out here last night," Thane replied quietly. "With my Pa gone, I thought it best."

Emma stopped rocking and opened her eyes to watch Thane. His expression was guarded and she found herself wondering what he was thinking.

Thane took the flapjacks from the pan and set them on the table. Propping the skillet next to the hearth to cool, he walked out the door. Before Emma could wonder where he had gone, he returned setting a jar of jam on the table.

"My jam?" she asked amazed. "Ya haven't eaten it yet?"

"Was savin' it fer somethin' special," he answered. Thane held his hand out to Emma, helping her to the table.

"Flapjacks are special?" she asked with a raised eyebrow.

The corner of Thane's mouth turned up. "No. But you walkin' around an' tryin' ta be useful means yer feelin' better. That's pretty special."

Emma returned the smile, then bowed her head to pray.

"Will ya pray out loud?" Thane requested.

"Oh," she answered in surprise. Back home, her father had always prayed. "Alright," bowing her head again, she began, "Father, who art in heaven, thank ya fer the food you've provided fer us. And thank ya fer the wonderful care you've provided fer me. In yer name, Amen."

"Amen," Thane echoed, but he did not immediately pick up his fork.

Emma watched him for a moment, confused, until she felt rude. Picking up her own fork, she forced all her attention on the food in front of her.

"Emma," Thane's voice was small when he finally spoke, "how can ya call what we've done here 'wonderful care'? My family has hurt ya, taken ya from yer family.. and barely given ya shelter from the outdoors."

Emma's fork froze on its way to her mouth. Thane kept his gaze down at his folded hands, keeping his eyes hidden from her. She lowered her fork back to her plate. "Well, ya've kept me warm, ya've provided clothin' fer me, an' ya stayed by my side fer the days I was healin'. Seems like it's everythin' God coulda asked of ya."

He looked up then, "Yer whole world changed from my Pa's thoughtlessness. How can ya forgive us so easily?"

"I forgive ya easily. Thane ya didn't do this," Emma paused before continuing. "Forgivin' yer Pa? That's a little more work. My mama used ta say if yer holdin' on ta a hurt, then it holds on right back. Soon yer life won't be yer own. Sometimes, I have ta ask God ta help me though. Forgivin' yer Pa took a couple days longer than it shoulda, but God got me through."

Emotions churned in Thane's stormy eyes. Confusion, anger, amazement and hurt flashed quickly in their turn. He nodded and looked down at his food. Picking up his fork, he began to eat.

Emma rose slowly from her chair and using a towel, pulled the coffee pot from the fire.

"I can get that," Thane insisted, pushing back his chair to stand.

A smile tugged at Emma's mouth. "I can lift a coffee pot. But I'll let ya get the dishes."

As soon as breakfast was eaten, Thane cleared the dishes. Disappearing into the bedroom, he brought back the promised sewing basket. He placed it and the freshly washed dress on the table in front of her.

"Thank ya," Emma said as she got right to work.

When Thane had finished scrubbing their few dishes, he disappeared into the bedroom again. This time he returned with brown package that was tied with string. He stood in the doorway for a long while, before he moved to her side. Kneeling next to her chair, he began, "Emma, I don't care what happens ta me, but I need ta know what ya want ta do. The best thing fer ya'd be fer us ta marry before I take ya home ta yer family," he looked down, "I don't really deserve ya. But it'd be the easiest way fer ya. If we marry, ya can go home iffen ya want. Ya can tell folks I abandoned ya... Ya'd get pity but not dishonor."

"What do YOU want Thane? Do ya want ta marry?" she asked hesitantly.

"I don't get choices. I must do what I can fer ya," came his firm reply.

Emma nodded in understanding. It was obvious to her that Thane felt trapped. Stuck with the need to marry her.

Standing, Thane hit the brown package against his thigh. The action seemed familiar to her somehow, but she could not place it.

"I wasn't gonna give this ta ya. Seemed too selfish of me, before. But now- now seems it may be kinda useful." Thane gently laid his package down on her lap and quietly left the house.

Surprised by Thane leaving so suddenly, she stared at the door for a moment before turning her attention back to the bundle in front of her. Emma pulled the thin twine that was used to hold the paper closed. Opening the folds of paper slowly, she found a dress length of a purple material. Her breath caught. It was the pale purple material from the mercantile. Letting her fingers brush gently across the folded material, she smiled. The scene from the store flashed through her mind. The way Thane had smiled in amazement at finding the purple material. "Oh Thane, thank ya," she whispered softly, to the empty room.

Emma wasted no time getting to work. First, she set about patching her dress. Fixing the tears from the night she was taken. Then using her old patched dress as a pattern, she traced the shape onto the purple fabric.

By the time the new dress was cut out, Emma was exhausted. She looked out the small window. The sunlight looked so inviting. Deciding that a break would do her good, she opened the door and went out to stretch her legs.

As she stepped outside, Emma was surprised to find it no brighter than inside the cabin. Indeed, when she turned around it seemed no brighter. Looking toward the small window, she saw a shaft of light coming from a tiny gap in the trees. Emma smiled at how perfectly the window was placed. In fact, looking around there were very few gaps in the trees. Very little sun shining through the dense leaves.

Turning away from the dark cabin, Emma saw a small hill where the sun was shining brightly down. The bright light among the darkness seemed to fill the area with such hope. She found herself headed for that light. The climb took more of a toll on Emma than she expected and she was forced to rest against a tree.

At the base of the tree, Emma saw the outline of a gravestone hidden among the tall grass. Curiously, she stepped away from the tree and knelt down in front of the stone. Gently, she pulled the grass and weeds to clear them away.

Emma was so focused on clearing the grass away, she didn't hear Thane approach until he knelt beside her. As he helped her work, Emma found her thoughts turning to their mothers. How Thane's Ma and her Mama both had love in their lives. Enough love that the husbands they left behind felt they couldn't replace it. As the sun shone on her face, Emma realized she wanted that. She wanted to live a life where she was loved.

"Thane, I want ta be loved," she said softly, breaking the silence of the trees surrounding them. "I want ta be loved like my Da loved my Mama. Loved like yer Pa loved yer Ma. Loved so much that it's hard ta go on without that love," her voice cracked. Emma paused to clear her throat. "Do ya think ya could ever have that fer me? Do ya think ya could love me that much? If yer not sure, then I jest want ya ta point me toward home. No one need know yer Pa was involved. No need fer ya ta feel guilty," she said softly, as tears slipped down her cheeks. She waited quietly for him to say something. Taking the silence for his answer, her chest felt full and began to ache - making it hard to breathe.

"Emma," Thane started slowly, "I've wanted nothin' more than ta marry ya since ya were a young girl. Since I watched ya sufferin' so young and tryin' so hard ta be brave. But I know that I'm not worthy of ya. I knew that then and I know it now. I feel so torn. I want ta keep ya with me. Ta protect ya. Ta take care of ya and never let ya go," Thane's voice was thick with emotion. Emma looked up surprised, joy filling her heart. Tears ran down her cheeks unnoticed. "I know ya need better than the likes of me. Yer better than anythin' I have ta offer ya," he reached up to tuck a loose curl behind her ear. "I tried ta be unselfish and jest think of what's best fer ya. I tried ta let ya marry James. Ta let him take care of ya. Give ya everythin' ya need. But I find that I jest can't. I can't live without ya anymore." His hands held her face gently as he wiped the tears from her cheeks.

Emma dared not to breathe for fear of breaking the moment.

Finally, she gave him a joyful smile and reached up to caress his wrists. "Well then, it seems we're gonna get married. I best be headin' back ta the cabin. I have a dress ta finish."

Smiling, Thane stood and held his hand out to help Emma. As she reached up to accept his outstretched hand, she looked at the headstone one last time. The etching caught her eye and caused her hand to freeze. Near the bottom of the stone, buried in the weeds was a date. Emma reached out and pulled the last few weeds away, exclaiming, "Why - yer Ma died before I was born. That's close ta 20 years ago."

Thane objected, as he knelt by Emma's side, "That's not possible! I had ta've been 10 or so when she died."

Emma leaned out of the way, so that Thane could move closer to see the year clearly. He traced his finger along the engraving. "1838," she confirmed quietly. "That's the year before I was born."

"Pa never clears around this stone. He's never wanted ta see it - too painful fer him. I never even knew these numbers were here," Thane spoke thoughtfully, as if he had forgotten that Emma was there. "My Ma died two winters before yer Mama did. It's why I was so taken by yer tears," Thane turned to her then. "What year was that?"

Emma cleared her throat softly before replying, "Mama died the summer of 1850. That was eight years ago." She studied his face carefully as she watched the confused emotions cross his face. Her breath caught as a memory passed through her mind. A memory of dark gray eyes in a young face. "Was that you? The little boy in town? The one who found the purple flowers fer me and then disappeared?" Thane gave her a subtle nod. "No wonder yer eyes looked so familiar when I saw ya in town. I dreamed about ya so often. Fer years I looked fer ya every time I went inta town. I jest never stopped ta think that ya'd grow up."

They both kneeled in silence, lost in their own thoughts as the minutes passed.

"Maybe this isn't my Mama's grave - maybe I jest assumed it was," Thane decided.

Emma shook her head, "It says Annabel Hawkins. That's her name. Maybe yer Pa got the year wrong? He did make the stone hisself."

Thane nodded slowly. Pushing to his feet, he again held out his hand to her. Emma accepted his help. Once on her feet, she didn't think to let go of his hand.

"Let's get ya somethin' ta eat," he said quietly, as he led Emma back to the cabin.

Emma didn't feel hungry but she didn't argue with him. Her busy morning was catching up to her and she was starting to feel sleepy. Thane had her sit in the rocking chair in front of the fireplace while he gathered their simple meal. As she let the fire warm her, she watched the flames flicker and wave. Her eyelids felt heavier and heavier, making it hard for her to keep them open.

"Emma?" Thane spoke softly. "I think ya should rest. Let's get ya inta bed." Emma felt his warm hand gently tug on hers.

"No," she denied. "I must keep workin' on this dress. My family will be worried. Jest give me a minute." Emma's words drifted off as she spoke.

Thane chuckled softly. Carefully lifting her, he carried her into the bedroom. "The dress'll be here when ya wake. Just rest."

Emma tried to protest as she felt a quilt being pulled up over her. But sleep pulled at her and she was soon sound asleep.

~*~*~*~*~*~*~*~*~*~*~*~*~*~

Emma's progress on her dress was slow. Rubbing her eyes again, she lowered the fabric to her lap and let her shoulders relax. A frustrated sigh escaped her lips as she leaned back against the rocker chair.

"Emma," Thane said softly. "Ya should rest. It's no use pushin' yerself so hard." He carefully took the unfinished garment from her fingers.

Turning toward him, Emma wished she could argue. But she knew that she was done working for the day. She didn't have enough energy to lift her arms one more time. Thane carefully slid the needle into the soft material to hold its place. Watching him drape it neatly over the sewing basket on the table, Emma sighed again.

The wind howled outside the cabin, making the flames flicker. Her thoughts turned to her family. Were they out in this wind looking for her? Or would the wind have made them head home? Tears filled her eyes in frustration.

"Are ya hurtin'?" Thane asked softly.

"No," Emma whispered thickly, past the ache in her throat.

"What kin I get ya?"

Emma shook her head slowly. "I'm alright. I jest wish I could tell my family that I'm fine. They shouldna be out there searchin' fer me. Not when here I sit. Safe and warm."

Thane stared into the fire. After a long silence, he turned toward Emma. "Jest give yerself one more day. Ya can rest. And finish yer dress," his voice sounded tired. Helpless. "Jest one more day. Then I'll take ya ta yer family."

Emma nodded her head, not trusting her voice to answer.

~Thirty~

Noises from the next room woke Emma the next morning. "Thane must be cookin' breakfast already," she thought as she opened her eyes. Pushing back the blankets, Emma swung her legs over the side of the bed. Smoothing her patched dress over her knees, she felt her face redden. If she was still wearing her dress, then Emma knew that Thane had needed to carry her to bed again.

Rubbing her hands over her eyes embarrassed, she prayed silently, "Please Lord let me regain my strength." Pushing to her feet, she headed for the door.

Thane looked up as she opened the bedroom door. "Good mornin'," he greeted with a small smile.

"Good mornin'," she answered. "Ya shoulda woke me. I can finish cookin'."

"Jest sit yerself down. I can cook," Thane stated. Emma started to protest, but he interrupted her. "Iffen yer gonna finish that dress taday, yer gonna need all yer strength fer sewin'. Jest sit yerself down."

Emma had to agree with what he said. Finishing the dress was her goal for the day. She needed to just concentrate on that. But her pride wanted to insist she could cook too. She had always cooked for everyone else. That had always been her job in the family.

With the thought of her family, Emma took in a long, deep breath. Slowly, she sank into the rocking chair. "I'll rest today.. because I need ta finish this dress. But don't think I'll be lettin' ya cook once we're--," Emma couldn't bring herself to finish the sentence. Getting married still seemed so strange. Shaking her head slightly, she started over, "If I didna need all my energy ta sew this dress, I wouldna let ya do my chores. Do ya understand?"

"Yes ma'am," Thane answered with a lopsided smile.

The corners of her mouth curled up in response to his words. "Why do ya still call me that?"

"What?" he asked, looking over at her.

"Ma'am," she repeated. "Why do ya still call me ma'am?"

Thane smiled softly. He turned back to the meat he was frying. "At first it was jest ta make ya smile," he admitted. "But I continued -- ta remind myself that ya were off limits. I was tryin' ta protect my heart from gettin' attached ta ya."

"Did it work?" Emma asked hesitantly, not sure she wanted to know the answer.

Thane shook his head with a sad smile.

Reaching for the plate on the table, he dished up her simple breakfast and set it on her lap. Filling another plate for himself, he sat down next to her. Moving the food around with his fork, he opened his mouth to speak. But then hesitated.

"Ya look tired," Emma spoke softly. "Did ya sleep last night?"

Thane looked up in surprise.

"No. I can see ya didna," she answered for herself.

Slowly turning back to his plate, Thane admitted quietly, "I spent the night prayin'."

Taking a bite of her food, Emma realized she didn't recognize the meat she was eating. Not wanting to sound squeamish, she decided not to ask. They ate in silence.

When Emma finished, Thane took her empty plate and stood to his feet. "I know I promised I'd take ya ta yer family tomorra. But I feel we should find a church ta marry first." Thane stood quietly at the washtub with his back to Emma. She wished he would turn so she could see his face. Taking a deep breath, he continued, "I know yer worried about yer family, and would rather go ta them first. It's jest - I spent a long time in prayer - I know it's not perfect. I jest think this is what God is tellin' me ta do." Thane turned then. His gaze pleaded with Emma to understand.

Emma smiled softly. "As fer God, His way is perfect," she repeated the verse her Mama had taught her.

"It doesn't seem perfect," Thane said, as he turned his attention back to washing the plates. "But I do think it's God's plan for us."

"I agree," she said with a nod. Rising to her feet, she gathered her sewing supplies together. She turned around just in time to see Thane carrying the rocking chair out the front door. Following him outside, Emma saw him set the chair in a small patch of sunshine.

Seeing the question in her eyes, Thane answered easily, "I think being outside will do ya some good. Besides we both know how ya love the breeze."

Laughing softly, her hesitation vanished. Emma sank into the rocking chair.

Thane set a log on end, near her knee, to hold her sewing basket. With one last glance, he turned and walked away.

Emma turned her attention to the dress in her hands. She was giving herself one last day to rest. One last day to rely on the help of others. She intended to use it well.

~Thirty One~

The sun shone warm on Emma's face. Enjoying the warmth in her sleepy state, she lay with her eyes closed, soaking it in. She heard the quiet squeak of the front door opening.

Slowly opening her eyes, Emma pushed up on her elbows and looked around the room. When her gaze fell on her finished purple dress, she realized what day it was. "Today will be my weddin' day," she reminded herself. A gentle smile lit up her face. It felt strange that weeks ago she had been dreading this day. That had been when she had been torn between Thane and James. Memories of James's happiness filled her thoughts and her smile faded. An ache filled her throat. Emma laid back down and covered her face with her hands. She could not bear to think of how disappointed James would be when she returned home married. "I couldna marry him now anyway," she reminded herself. But the ache filled her chest anyway and made it hard for her to breathe. "It would hurt too much ta have others lose respect fer him. I could never do that ta him. I could never expect him ta take on my ruined reputation," she reminded herself silently.

Pushing away all thoughts of James, she sat up. Emma stood to her feet and headed for the water bowl. The water, Thane had brought in the night before, had cooled over night. The coolness felt good as she splashed it onto her face and neck. She patted the water away on the waiting towel.

Taking off the borrowed nightgown, she folded it carefully. Emma pulled on her patched dress. Deciding she would wait to make her hair fancy until after breakfast, she went in search of the outhouse.

Thane was already filling the washtub and had a fire going. There was meat frying in a skillet and biscuits on the table.

Emma hurried with her outdoor needs and returned to the cabin to help.

When they sat down to eat their meal, Emma said a simple prayer, "Father, who art in Heaven, Bless this food you have provided fer us. And Bless this day and all its events. Amen."

"Amen," Thane echoed sincerely.

They both ate silently for a few minutes, before Thane spoke. "I figure ta go on inta Charlotte today. Neither of us are known there. Should be less chance of someone objectin'," he explained simply. "We'll have ta stay in town fer the night, most likely. Then we'll head back ta yer Da's farm in the morning."

Emma nodded in understanding.

"Do ya wish ta change anythin'?" Thane asked softly.

The question surprised Emma. She couldn't remember a time when she had been asked to approve anything. "No, seems like a sound plan ta me," she stammered.

With that settled, Thane turned his attention back to eating. As soon as breakfast was over, he headed out to take care of some last minute chores.

Emma cleared the table and scrubbed the dishes. She wiped down the table, then turned to give the floor a thorough sweeping. When the board in the corner flipped over onto its side, Emma could see the hard packed dirt underneath. "Oh," she said in surprise. "The floor boards are jest settin' on the ground." She turned toward the door and realized there were no steps into the cabin. "I wonder why I didna notice before," she said curiously.

Satisfied that the room was clean enough, she turned her attention to the fire. Breaking apart the coals, she ladled dish water onto them. Since they would likely be gone for several days, she wanted the fire to be completely out.

Going back to the room, she gently closed the door. Pulling off her patched dress, she folded it neatly. Stacking it with the nightgown, Emma wrapped them both in brown paper and she tied it closed.

Emma slowly slipped into her beautiful new purple dress. She marveled at its softness. Since it was to be her wedding dress, she had taken the time to add extra tucks and fullness to the sleeves. Emma never wanted frivolities on a dress before this one, but she had found it fun to make it extra pretty.

Emma brushed her hair out. Carefully, she wound it around and pinned it in place. Without a mirror, she had to arrange it by touch.

One last check to make sure all the food was put in the cellar and Emma stepped outside with her packed clothes.

When Thane caught sight of Emma, he froze. "Ya look beautiful," he said softly.

Emma felt her cheeks flush with color. She twirled slowly to cover her embarrassment. "This material is perfect. It was so easy ta sew." When Emma stopped turning, Thane was still staring at her. Realizing he was being rude, he gave her a shy smile and reluctantly went back to his work.

Glad that his attention was off her, Emma stepped closer to see that Thane was tying down a load of furs behind his saddle. The furs were mostly coyote and fox. When Emma raised her eyebrows at them curiously, he explained, "I will need ta finish up some business I had with a man in the valley. He was tired of losin' his calves and chickens ta coyotes. Pays me per hide. Thought I'd deliver 'em tomorra. I figure we'll need some money ta set up a pantry here. And fer some repairs," his embarrassment at the state of his cabin was evident.

Emma sat down on the stump to rest while he worked. She was already exhausted from all her hurried chores.

When Thane was finished, he secured her wrapped clothes behind the saddle and lifted her up. As her knee looped around the saddle horn, a memory flashed through her mind of her hands locking into a black mane. Running her fingers through the reddish brown mane in front of her, she commented, "I thought yer horse was black?"

Thane climbed up and settled behind Emma. "My Pa's horse is black. Mine is the sorrel." He clicked to get the horse moving. "The black is the one ya rode here on," he added softly.

Emma nodded, the memory making more sense.

The trip to Charlotte was made mostly in silence. They travelled down the creek for a ways and then crossed into the trees on the other side. The downhill slope made Emma's ride uncomfortable. Not being used to riding a horse, she didn't know if she should lean back into Thane or forward. But leaning forward gave her the feeling she could fall off. Finally, Thane put his arm around her waist to keep her steady. Emma relaxed against him, and she started to look around her.

Once they reached the level road, Emma's exhaustion and the gentle rhythm of the horse caused her to fall asleep. Almost immediately, her head fell to the side and she startled awake. Thane turned Emma's body slightly in the saddle and she settled her head under his chin, against his chest. She fell asleep again and didn't wake until he called her name. Telling her they had reached Charlotte.

Emma watched the busy town through her sleepy eyes. The horse walked through the streets, ignoring the chaos around it. Thane rode straight to the blacksmith's shop. He hopped down and then reached up to lift Emma down. Emma's legs and back complained as she straightened. She groaned as she turned to follow Thane inside. Thane walked over to the blacksmith to inquire if he would look after the horse and feed him while they were in town. The blacksmith said he would be glad to keep the horse, taking Thane's offered coin.

"Can ya point us in the direction of the parsonage?" Thane asked.

The man's smile faded as he looked from Thane to Emma and back to Thane. "It's the little house next ta the church. Can't miss it."

"Thank ya," Thane stated with a nod.

The smell of the blacksmith shop brought memories of James flooding back to Emma. Guilt filled her for the second time that day. The emotions tightened her chest for a moment. "Lord, if this is yer will, please be givin' me the strength ta get through this day," she silently prayed in desperation. Slipping her hand through Thane's bent arm, she felt a peace settle through her. They walked toward the parsonage.

The parsonage was situated next to the church. The blacksmith was right, they couldn't miss it. Their steps slowed as they climbed the steps to the simple house. Emma looked up at Thane when he paused in front of the door. Finally, he stepped forward to knock.

It was opened almost immediately by a middle aged woman. "Hello, may I help ya?" she asked cheerfully.

"Yes ma'am," Thane removed his hat as he spoke. "My name's Thane Hawkins. We've come ta see the Parson. Is he in?"

The woman stepped back, opening the door further. "Come on in. Pastor Barton is jest eatin' his dinner. Won't ya join us?"

"We wouldn't want ta impose," Thane replied.

As they entered the tiny kitchen, the pastor stood up from the table. The men greeted each other with a handshake.

"My name's Thane Hawkins, sir. This here is Emma Wells. We're wonderin' if ya would marry us today, sir," Thane's voice sounded calm, but Emma could tell from the stiffness of the arm she was holding onto, that he was uneasy.

The Pastor's smile faded for a moment before he forced it back onto his face. "Sit down and join me while I finish my stew. Ya can tell me why yer needin' ta be married taday, while we eat."

Thane hesitated slightly before pulling out a chair for Emma to sit in. Sitting in the chair across from the Pastor, he began to tell their story. "Ta be honest, sir, Emma has found herself in my care while she recovered from an injury." Looking down uncomfortably, he continued, "Since there were no others with us, we'll need ta marry before I can return her home. I imagine her family is worried, so we'd like ta marry taday."

The Pastor nodded his approval at Thane's honesty, as he continued to eat his stew. After considering the words in silence for several minutes, he replied, "Why don't ya eat a bowl of my wife's delicious stew first. Yer Emma looks exhausted. I need ta check in with the Sheriff, as we do with all out of town weddin's. When I return, ya can be married right here. The church is full of school children right now, so this won't be a church weddin', I'm sorry ta say."

Thane nodded his head in understanding.

Pastor Burton slid his chair back, placed a gentle kiss on his wife's cheek and headed for the door.

The Pastor's wife was ready with bowls of hot stew. "My name's Harriet. Relax and eat. Then I'll help Emma get freshened up," she informed them in a friendly voice.

Emma's hand shot up to her hair. She could feel some of her curls had come loose and were sticking out. "It must be from leanin' on Thane," she thought embarrassed.

They ate in silence. Then Harriet showed Emma to a small room with a wash bowl and a small mirror. Emma started to fix her hair, when Harriet stepped forward and took the pins from her hand. "Sit down dear." Emma released a sigh of relief. The long horse ride had drained her strength, leaving her feeling mildly dizzy. She wasn't sure she could have held her hair up long enough to pin it.

Harriet carefully brushed out Emma's hair. Twisting and arranging. Finally, the pastor's wife pinned it firmly into place. When Emma looked in the mirror, she couldn't believe how lovely her hair looked.

"Are ya in any danger Emma?" Harriet asked quietly.

Startled by the question, Emma turned toward the older woman. "From Thane? No ma'am. He rescued me from the man who attacked me. Now he jest finds himself responsible for me," Emma replied just as quietly. "He has been very honorable."

Looking relieved at her answer, Harriet led her back into the main room. Thane was deep in a conversation with a young man, when they entered. When he saw her, Thane's face flooded with relief. Immediately, he came to stand by her side.

"Miss Wells says she has agreed ta this weddin'," Harriet told the other men in the room.

Emma looked at the older lady in surprise. She suddenly realized the reason behind Harriet offering to help her freshen up. When Emma turned her attention back to Thane, she noticed he did not seem surprised.

The Pastor nodded to his wife, acknowledging that he heard. The other man stepped back momentarily to look at the two of them. Then holding Emma's gaze, he spoke, "Miss Wells, I'm Sheriff

Bradley. This man claims you suffered from a blow ta the head. That he nursed ya alone in his cabin and now wishes ta marry ya. Ta save yer honor." The sheriff paused as his gaze passed between the two young people in front of him. "Do ya agree this is true?"

Emma and Thane had agreed ta tell the simple truth of the situation for now, but she felt it sounded so cold with no mention of their love. "Yes sir," she answered without giving away her feelings.

Harriet spoke up once again, "I saw a nasty gash and bump myself, while repinnin' Miss Wells's hair. Seems ta confirm they're tellin' the truth."

Sheriff nodded. "Miss Wells, how did ya come by that blow?"

Emma looked up to Thane in question, but Thane was still watching Sheriff Bradley. "My Pa gave it ta her, sir."

Again the single nod. The sheriff was silent for a long time before continuing, "I'll stay ta witness the weddin'. Then we'll send word ta Sheriff Granger in Vermontville. I've had several notices sent from him updatin' me on the search fer this young lady."

Emma felt a lump form in her throat.

"I'd planned on takin' her there first thing in the morn," Thane informed the sheriff, turning to Emma, "Maybe we should continue on taday?"

Harriet commented, "I'm not sure Emma'll make it taday without some rest. She's almost dead on her feet."

Thane studied Emma closely and noticed how tired she looked. "Ya can sleep on the way there?" he suggested.

Emma was torn. She wanted to continue on but she was suddenly not sure she had the strength to face her family today. She forced herself to nod.

Sheriff Bradley cleared his throat, "Let's continue with the ceremony and discuss it after. I think gettin' notice ta her family tonight will do."

Thane looked to Emma for her decision. She nodded slowly.

Harriet took Emma's hand, guiding her over to the fireplace. Thane stepped next to her and took both her hands in his. He smiled down at Emma, as the Pastor stepped in front of them.

Opening his Bible, Pastor Barton began to read, "Will you, Thane Hawkins, have this woman ta be thy wedded wife, ta live together after God's ordinance, in the holy estate of matrimony? Will ya love her, comfort her, honor and keep her, in sickness and in health; and forsaking all others, keep thee only unto her, so long as ye both shall live?"

Thane looked down into Emma's eyes. He cleared his throat, but it still sounded thick with emotion as he answered, "I will."

Pastor Barton's mouth turned up at the edges. His eyes flickered to his wife beside Emma. Looking back to young bride, he began again, "Will you, Emma Wells, have this man ta be thy wedded husband, ta live together after God's ordinance, in the holy estate of matrimony? Will ya obey him, serve him, love, honor and keep him, in sickness and in health; and forsaking all others, keep thee only unto him, so long as ye both shall live?"

Emma felt her eyes fill up with tears. Blinking them back, she answered, "I will."

"Thane, take Emma's hand in yers and repeat after me," Pastor Barton instructed. "I, Thane Hawkins, take thee, Emma Wells, ta be my wedded wife.."

Clearing his throat, Thane echoed the Pastor's words, "I, Thane Hawkins, take thee, Emma Fern Wells, ta be my wedded wife,"

"Ta have and ta hold,"

"From this day forward,"

"For better, or worse, for richer, for poorer,"

"In sickness and in health,"

"Ta love and ta cherish, till death us do part,"

"According ta God's holy ordinance,"

"And thereto I plight thee my faith."

As Thane's voice repeated the words, his voice thickened with emotion. Emma felt tears fall down her cheeks.

When Pastor Barton turned to her, he smiled broadly. "Emma, take Thane's hand in yers and repeat after me."

"I, Emma Fern Wells, take thee, Thane Hawkins, ta be my wedded husband,"

"Ta have and ta hold,"

"From this day forward,"
"For better, for worse, for richer, for poorer,"
"In sickness and in health,"
"Ta love, cherish and ta obey, till death do us part,"
"Accordin' ta God's Holy ordinance,"
"And thereto I give thee my faith."
Emma's voice quivered as she repeated the words that joined her life with Thane's forever. Peace filled her. Finally decided, her future held no more questions. Tears flowed slowly down her cheeks.
"I now pronounce ya husband and wife," Pastor Barton called joyfully. "Thane, ya may now kiss yer bride."
Thane's gaze flickered down to Emma's lips and then back up to her eyes, shyly. He lowered his lips to hers in a short, shy kiss. This shy kiss brought a boisterous laugh from the sheriff and he clapped his hand down on Thane's shoulder in congratulations.
Emma looked toward Harriet and noticed the other woman's cheeks were wet, with tears, as well. Before she could comment, she felt something slide onto her ring finger. Looking down at the simple gold band around her finger, she gasped.
"This was my Ma's ring. It was passed down ta her, from her grandma. I'd be honored if ya'd wear it," the uncertainty in Thane's voice made Emma look up into his eyes.
"Thank ya," she said through her choked voice. "It's beautiful."
He pulled her unexpectedly into his arms and crushed her to his chest. The laughter from the sheriff, brought their attention back to the others. Thane slowly released Emma, so they could turn to accept congratulations from them.
As Harriet wrapped Emma in a motherly hug, she whispered in her ear. "There is much more than honor in that boy's heart. He loves ya dear. That's fer sure and fer certain." Pulling back in surprise, Emma saw the tears in the older woman's eyes again. She felt herself smile and hugged her again.
Turning toward the other gentleman, she accepted both of their wishes of joy, as she held onto Thane's arm.
As Thane shook the sheriff's hand, the other man's face hardened into a decision. "Thane, would ya accompany me down

ta the jailhouse? There is somethin' I'd like ta discuss with ya while I record yer marriage."

Thane nodded slowly. Emma could feel the relaxed arm she held, tense up.

"Mrs. Hawkins can stay here with Harriet if she wishes," the sheriff said with a smile.

"I'd like ta go with Thane," Emma stated firmly, even though she would have preferred to sit down. She felt uneasy about being separated from him.

Thane tightened his hold on the hand Emma had tucked in his elbow. "She'll come with us."

Emma turned to Harriet, "Thank ya fer all yer help today."

"It was my pleasure, Emma," Harriet assured her. Giving her hand a squeeze, she offered, "We have an extra room, if ya'd like ta stay here tonight."

"We wouldn't want ta put ya ta any trouble," Thane started but was interrupted.

"Nonsense," Pastor Barton laughed. "Harriet loves ta fuss. We'll have a room ready fer ya when ya return."

Thane nodded. "I'm much obliged ta ya both. Hadn't much looked forward ta takin' Emma near the hotel."

They turned to follow Sheriff Bradley out the door and up the street to the jailhouse.

~Thirty Two~

Sheriff Bradley sat at his desk and pulled out a ledger. He diligently filled in the information. ".. married this day in September..," he murmered.

"September?" Emma gasped. She looked to Thane to explain. "How long did I sleep?"

Thane squeezed her hand. "Pretty near a whole week. Ya had me worried."

"I thought it was a couple days," she muttered.

The drawer of the sheriff's desk was slammed shut, bringing their attention back to the lawman. "I suspect that there is much more ta yer story than yer willin' ta tell me. I was witness ta more than a marriage brought together by honor," the sheriff stated, smiling at their embarrassment. "But that isn't why I brought ya here." Standing up and walking around to the front of his desk, he sat on the edge. "I thought ya looked familar ta me. I jest couldn't place it at first."

Thane reached out to take the sketch the sheriff offered him. The paper was yellowed with age, but the face was Thane's face. Emma let out a gasp.

"In 1849, we had a woman brought into town. A traveler had found her wanderin' sick and delirious in the snow," the sheriff began. "She claimed that she'd been kidnapped and forced ta marry. That this man had other victims.. a mother and a son. And that he'd abandoned her at last."

"That can't be Thane. In 1849, he'd have been a lil' boy," Emma said firmly.

"Yes ma'am. I'm aware that this can't be yer husband," confirmed the lawman. "But the strikin' resemblance, leads me ta believe it may be his Pa."

"My Pa?" Thane asked shocked.

"The description says blue eyes.. yers are a dark gray," he pointed out. "But the similarities are strikin' in all other ways."

Emma stared at the sketch amazed that Thane's Pa had ever been that attractive. The years of bitterness had changed that.

Thane found his voice, "My Ma died about 10 years ago, I would've known if he abducted another woman."

Sheriff Bradley leaned forward from his perch on his desk. "Miss Clara claimed she cared fer this man's baby until he was near grown."

"No. My Ma died. We got snowed in on a hunting trip. It was bad. We stayed gone fer pret' near a month. When we returned the cabin had been shredded by coyotes or wolves lookin' fer any shred of food. Pa said they must've got Ma. That was in--," Thane looked to Emma in question.

"Ya said two winters before the summer of '50. So either late 1848 or early 1849," she answered softly.

"That was probably Miss Clara," the sheriff confirmed.

~Thirty Three~

Thane stood completely still.

"Would ya like ta talk ta Miss Clara?" Sheriff Bradley asked. "Maybe that would clear things up."

Thane and Emma looked up at the same time. "Talk ta her," Thane echoed in confusion. "She's here?"

The lawman nodded. "She didn't know how ta go back fer the boy. Fer you. So she stayed on as our school teacher. It was her profession before she was taken by yer Pa."

Thane didn't move. He just stood silently in shock. Emma slid her hand down his arm into his fingers and squeezed. He looked down at the tiny hand and then up into her eyes. Emma lost herself in his gray eyes. The confused emotions, flashing through his eyes, made her throat hurt.

"I must get Emma home first," Thane spoke finally. He cleared his throat before continuing. "Once she is settled, I can return ta talk ta this Clara."

"But Thane yer so close," Emma argued.

"Emma, yer family'll be beside themselves with worry," Thane said.

The Pastor spoke up from doorway, "Emma, why don't you write a letter ta your father. We'll make sure it's delivered today with the letter ta the sheriff in Vermontville," he suggested.

Emma looked at Thane, raising her eyebrow in question.

"Do ya think that will reassure them?" Thane asked.

Emma nodded. As much as she wanted to see her family, she knew that Thane needed to have his questions answered.

The sheriff went back to his desk and sat in the chair. He pulled writing supplies out for her. Rising, he offered Emma the chair.

Emma squeezed Thane's hand once before releasing it and went to sit down. Staring down at the blank sheet of paper, she felt her heart race. "How much should I tell them?" Emma wondered nervously. Taking a slow deep breath, she sent up a silent prayer for guidance. Peace settled over her. "I'll jest let them know ta stop lookin' fer me," Emma decided. Picking up the pencil, she began to write slowly and carefully.

> *Dear Da,*
> *I am safe.*
> *I am sorry to have caused so much trouble. I will explain the situation when I get home to the farm. Because I have found myself alone in the company of a young man, we feel the only solution is to marry before he returns me to you.*
> *Unexpected business has come up and it will keep us from coming home today. But we will follow this letter in a day or two.*
> *Give everyone my love,*
> *Your loving daughter,*
> *Emma*

When Emma finished her letter, she read it through, once more, before handing it to the pastor. "Do ya think it'll relieve their worryin'?"

The pastor scanned the letter and nodded in agreement. Returning the paper to Emma, he turned to Thane. "Why don't you and yer wife return with me, ta the parsonage, until school lets out. Sheriff Bradley can escort Miss Clara over when her teaching duties are over," Pastor Barton suggested. "Ya can leave the letter here for the sheriff ta arrange delivery."

Emma folded her short letter and sealed it.

The sheriff nodded, "Let me jest round up my deputy. I'll send him ta Vermontville as soon as he can be ready." The sheriff left the building with the pastor.

The jailhouse was left silent as Emma stood next to Thane. Watching his face, as he stood there in shock, she reached out to touch his arm gently.

"Emma. What if it's true?" Thane asked quietly, as he lowered himself down into the chair she had just risen from. "What if everythin' I knew was all a lie?"

Exhausted from all the excitement, Emma did not know what to say or how to comfort him. So she knelt on the floor, near his knee, and curled her hand into her husband's huge one. "My husband," she said silently. "How different that sounds." A soft smile touched her lips as she leaned her head against Thane's knee. "That'll take some gettin' used to."

~Thirty Four~

Harriet refilled Emma's cup with hot coffee. She would have refilled Thane's as well, but his cup was still full. His thoughts were so preoccupied, he had done little more than hold it. His coffee had long since cooled.

Emma sat next to her new husband at the parsonage table. Exhaustion was taking its toll on her but she refused to leave Thane's side. It had been such a busy day, and all the confusion was making her head hurt. She massaged her forehead, hoping for some relief. She looked toward the clock, hoping the hands had moved since she had last looked. "Should only be a few more minutes," she thought thankfully. Leaning her head into her hand, she allowed herself to close her eyes.

"Emma, are ya sure ya won't rest? Ya look wore out," Harriet commented for the third time.

Emma shook her head as she looked up. "No thank ya Harriet. I'll be fine."

Thane turned his head toward her. He reached for her hand and squeezed it, "Ya feelin' alright?"

"My head is jest hurtin' again, is all," she admitted quietly.

"Ya should rest," he insisted, studying her face closely.

Before she could protest, they heard the front door of the house squeak open. The pastor's voice could be heard talking softly.

Thane stood to his feet and Emma found herself tucked behind him, holding tightly to his arm.

"Nathaniel?" asked a timid voice.

"No, Miss Clara. This is Thane," Sheriff Bradley replied.

"Thane?" came Clara's voice again, surprised.

Thane's grip on Emma's side tightened. "Ma?" his voice broke on the single word. Emma wanted to peek around her husband to see the person belonging to the timid voice, but the tension in Thane's body kept her frozen in place.

"It's me," the small voice quivered with tears. "Oh, my boy."

"But how -? How are ya here?" Thane sounded so confused and unsure. "Why are they callin' ya Clara? Yer name is Annabel."

"No, it's always been Clara," the voice corrected. "Yer Pa called me Annabel whenever he'd been drinkin'. I stopped correctin' him after the first few years. The rest of the time, he didn't call me anythin' at all."

The sheriff's voice interupted sounding perplexed, "Do ya know what Annabel's family name was?"

Emma saw Thane shake his head.

"Preston, I believe," Clara answered. "I found her journal in her trunk once."

"Annabel Preston?" the sheriff asked again, astonished.

Emma's curiosity got the better of her then and she peeked around Thane's arm. The lawman was the first person Emma saw. He looked very deep in thought as he slipped from the room. No one else seemed to notice him leaving.

In the center of the room was a petite dark haired woman. Sections of her hair were graying, but she still possessed a simple beauty. She gave a small gasp, when she noticed Emma. Turning in alarm to the pastor, Clara stammered, "Who -?"

Pastor Barton patted Clara's hand and spoke softly, "Thane and Emma came into town, ta marry, today."

"Freely?" Clara's voice squeaked.

"Yes, I married Thane freely," Emma confirmed softly.

"Pa took her," Thane explained. "It's the only thing we could do."

Clara sat down hard in the straight back chair behind her. "Oh dear."

Thane stepped forward then, pushing Emma back behind him. "I don't understand," he stated confused. "Yer the Ma I remember. Yer the only one I remember. Yer the one I cried fer when ya died."

Emma ached for Thane, ached for the confusion in his voice. But all the emotions weren't helping the pain in her head. The throbbing began to pound loudly in Emma's ears. She leaned her head onto Thane's back, her fingers wrapping around the ones holding her back.

"Yer Pa said that yer Mama died a few weeks after ya were born, from a fever," Clara's timid voice explained. "I met Nathaniel.. I met yer Pa when I was a young school teacher up north of here. He had called me Annie that day, mistaking me fer yer Mama." The room was filled with a long silence. "He returned fer me that night. Told me ta pack my bag. I was foolish enough ta think it would work out. By the time I realized he would never love me, I was so attached ta ya that I couldn't leave ya."

"But ya did leave," Thane stated. "Ya let me think ya had died."

"When ya didn't return from yer trappin', I thought yer Pa had left me there. I ran outta wood ta keep me warm and then I got sick," Clara's voice pleaded for understanding. "I left ta get help."

Some of the tension left Thane's back. "We ran inta a storm that seemed ta never end. When we returned, the cabin had been tore apart by a wild animal. We thought ya died. Pa even buried-," Thane suddenly stopped. "No, that grave musta already been there."

All the information swam around in Emma's head as Thane fell silent. All his questions seemed to be answered but the throbbing in Emma's head made it hard for her to concentrate. Closing her eyes, she rubbed against her temple. Her world sway slightly. "Thane?" Emma said softly. He turned to her and seemed to know what she needed without her having to say anything else. She felt herself lifted carefully and held close.

"If ya'll forgive me, I need ta find a place fer Emma ta rest," Thane stated. Relaxing into his arms as they pulled her in tight, Emma felt sleep tug at her. Harriet was speaking to Thane, but Emma didn't try to listen. She sighed as she fell asleep.

~*~*~*~*~*~*~*~*~*~*~*~*~

"I think ya should've let her rest fer a couple more days before makin' this journey," Harriet chided.

"I didn't have a choice. She has family and a - and friends that are worried about her," Thane's voice said softly. "She couldn't rest knowin' they were out there lookin' fer her." A cool cloth dabbed at her forehead.

"She is blessed ta have such a carin' young man," Harriet stated.

"No," Thane denied fiercely. "She's a blessin' ta me, but she'd be much better off without me in her life."

Silence surrounded Emma as she slipped back into sleep.

~*~*~*~*~*~*~*~*~*~*~*~*~*~

"Thane?" Emma called quietly into the surrounding darkness.

"I'm here," he answered quickly. She felt his weight on the bed next to her. "How's yer head?"

"My eyes are hurtin' some," she answered. "Where are we?" Trying to sit up, Emma felt her shoulders lifted off the pillow.

"We are at the parsonage with the Pastor and Harriet," Thane said cautiously, concern showing in his voice. "What are ya needin'?" A cool cloth was pressed gently over her eyes.

Emma felt herself sigh, and leaned her head against Thane's chest.

"Emma?" Thane asked again.

"Hmm?" Emma couldn't remember what she needed. She fell back asleep.

~*~*~*~*~*~*~*~*~*~*~*~*~*~

A soft chuckle woke Emma from her sleep. Confused, she couldn't place where she was at first. Opening her eyes, she saw Harriet smiling down at her. Emma tried to sit up and found that she couldn't move. Her arms were pinned by her sides. She turned her head slightly, and saw the sleeping body of Thane. Her head was leaning against his chest. He had propped pillows behind his back and sat on top of the blankets that were wrapped around her.

Harriet's soft laugh brought Emma's attention back around. "He insisted he would sleep on the floor, even though yer married now. Somehow ya changed his mind."

Emma's cheeks flushed. "I woke up hurtin'," she insisted. "He musta fallen asleep while tendin' ta me."

"Not surprisin'. He hasn't slept since ya both arrived," Harriet patted her cheek gently. "Jest rest Emma. Enjoy these quiet moments." With another smile, the pastor's wife turned to leave the room, closing the door quietly behind her.

Emma turned her head back to lay against Thane's chest. She could hear his heartbeat against her ear. The relaxing rhythm of his breathing lulled her back to sleep.

~Thirty Five~

The next few days weren't very eventful for Emma. Everyone insisted she stay in bed and rest. Thane sat next to her bed during the day, keeping her company while she was awake.

Every evening, Clara came to eat the evening meal at the parsonage and visit with Thane.

Emma couldn't tell how he was dealing with all these changes in his life. When she would ask Thane how he felt, he would carefully change the subject.

Harriet came to sit with Emma on the second day. Thane decided he should deliver his furs while she was resting. He insisted it would make their ride, to her father's farm, easier on her. Thane stood in the door to their room for a long time, looking torn. Finally, he turned and left her alone with Harriet.

Emma did not want him to leave her.

The Pastor's wife tried to cheer her up. As she rocked and knitted, she spoke softly about their small congregation. She told Emma story after story of happenings amongst the set of quiet people. Gradually Emma relaxed. Listening to the stories, she couldn't help but enjoy herself.

After they had eaten lunch, Emma sighed, "Why am I not gettin' any stronger?"

"I think ya jest over did it," Harriet stated calmly. "Doc said it was common with bumps ta the head."

"The doctor was here?" Emma asked shocked.

The older lady nodded, "We sent for him after ya fainted that first night. He insisted ya stay in bed until your head felt clear."

"I fainted?" Emma moaned, covering her face in embarrassment. "When did I become so weak?"

Harriet chuckled. "I think ya are entitled. Ya took quite a blow. That bruise covers most of the side of yer head. Yer young man was astonished at the size."

Emma nodded her head in understanding. Thane's feeling of guilt for her injuries had increased. The doctor's examination explained a lot to her. "He seems ta think he coulda stopped his Pa somehow. And I was so angry at first. I know that didna help."

~*~*~*~*~*~*~*~*~*~*~*~*~*~*~*~

Thane returned that evening after supper. He looked exhausted when he came in to check on Emma.

"How are ya feelin'?" he asked her softly.

"Much better today. I had no dizziness when I got up ta visit the outhouse," Emma stated. "I'm ready ta travel on when you are."

Thane leaned his elbows on his knees. "Let's take it slow. Maybe ya can get up and about fer a bit in the morn? See how ya do?"

"I can't stay in bed forever," she insisted.

Letting out a sigh, Thane scrubbed his hands over his face before balling them into fists in his hair. The strain had taken a toll on the man in front of her.

Emma felt guilty for her words. "I'm sorry Thane. I'll take it slow fer another day, if it'll make ya feel easier," she spoke softly.

"I'm the one who's sorry, Emma. I'm sorry for everythin' my family has put ya through. Ya can't understand what it's like havin' a family that ruins everythin'. Yer so good. And yer family is so lovin'. Ya can't imagine what it's like," Thane paused and then looked up into her eyes. "I'm not sure why God brought ya inta my life. What good could it possibly do ya? My family has ruined yer life. And now I'll be takin' ya from a farm, where ya're safe and warm? Ta where? Ta a leaky cabin in the woods? I won't do it Emma... I won't take ya there ta die," his voice broke on the last word and he paused to clear his throat. "I won't take ya back there. Ya're too good fer that. Ya're far too good fer me and my family."

Emma reached for his hand through her tears, "Yer wrong. I'm right where I need ta be, right by ya. Yer family is now my family. An' I'll follow ya wherever ya take me. Even if it's ta a leaky cabin," she cleared her throat gently. "I'm sorry I canna be more of a comfort ta ya while ya're dealin' with all of these surprises. With findin' Clara. I wish I was able ta be up and about. But Thane, yer family did NOT ruin my life."

"My Pa put ya in that bed. The doctor said he could've killed ya," Thane's voice quivered. "He almost ruined everythin', Emma. I never should've told him about ya. This's all my fault." He leaned his head back down into his hands, pressing his forehead against the small hand he grasped between his.

"Thane," Emma said softly. "None of this is yer fault."

But Thane did not reply. He kept his face pressed against the palm of her hand. With her free hand, Emma reached over and ran her fingers through his hair soothingly. She only stopped when sleep closed her eyes.

~*~*~*~*~*~*~*~*~*~*~*~*~*~

The next morning, Emma was propped up in her bed. By midday, she had felt no dizziness so she was allowed up to eat a meal in the kitchen.

"Since Emma's head is healin', we'll be takin' our leave in the mornin'," Thane stated while they ate. "We are much obliged ta ya fer lettin' us stay on this long."

Pastor Barton nodded his head in understanding. "Was our pleasure havin' ya both here. I know my Harriet has had fun pamperin' yer Emma."

Harriet studied Emma's face, "Are ya sure yer up fer the trip?"

Smiling, Emma answered, "I'm ready. My family'll be anxious ta hear from us."

After dinner, Emma was escorted back to bed for a rest, while Harriet cleaned up the meal. Emma wanted to protest, but she did feel a little tired. Thane promised to take her for a short walk if she complied. Within minutes of putting her cheek to the pillow, she felt sleep claim her.

When she woke, Harriet straightened Emma's hair for her and helped her dress. Thane tucked her hand through his elbow and took her for the promised walk. He headed toward the school to collect Clara for supper.

"Ahh Emma, yer up outta bed," Clara exclaimed surprised.

Emma felt her pride sting at the comment. She didn't want Clara to think she was a weak person. Taking a deep breath, she released it slowly in a sigh. "Forgive my pride, Lord," she prayed silently. Smiling at Clara, she agreed, "I've finally been allowed up."

Thane chuckled softly, "Emma would've been up yesterday if I'd allowed it. She isn't used ta bein' still this long, I fear." His defense of her character warmed Emma's heart and she squeezed the arm she was holding. He gently squeezed back. "We came ta see if ya'd join us fer one last meal at the parsonage. We'll be returnin' ta Vermontville on the morrow."

"Oh," Clara said surprised. "I'd hoped you'd stay around longer. Stay on until the trouble blew over."

Shaking his head, Thane replied, "Emma won't rest easy until she's assured her family that she's fine. An' I have weeks of work ahead gettin' the cabin ready fer Emma ta stay in before winter hits."

Emotion clouded Clara's face, before she nodded. She took Thane's other arm and they continued their short walk. When they reached the last house before the edge of town, Thane carefully turned and headed back to the Parsonage.

~~*~*~*~*~*~*~*~*~*~*~*~*~*~*~*~

As Emma lay in bed, she could hear the men talking in the kitchen. Just before she drifted off, she heard Thane ask, "Pastor.. In the Bible, Emma read ta me about Ruth. She gave up everythin' ta follow her dead husband's mother, when she wasn't expected ta. Then she married the man, Boaz, ta give that mother security. It tells of what a blessin' she is ta the mother and ta Boaz. With all that she gave up.. of her own choice. Why wouldn't God be also blessin' Ruth?"

Emma listened closely for the answer, but all she could hear was silence for a long time.

"Yer speakin' of Emma," the pastor commented gently. "Yer wantin' ta know why God would put that wonderful young lady through all this... when ya can see no blessin's in it fer her."

Emma's throat choked up with emotion. She could hear the same emotions in Thane's voice when he spoke. "Emma's been the brightest light in my world -- Pushin' back the shadows. Never askin' fer anythin' in return. She told me she'll go where I go.. and said she'll accept my family as hers," she heard the hurt in his bitter laugh. "My family? My Pa almost killed her. What blessin's could there be in store fer her?"

Pastor Barton cleared his own throat. "When ya walked through my door four days ago, I admit I was thinkin' the same thing. But then I remembered that God promises us that He has a plan fer each of us.. A plan that promises not ta bring harm ta us. We can't question that plan. We jest need ta have faith in it. Need ta have faith He'll be blessin' that young wife of yers," he reassured. "And as fer Ruth. She had blessings. Ya jest have ta look ta see them."

Emma's eyes filled with tears. After all of the hurt that Thane had dealt with over the last couple weeks, his thoughts weren't about himself. "He jest wants blessin's fer me," she whispered past the soft smile on her lips.

The conversation, she had overheard, was still repeating itself in Emma's mind, when Thane came in and settled into his bedroll on the floor.

~Thirty Six~

The next morning, Thane packed up their few belongings and the cold dinner from the pastor's wife. After climbing up into the saddle, he lifted Emma into his arms and they rode out of town. The four days they had spent in Charlotte seemed like an eternity to Emma. She was anxious to see her family again, but an uneasiness filled her as they travelled closer to her home. She began to worry that her family would blame her for wandering so far from the farm.

Shaking her head to clear away the nagging concern, Emma turned her focus on the passing scenery. She tucked as close to Thane as she could to ward off the chill of the morning. As the morning moved on, the chill disappeared but the sun never peaked through the clouds.

They stopped midday to eat the cold dinner Harriet had packed. When they climbed back into the saddle again, Emma fell asleep almost immediately. She slept peacefully against Thane's chest until he gently woke her.

"Emma," Thane called softly in her ear. "Emma? I need ya ta wake up. Emma?" She felt a gentle shake. "We're almost ta yer Da's farm. Open yer eyes fer me."

Emma yawned and tried to open her eyes.

"There ya go," he said softly. "I thought ya might want ta be awake when we get there."

Emma nodded her agreement. She turned slightly, so that she was facing the road. She could see the turn off for the farm up ahead. They were very close.

The horse continued to walk calmly around the bend to her family's farm. The animal had no idea how nervous Emma suddenly felt. "What if Da's angry with me?" she thought.

As they came to a stop in the farmyard, her father stepped out of the barn to meet them. The happiness that lit up his face made Emma's throat hurt.

Thane's arm tightened around her waist before he released her to slide down off the horse. Reaching up, he lifted Emma down, and smiled nervously at her.

Emma squeezed his arm in return. Then turned toward her Da. Her father closed the distance in a few steps and pulled Emma into his arms, hugging her tight around her shoulders. "There ya are my Emma girl," his voice sounded choked, as he pressed a kiss to the top of her hair. When he finally stepped back from her, he looked over her shoulder at Thane. His eyes darkened.

"Da, I want ya ta meet Thane Hawkins, my - my husband," Emma introduced quietly, hesitating slightly over the strange word.

Emma saw her Da's jaw flex. "So ya've made her an honest woman at that."

"Da-," Emma protested.

Thane's eyes flashed. "Sir, yer daughter is still as -innocent- as when I found her."

Da looked at Emma quickly, surprise and doubt showing in his eyes. He turned back to Thane, "Why?"

Thane rubbed the back of his neck. "In case ya didn't agree with my decision, sir. She would remain untouched," he explained, clearing his throat.

Emma was startled by the thought that her Da could reverse her marriage. The peace she had found, knowing that everything was decided, was starting to crumble. She looked back and forth between the two men beside her.

Thane continued without noticing her distress, "Emma couldn't come back here unmarried. And I couldn't wait fer yer decision if it'd leave her open ta talk. She's too good fer that. But I wasn't sure ya'd agree. So I continued ta sleep on the floor even after the weddin' until she had yer blessin'."

Da nodded. Continuing to stare at Thane, he squeezed Emma's arm. "How did ya come by my daughter?"

Emma tried to answer for Thane, "He found me after I'd been injured -."

"By my Pa," Thane interrupted her. He squared his shoulders and his face was stone cold, showing no emotion but determination. On the ride from Charlotte, Thane had told Emma that he wanted the truth to be told from the beginning. That he was tired of living in the shadows of lies. "He'd been drinkin' sir and gave her quite a lump."

Emma saw her father's jaw flex again, as his grip on her shoulders tightened. "Why didna ya bring her straight home?"

"Da...I was unconscious and `twas the middle of the night," she put her hand on her Da's arm. "He was tryin' ta figure out what was goin' on."

"At first my only thoughts were gettin' her well enough ta get her home," Thane paused. "But she slept for days. By then-."

Her Da turned to look at her again. The anger in his face slipped away slowly. Only concern remained. "By then, her reputation was in question," he confirmed. Suddenly, something dawned in her father's eyes. He turned back toward Thane again. "Did ya say Hawkins?"

Thane nodded, "Yes sir."

"Wasn't it yer Pa that took the Preston girl years back?" Da's eyes narrowed. Emma saw his jaw was flexing again.

"My Pa has done many things that I don't know of sir. All I do know is that he loved Annie Preston enough ta marry her and enough ta drink himself stupid every day after her death," Thane answered, sounding exhausted.

"It's his Ma, Da," Emma said softly.

She could tell her father was thinking about something. While Emma didn't know what it was, she hoped he wouldn't ask Thane anymore questions about his past. Thane was still unsure of how to take any of the news he had learned in Charlotte. Emma's heart ached to see him defending a family that lied to him.

"EMMA!"

She turned toward the voice, just in time, to see James jump down off his horse and run towards her. Emma was completely unprepared as he wrapped his arms around her waist, lifting her up off the ground. His face buried into her neck, leaving her arms to fall around his shoulders. He squeezed her so tightly she could barely breathe. Surprised by her own emotions, she felt her eyes fill with tears.

"Jest give him a minute Mr. Hawkins. And then I'll have him let go," Emma heard her Da say from, what seemed to be, far off.

"No," James declared against her neck. "I'll never let go of her again." His arms tightened around her ribs in emphasis.

"James boy," Da started. He stopped to clear his throat. "Yer holdin' another man's wife."

Emma felt James freeze. Slowly, he lowered her to the ground but did not pull his arms away. Confusion showed on his face. "What?" He looked down at Emma. At her tear filled eyes. She thought she saw his eyes fill with tears of his own. "I'm not understandin'."

Emma turned to her father. "I sent ya the letter explainin'," she stated, through the burning of her throat.

Da met her eyes. "Saw no reason ta tell anyone until I saw ya first. 'Til I knew fer sure and fer certain ya were married. So I jest told everyone the letter said ya was safe."

She turned back to James, starting to feel uncomfortable with his arms around her. She tried to step back but he kept his strong arms locked around her. Emma knew that she would be no match for the strength in his arms as he pulled her close again.

"Let's give 'em a couple minutes, Mr. Hawkins." Thane must not have agreed with him. After a pause, Da insisted, "Ya'll have her fer the rest of yer life. Give him 5 mins. That's a short time fer him ta settle his feelin's. We'll jest be in the barn - We'll be able ta see 'em."

Emma held her breath as the footsteps led away.

"Yer married?" James asked softly as soon as they were alone. His voice sounded gravelly with emotion. He loosened his hold on her, so he could see her face.

But Emma couldn't look up at him. She couldn't bear to meet his eye. Unable to utter a sound, she just nodded - barely noticeable.

"No," James choked out. "Why?" He pulled Emma back into his arms, lifting her off the ground again. His strong arms were wrapped around her ribs so tightly, she could barely move. He breathed in the scent of her hair. Suddenly, James stiffened. "Has he touched ya?" he asked.

Emma shook her head, "No."

She felt him relax again and gathered her closer. "Why didn't ya come home first? We could've been married right away."

"James ya willna want me now," Emma interrupted. "Not when ya think about it. All the talk there'll be about me bein' gone so long. Yer too good fer that. Ya don't deserve it."

"Yer wrong!" James insisted. "I love ya, Em. I've never wanted anyone else in my life. Not since the moment I saw ya."

"Why?" she pleaded. "Why me? There is nothin' special about me."

James lowered Emma to the ground again. "Ya don't know?" Slowly he lifted his hands to rest on either side of her head. "Emma -," he started to explain. But as his fingers grazed the lump above her ear, she flinched. James froze, "Ya alright?"

"Yeah," Emma said softly, raising her hand carefully to feel the sore spot. "Jest my healin' isn't quite done, I suppose."

James turned her head to the side. Gently moving her hair aside, he revealed the healing bruise. His breath caught. Everything in Emma's world stood still for a moment. After a long quiet moment, she felt a soft kiss pressed to the side of her head. Just above her ear.

Before Emma could react to the kiss, an angry growl erupted from James's chest. Surprised by the sudden change in him, she barely had time to catch his arm before he could storm off toward the barn. "Let go Emma! I'm gonna let him hit someone his own size."

"Thane didna hit me, James," Emma insisted, shaking her head to emphasize her words. "He was jest there ta take care of me. He protected me."

"This is his fault, Emma!" James argued angrily.

"No James-- it's mine!" she insisted, more tears flowing down her cheeks. "It's my fault."

James turned back to her in question. "Yer fault?"

"If I hadna had doubts and fears, I wouldna gone walkin' that night. The fault is mine. All mine," she explained quietly. Tears filled her eyes and ran down her cheeks.

"Doubts?" James took her head in his hands again, gently this time. His thumbs wiping at her tears. "Why were ya not tellin' me?"

"Ya didna ask. And ya were so happy," Emma whispered as her chest began to ache. "I take all the blame fer this."

"I don't blame ya, Em," James whispered. He pressed his lips against her forehead. Then carefully, he leaned his forehead against hers.

Emma fought to breathe through all the emotions. The ache filled her chest. She reached up to grip James's wrists. Holding on to the strength she could feel beneath her fingers.

"Please don't go with him, Emma. I love you," tears choked James's strong voice. "What will I do without ya? Yer my whole life. Jest stay with me, please? We'll figure somethin' out, I promise. Jest please stay. Stay with me." He reached down to pull her back into his arms.

Emma stepped back. Just out of James's reach. She wrapped her arms around her chest tightly, as her tears flowed freely down her cheeks. The ache in her chest had expanded until it felt like she was breaking apart.

"By law, she is Mr. Hawkins's wife, James," Emma's father intervened gently. Emma was surprised he was so close. Through her tears, she had not heard him approach. "She has ta go with him."

Thane stepped in front of her then, gently pushing her behind him. His arm wrapping around her side and pulled her up against his back. Curling her fingers into his shirt, Emma leaned her head against his back.

James stepped forward angry, "Let go of her, ya -," but his angry words died on his lips and he froze. "Did ya say Hawkins?" The odd question brought Emma's gaze up. James looked questioningly from Emma to her father. Emma's father nodded firmly.

An astonished laugh burst from James. "Thane Hawkins?" James met Emma's gaze, tears filled and overflowed his eyes as he stared into her confused ones. "He gets everythin' then? My whole world?" James stepped backwards, stunned. "He gets everythin' and I'm left with nothin'." Taking several more steps backwards, he kept his eyes locked on Emma. Finally, he turned and strode to his horse. Mounting with one smooth motion, James rode off.

As he rode away, sobs rose from Emma's chest. She could no longer control the emotions running through her. Familiar arms gathered her close and she cried. She cried for all the hurt she had caused James. She cried for all the worry she had caused him and her family. She cried until all the sadness was gone.

When she was finally calmer, Emma stood quietly with her head pressed against Thane's shirt. Thane turned to her father and asked, "What does Hawkins mean ta ya, sir?"

Her father's attention was on Emma. He continued to watch her quietly before replying, "Ya'd best be comin' in and sittin' fer awhile."

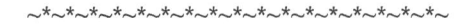

~*~*~*~*~*~*~*~*~*~*~*~*~

Emma watched the flames come to life in the cookstove. Closing the door, she slid the coffee pot forward. The menfolk still hadn't come in from putting the horses away. Restless, she looked out the window one more time before she went to sit in a chair at the table.

"What am I doin'?" Emma scolded herself. "I can be washin' up these dishes while I wait." Grabbing a bucket for water, she went out the back door to the well. By the time she had hauled up enough water to fill her bucket, Emma was exhausted. Pressing the back of her hand to her forehead, she took a deep breath and then carried it back inside.

As soon as she opened the door into the kitchen, Emma felt the bucket lifted from her hands. "What're ya doin', Emma?"

Emma looked up startled by Thane's angry words, but the worried look on his face put her heart at ease. She let him lead her to a chair. "I was jest gonna wash the dishes," she stated simply.

"I'll get 'em," Thane offered, taking the bucket over to the wash stand.

"Leave 'em," Da told Thane. Nodding in Emma's direction, he asked, "What did the doctor say?"

Putting the bucket down, Thane brought Emma a cup of water. "He told her ta take it easy for a couple weeks," he answered. Pulling out a chair, he sat next to Emma. "Said if she doesn't-- if she works too hard--, the faintin' will come back."

"I already took it easy," Emma insisted.

"Last time ya took a long ride on horseback, ya fainted dead away, Emma," Thane reminded her.

Impatiently, Emma pointed out, "My head was still pounding that day. It doesn't hurt today. I'm jest tired."

Her father's chuckle surprised her, "Ya got yer work cut out fer ya, Mr. Hawkins, if ya plan on makin' her rest."

A smile touched Thane's mouth. "Yes sir, I do." With a gentle squeeze of Emma's hand, Thane turned toward her father. "I'd be obliged iffen ya'd explain how ya know my name, sir."

Da nodded once and took his seat across from them. "I knew yer Mama. Annabel and her parents travelled out in the same wagon train we did. She was such a joyful girl. Ya look a lot like her. She had the blackest hair we'd ever seen. And the same gray eyes as yers too," he paused to look at Emma, before returning his attention to Thane. "But yer Mama was a headstrong girl. Lily said she argued with anythin' her father said ta her. One morn, William came ridin' over at first light. Said they'd woke ta find Annie gone. We searched fer weeks. No trace of her was ever found."

When Da paused, Emma heard the coffee boiling. Sliding her chair back, she quietly got cups and filled them with coffee.

"Then one day, Emma's Mama was over visitin' with Mary, when Annie walked in. Annie announced she was havin' a baby. When her Father came in from searchin' again and found her there? He started ta yellin'. Lily said Annie insisted she had left a note explainin'. But neither of her parents believed her. Annie left in tears. By the time William calmed down enough ta regret his words, Annie had again disappeared."

Emma silently handed Thane and her father a cup of coffee, then sat back in her chair without making a sound.

"When word came that Annie died soon after her baby was born. William closed up that house and left," Da took a swallow of coffee. "We haven't heard from the Prestons since. When James wrote ta them, asking them if they were interested in selling their farm, Mary wrote back sayin' she's decided ta return. She wanted ta search fer Annie's baby--, her grandson. She wrote ta the sheriff in all the cities, hereabout, askin' fer information on Annabel Preston's baby. The day Sheriff Granger rode out ta deliver Emma's letter, he announced that the grandson had been found. A Thane Hawkins from Charlotte."

"How did they know it was me?" Thane asked bewildered.

Emma searched Thane's face, wondering why he didn't remember Clara telling him. "Clara told the sheriff yer Ma's name was Annabel Preston. She told him that first night."

"Did she?" Thane asked.

"Right before I -," she started.

"Before ya fainted," he finished, nodding.

Da waited for a moment, before he continued. "Sheriff Granger never mentioned ta us that Mr. Hawkins being found and yer letter were connected."

The sound of horses approaching, brought Emma to the window again. She recognized her brothers as they jumped down from their horses and ran for the door to the cabin. She had just enough time to open the door before Mark was there, picking her up. Hugging her tightly, her brother twirled her around in a circle with a laugh. "Yer back!"

As he set her on the floor, Seth leaned in for a fierce bear hug. A groan escaped Emma's mouth.

"Be careful," Thane commanded protectively and the room froze.

"Who are you?" Mark demanded, as he stepped in front of Emma.

Emma's father stood up, gesturing toward Thane. "Mark and Seth, this is Thane Hawkins, Emma's husband."

Mark stood frozen in his shock.

"Husband?" Seth asked, equally as shocked.

Emma stepped around her brothers. "Yes, he's my husband. He took care of me until I was well enough ta travel. Then he married me ta save me from talk," she finished softly.

"My Pa gave her a nasty blow ta the head. She was asleep fer days. Too many days ta be seemly. Marriage was her only option," Thane explained further.

"That won't be necessary. James will be marryin' her-," Mark retorted angrily.

Emma interrupted her older brother, "It's too late fer that now, Mark."

"No! It's not too late. It's easy enough ta fix really," Mark corrected her.

Looking toward her father in question, Emma asked, "How can ya fix a marriage?"

But her father wouldn't meet her gaze, so Thane answered. His voice was low and cautious, "By hangin' me."

"Hangin' ya?" Emma gasped. "But why?"

"Why?" Mark retorted angrily. "Em.. it'd fix everythin'."

A voice from the doorway spoke up then. "I'll be the one decidin' if anyone'll be hangin' taday," Sheriff Granger stated. He stood still, studying Thane closely.

"Ya can't hang him! He's done nothing but protect me. He didn't hurt me.. that was his Pa," Emma felt tears fill her eyes. "Why would ya hang him?"

Thane stepped forward to grab her arm, as Emma swayed slightly. Mark moved so quickly, Emma didn't know what really happened. She felt Thane's arm pulled from hers and she rocked backwards into Seth.

"Don't EVER touch my sister," Mark growled, as he leaned his forearm into Thane's neck. Thane's back was pressed against the wall of the cabin.

Thane seemed equally as angry. "Yer sister isn't well. She needs ta sit down."

"Mark," came her father's stern voice. "Leave him. The marriage stands as it is."

"Da, ya can't LET him have her. What about James?" Mark demanded furiously.

"Let it be, boy," Da warned.

Mark released Thane and stormed out of the cabin. The door slammed behind him.

Emma felt a chair placed behind her legs. Slowly, she sank into it. Sheriff Granger stepped forward then. "Emma? I need ya ta tell me exactly what happened the night ya were taken."

Exhausted, Emma explained how she had walked to the abandoned farm along the creek. She explained how Thane's Pa had stepped from the shadows, surprising her. Her voice quivered as she described waking up in the little cabin. She explained how Thane had kept his father away from her. How he nursed her while she slept. Finally, she told them about their simple wedding in Charlotte. On the verge of tears, she left out everything except the bare details.

Sheriff Granger nodded in understanding while she talked. When she finished, he remained quiet for a couple minutes. "I see nothin' ta charge this Mr. Hawkins with," he stated finally. "Seems he's done an honorable thing here. I will send out inquiries ta the whereabouts of Nathan Hawkins, though."

Emma breathed a sigh of relief.

Da offered the sheriff a chair and a cup of coffee. After the sheriff had taken a swallow, he glanced over at Thane. "I see no reason fer ya ta wait fer Mary Preston ta arrive. The letter I received states the farm will be yers. That's good enough fer me."

"Wait fer Mary Preston?" Thane echoed, confused. "Fer what? What are ya meanin'?"

The Sheriff nodded, "Mary Preston is yer Mama's Ma.. yer grandma. She owns the abandoned farm ta the West of here." When Thane didn't give a reply, the lawman continued. "She is travelin' here ta find ya.. ta give ya the farm."

Thane turned to look at Emma. The confusion in his eyes caused her to reach over and take his hand. "I'm not understandin'," Thane repeated to Sheriff Granger.

The sheriff's mouth relaxed into a smile, amused at the young man's confusion. "The farm that borders this farm, is yours. You and yer bride can move in whenever ya want."

"Mine?" Thane repeated. "It can't be mine."

Laughing outright, Sheriff Granger repeated the story that Emma's father had told them earlier. Repeated the fact that Mary Preston was on her way to their small town to look for her grandson.

"In the law's eyes, the letter in my desk at the jailhouse is enough for me. You can move inta the house whenever yer ready."

Thane stood then and walked to the window, looking out. "I have a farm?" Disbelief laced his words.

"Yes Mr. Hawkins," the sheriff confirmed.

Thane leaned his arm against the wall above the window, looking out the small panes of glass. He looked so overwhelmed that Emma wished she could go to him. But she was too tired.

Da spoke up then. "I think ya should stay here tonight," he suggested. "Emma looks exhausted. And that farm is a sight. It'll be better tackled in the morn."

Thane turned to look at Emma again. The confusion in his eyes faded to concern. "Ya need ta rest."

Emma nodded weakly. Rising to go to her room, Thane was immediately at her side. "My room's upstairs," she explained.

Seth stepped forward then, "I can take her up," he offered.

Not bothering to respond to her brother, Thane lifted Emma easily into his arms. She leaned her head against his chest, letting her eyes fall shut. Carefully climbing the steep steps, Thane paused at the top.

"It's the room straight ahead," came Seth's voice from below them.

Thane carried Emma into her room and lowered her down onto the bed. She felt her shoes being removed and heard them hit the floor. A quilt was pulled over her and settled under her chin. When fingers trailed down her cheek, Emma opened her eyes. Thane's face was inches from hers. So close she could see the tears pooling in his beautiful gray eyes.

"Emma. We have a farm. A farm," Thane's voice still held disbelief. "Maybe we won't have ta go back ta the cabin. A farm. Maybe I'll be able ta keep ya warm this winter," his soft spoken words were gruff with emotions he couldn't hide.

Pulling her hand out from under the blanket, Emma reached up to smooth Thane's hair from his eyes. "God is blessin' ya fer bein' so faithful. He is blessin' ya," she stated with a smile.

"I want Him ta be blessin' you," Thane whispered, caressing her cheek lightly.

"God blessed me with you," Emma said. A tear escaped her eye. "Yer all the blessin's I need."

Thane's thumb wiped the tear away. He leaned forward to kiss her forehead gently. Pulling back slightly, he looked down into her eyes. "A farm, Emma. Can ya believe it?" he repeated with a smile.

Emma laughed softly. Wrapping her arms around his neck, she hugged him. Thane's arms slipped around her, pulling her close. She heard his laugh echo against her neck.

Eventually, Thane loosened his grip on Emma. "Ya need ta rest," he stated as he laid her back against the pillow. "I've some questions fer the sheriff before he leaves." Standing, he tucked the quilt around her again and headed for the door. Thane paused in the doorway to turn back to her. "I'll check back on ya after awhile," he promised with a smile. Then he pulled the door closed behind him.

The sight of Thane so happy filled Emma with joy. She felt a smile touch her lips. A farm. "Thank ya Lord. Thank ya fer blessin' him. Fer blessin' us," she prayed silently.

Closing her eyes, Emma drifted off to sleep.

~Thirty Seven~

"I don't even know where ta start," Emma stated, a little overwhelmed. She walked slowly through the room. Dust coated everything with a thick blanket. Picking up a small box, she wiped the surface with her hand, revealing an engraving on its lid.

Light poured through a door on the far side of the main room. Setting the box down, Emma walked toward it. As she stepped through the doorway, she let out a gasp and she took a step back out of the room. A thick tree limb stuck through the roof. The way the branch was dried and falling apart, Emma decided it had been there for awhile.

Thane stepped up behind her. "Hmm.. Didn't see that from outside."

"This must be the back of the cabin," she pointed out. "Well I guess we might as well start here."

"Let me get the tree out of the way and then I'll get that feather tick outside ta air out," Thane offered.

Examining the mattress, Emma wrinkled up her nose. "Not sure airin' will do it any good. The holes are one thing, but that black rot looks ta be all the way through the feather."

Thane chuckled. "Perhaps yer right." Looking up through the hole in the roof, he took in a deep breath. "I'll get ta work closin' this in before I do anything else."

Emma rolled up her sleeves as she stepped further into the room. "I can get these littler sticks outta yer way." As she moved a stack of decaying branches, a raccoon lunged toward her hissing. Startled, she let out a strangled scream and tried to retreat. Her foot caught on something behind her and she felt herself falling backwards.

Thane caught her before she hit the floor. Lifting her, he swung her quickly through the doorway.

Emma clung to his arms for a second before a laugh burst from her lips. Thane chuckled along with her and gathered her to his chest. When Emma's heart quit racing, she lifted her head to look up into Thane's eyes. "Maybe we should get rid of our guest BEFORE we do anything else?"

Thane nodded his head in agreement but did not answer her. He brushed her tussled hair away from her face. Emma felt her breath catch as she realized how close his face was. His fingers slowly brushed down her cheek bone, but his eyes never left hers. Slowly he lowered his face to hers until she could feel his breath on her cheek. When he hesitated, Emma turned her face, her lips brushing shyly against his. Neither of them moved for fear of breaking the moment. Finally, Thane slide his fingers into her hair and brought his lips down gently upon hers. Then Emma closed her eyes and was lost in his embrace. His kisses falling on her eyelids, cheeks and her jaw line. Her arms found their way around his neck and he pulled her close, holding her tightly in his arms. "I love ya, Emma," Thane whispered against her neck. Pulling back a little, he gazed down into her eyes. "I love ya, Emma Fern Hawkins," he repeated, with a smile full of awe.

"And I love you, Mr. Hawkins," Emma replied softly. She let her fingers brush his hair back from his face.

A shriek from the raccoon startled Emma, making her jump again. Thane chuckled as he brought her back to his chest. "I'd best be gettin' rid of our guest."

"Thank ya," she said. Pulling away from him reluctantly, Emma sighed. "I guess I best get ta work too. If we're ta have a bed big enough fer the both of us ta sleep in tonight."

Thane froze, his fingers still wrapped around her arm. She looked up shyly to see his expression. "Ya sure?" he asked.

Emma saw the uncertainty in his eyes. But she also saw a shy hope growing in them. Emotion caught in her throat making her unable to speak. Instead, she stood on her tiptoes to kiss his cheek before fleeing the room.

Several minutes later, Emma was concentrating on finding rags and a scrub brush, when the gun went off. Her hand flew to her mouth in surprise. When Thane emerged from the bedroom a few seconds later, she felt foolish. "Of course ya had ta shoot it," she laughed embarrassed.

Thane laughed with her. "I tried ta talk him inta jest leavin' but he wouldn't hear of it." With another smile, he asked, "Ya up ta cookin' him?"

Wrinkling her nose, Emma nodded. Raccoon wasn't her favorite, but she knew better than to waste meat. "I'll find a pot ta get him a soakin'."

"I'll clean 'im fer ya," Thane said as he walked out the front door.

A pot was found easy enough. Getting it clean was another story. When her task was finally done, she located the salt she had brought with them. She took the pot and the salt out to Thane.

They worked all through the day. After clearing the room of all the debris, Thane started covering the hole with boards. Knowing he could add shingles the following day, he then went back inside to help Emma. Wrestling the feather tick out of the cabin, they decided that it had indeed been wet for far too long. It would need to be burned. He swept the remaining leaves and dirt from the room, while she wiped the dust from the other furniture.

In the smaller room, they found another feather tick. This one was dusty but intact. Again, Thane wrestled it out of the cabin so he could beat the dust out of it. When Emma returned to the smaller bedroom, she saw a couple trunks pushed up along the far wall. She bent down to open the larger of the two and found a stack of quilts. Grabbing a few, she headed back outside to air them out. Hanging them over the railing, she quickly ran out of room. Looking around the yard for another space, she headed for the fence by the barn.

"I need ta add rope ta our list. I'll be needin' it iffen I want ta hang clothes ta dry on wash day," Emma told Thane, when he came over to help her spread the quilts. "When I find paper, that is," she finished with a smile.

When they were done outside, Emma headed back in to the kitchen. She swept the table and washstand off, finding it easier than wiping them down. Thane brought in a bucket of water to fill the wash tub.

"We'll need a new bucket too," he said with a smile. "Only thing holdin' this one together is my hands."

Thane cleaned the ashes and debris out of the hearth. Climbing onto the roof, he made sure the chimney was clear so it would be ready for supper. Emma scrubbed down every surface in the kitchen, and then turned her attention to the dishes she found.

When Emma decided the cooking area was clean enough, she set about peeling some vegetables. Thane had already started a fire for her. So when Emma had everything cut up and in the pot, there were enough coals to put the stew on to boil.

While they let the stew cook, Thane brought the feather tick back into the cabin. Emma followed with the bedding. They took turns stoking the fire and checking the stew, while they moved their belongings into the room.

When the bedroom was all set, Emma brought a chair closer to the hearth, so she could rest.

"I'll have ta make a trip ta the cabin ta bring the rocker," Thane commented, kneeling next to Emma for a moment.

Emma smiled at his thoughtfulness, imagining how nice a rocker would be at that moment. Leaning forward, she stirred the stew.

When the meat was pulling away from the bone, Emma announced that it was time to eat. She dished up a bowl for each of them. Filling cups with water, she sat down across from Thane.

It felt strange to sit across from each other at the freshly scrubbed table. It was the first meal they had eaten alone since they were married. Emma could feel Thane watching her but felt too shy to meet his gaze. When she ate her last bite, Emma slowly looked up toward her husband. A happy smile lit up his face. Sliding his chair back, Thane carefully walked around the table to her side. With a graceful movement, he pulled his wife to her feet. Putting an arm behind her knees, he lifted her easily into his arms. Her arms looped around his neck and she ran her fingers through his hair. His eyes never left hers as he carried her to their bedroom.

~Thirty Eight~

Emma looked down at the broken latch in her fingers. Laughter bubbled up from within her.

"What d'ya find that's so funny?" Thane asked curiously as he came up behind her.

Holding up the latch, she replied, "One more thing ta add ta our list."

Thane watched her happy face as he stepped closer to her. Slipping his arms around her waist, he pulled her close and smiled down at her. He leaned forward and Emma knew he intended to kiss her again.

The sound of a throat clearing stopped them. Looking toward the barn entrance, they saw Mark standing there. The look on his face took the smile from Emma's and she stepped away from her husband. Seth stood a little ways behind his brother, looking uncomfortable.

"Sheriff rode out this morning with the letter he told ya about. The one he received from yer Ma's family, Mr. Hawkins. Seth and I were on our way here, so we said we'd deliver it ta ya," Mark stated.

Thane stepped forward and took the offered letter.

"Mr. Hawkins, I would like ta speak ta my sister," Mark requested, without turning his attention to Thane.

Thane gave Emma a questioning glance. When he saw her small nod, he turned to leave. He walked all the way to the house, but sat on the steps where he could still see his wife.

Mark moved closer to Emma, "James's world has fallen apart and yer here.. smilin' and laughin'?" The anger in his voice made her take a step back. "Take care Emma or others'll think ya asked fer this."

"Mark?" Seth spoke softly in a warning tone.

Mark held his hand up to his brother to keep him from interrupting, but his eyes softened. "I know yer jest tryin' ta make the best of yer situation. Yer happy soul lookin' fer the good in everythin'. Jest try not ta enjoy yerself too much around others."

Emma's eyes filled with tears.

"Jest fer a little while, Em'," Seth added softly. Reaching out, he took the metal pieces from her hand, asking, "What's this?"

She looked down at the forgotten latch. "The stall latch broke in my hand. I was goin' ta use the stall fer my chickens," she explained. "Everythin' is so old -- it's all fallin' apart."

Mark took the latch from Seth and studied it. "I'm headin' ta town ta see James this evenin'. I'll see if he can fix it."

"No," Emma burst out, shaking her head. "Ya canna ask him." She reached out to take the latch back, but her brother held it out of her reach.

"Why?" Mark asked confused.

When she didn't answer, he continued, "Ya didna think he'd be blamin' ya? Yer our family and we'll still be lookin' after ya," Mark stepped closer in emphasis.

"Why didna ya jest come home first Emma?" Seth asked confused. "Why did ya marry without talkin' ta us first?"

Emma's voice cracked. "I was alone in the care of an unmarried man fer more'n a week. It was the only choice I could make. Thane said he would honor my choice, but I knew - I knew no one'd want me after that."

"Yer wrong Em! James loves ya - he'd take ya still," Mark insisted angrily. "He's so lost without ya."

"Mark," Seth cautioned his brother softly.

Mark put his hand up to again stop his brother's words.

Mark's angry words had gotten Thane's attention. Before Emma knew it, Thane had stepped in front of her. He wrapped his strong arm around her, keeping her behind his back.

"Get away from my sister," Mark growled.

"Don't ever yell at her, ya understand?" Thane stated, quietly but firmly. The barn stood quiet as the two men faced each other.

"Emma's still a part of our family and will be always. We'll keep on lookin' out fer her. She doesn't belong with ya and we all know it," Mark stated angrily, but kept his voice quiet. Stepping toward Thane, he continued, "And don't ever come between me and my sister."

Thane didn't move from where he stood. "Yer sister's my responsibility now. I'll protect her from anyone who'd harm her.. even her brother," he stated firmly.

Mark's jaw flexed. "I'd never hurt my sister," he growled. With one last hard stare, he turned and strode away. He walked past the wagon and down the drive.

Seth cleared his throat nervously. "Da sent us over with some chickens and such. Do ya want me ta help unload 'em? Or jest leave ya the wagon."

Thane dropped the protective arm he had around Emma. "I'd be honored with yer help Seth. Thank ya."

They all walked to the wagon. A hog was tied to the rear of the wagon. The back was full of crates and baskets. Chickens clucked to each other as Emma looked through the baskets of vegetables. The same vegetables she had harvested with Thane only weeks before.

Thane and Seth carried the crates of chickens to the stall Emma had cleared for them. Emma followed with an armload of straw from the wagon.

When the wagon was cleared, Thane turned to Seth. "Thank ya fer yer help, sir," extending his hand to Emma's younger brother, to shake his.

Seth hesitated for only a moment before accepting it. Turning to Emma, he took her hands in his and squeezed them gently. "Mark's jest upset Em. He'll come around." Brushing his clothes off, he walked back toward the wagon. "I must git back now. We need ta finish gettin' the crops in." Seth climbed up into the wagon seat before turning back to Emma. "Da said he'd be by Sunday mornin' with the wagon. Doesn't want ya overdoin' it. He asked iffen ya'd both plan on comin' ta dinner after service?" Seeing the nod from Thane, Seth clicked to the team and led them down the drive.

Emma leaned her head back against Thane's chest, as she watched Seth drive away. "Are ya alright, Emma?" Thane asked softly.

She nodded slowly. "What am I gonna do?"

"We are gonna take one day at a time. The Bible says there is a time ta rejoice and a time ta mourn. Might be ours is gonna mix a little," Thane said with a lopsided smile. Turning Emma to face him, he put his hands gently on her cheeks. He smiled as he continued. "All I know fer sure is that I love ya, Emma. And I'll spend the rest of my life showin' ya how happy I am."

Emma raised her hands to cover the fingers cradling her face. Thane lowered his lips to hers. She closed her eyes to cherish the gentle kiss, until Thane reluctantly pulled away.

"Let's go finish our list," he said with a smile.

Hand in hand, Thane led Emma back into their home.

~Epilogue~

October 4, 1858

My dear Thane,

    I hope this letter finds you well.
    I am overjoyed to have found you at last. I received the letter Sheriff Granger sent. He explained that you and your young bride have moved into the cabin. This is wonderful.
    I am getting my affairs in order here in Detroit. My hopes are to be finished packing and on my way to Vermontville before long. I wish to make it before the snow flies.
    I would very much like to stay with you until another place can be found. We have much to learn about each other.

With Love,
Mary Preston

Jules Nelson *grew up in northern Michigan, the middle child of seven. With these siblings, she confidently explored the world around her. She spent much of her childhood making up stories and writing them down. The characters in her stories so real to her that they seemed to come alive.*

Jules has lived much of her adult life in Missouri, where she enjoyed a life rich in culture. With her husband Chad and their two children by her side, Jules continues to explore the world around her.

Recently, Jules has moved home with her family. With the slower pace of life in rural Michigan, the characters in her stories have come back to life.

Visit Jules Nelson's website to follow her current projects!
julesnelson.net

~Acknowledgements~

I want to personally thank everyone who helped me with the developing of **Shadows**...

Thank you Chad... my rock... for your constant support and patience through this long process. I love you!

Thank you to my Biggest Fans.. my parents... Grant and Gail Olmsted. Your support throughout my lifetime means the world to me.

Thank you to my siblings... Andy, Tammy, Paul, Dan, Dave and Mark... You have been the best supports a person could EVER ask for. Even though I only used one of your names, each of your personalities went into the creation of "Mark"... I love all of you!

Thank you to my Team. Jill Hulsey, Sabrina Nelson (my baby girl), Carol Nelson, Jane Ann Olmsted, Tracy Kutchuk, Shannon Webb, my own dear Da (Grant Olmsted), Jamie Cowden, Anne Baker and my own brother Mark. These wonderful people took time out of their busy lives to Read, Edit, Advise, Encourage and/or Criticize this book. Love you all!

Thank you to my Olmsted Girl Fan Club... Melanie, Meghan, Carmen, Madison and Alisa. A more amazing set of nieces, I will never find.

A special thank you to my Melanie. Without your constant nagging, persistent encouragement... I may never have finished.

Thank you to everyone who has ever read one of my creations.. and encouraged me to create another. Without all of your encouragement, I may never have had the confidence to publish **Shadows**.

And last but not least...Thank you to my Uncles James Kuhlman, who lent his name to one of my favorite characters. My Uncle passed away, unexpectedly, during the editing of Shadows.. He will be missed but not forgotten.

~References~

Jeremiah 29:11 NIV
*"For I know the plans I have for you," declares
the Lord, "Plans to prosper you and not to harm
you, plans to give you hope and a future."*

Luke 2:19 NKJV
But Mary kept all these things and pondered them in her heart.

2 Samuel 22:31 NIV
*As for God, His way is perfect: The Lord's word is
flawless; He shields all who take refuge in Him.*

Ecclesiates 3:1-14 NKJV
*To everything there is a season, A time
for every purpose under heaven:
A time to be born, And a time to die;
A time to plant, And a time to pluck what is planted;
A time to kill, And a time to heal;
A time to break down, And a time to build up;
A time to weep, And a time to laugh;
A time to mourn, And a time to dance;
A time to cast away stones, And a time to gather stones;
A time to embrace, And a time to refrain from embracing;
A time to gain, And a time to lose;
A time to keep, And a time to throw away;
A time to tear, And a time to sew;*

A time to keep silence, And a time to speak;
A time to love, And a time to hate;
A time of war, And a time of peace.
What profit has the worker from that in which he labors? I have seen the God-given task with which the sons of men are to be occupied. He has made everything beautiful in its time. Also He has put eternity in their hearts, except that no one can find out the work that God does from beginning to end. I know that nothing is better for them than to rejoice, and to do good in their lives, and also that every man should eat and drink and enjoy the good of all his labor – it is the gift of God. I know that whatever God does, It shall be forever. Nothing can be added to it, and nothing taken from it. God does it, that men should fear before Him.